Quotations of a B

Studies in Austrian Literature, Culture, and Thought

Translation Series

Evelyn Schlag

Quotations of a Body

Prefatory Note by
Claire Tomalin

Translation and Afterword
by
Willy Riemer

ARIADNE PRESS
Riverside, California

Ariadne Press would like to express its appreciation to the Austrian Cultural Institute, New York and the Bundeskanzleramt - Sektion Kunst, Vienna for their assistance in publishing this book.

Translated from the German
Die Kränkung
©1987 S.Fischer Verlag, Frankfurt am Main

Library of Congress Cataloging-in-Publication Data

Schlag, Evelyn, 1952-
[Kränkung. English]
Quotations of a body / Evelyn Schlag ; prefatory note by Claire Tomalin ; translation and afterword by Willy Riemer.
p. cm. -- (Studies in Austrian literature, culture, and thought. Translation series)
ISBN 0-57241-050-7
I. Riemer, Willy. II. Title. III. Series
PT2680.L37K7313 1998
833'.914--dc21 97-6990
CIP

Cover Design:
Art Director, Designer: George McGinnis

Copyright ©1998
by Ariadne Press
270 Goins Court
Riverside, CA 92507

All rights reserved.
No part of this publication may be reproduced or transmitted in any form or by any means without formal permission.
Printed in the United States of America.
ISBN 0-57241-050-7 (paperback original)

Prefatory Note

Evelyn Schlag's delicate and dreamlike narrative is about the friendship between two women writers. Each of them is living out difficult and painful days as she tries to work and struggles with an unsatisfactory love affair. One inhabits a wintry northern landscape, the other a southern villa, yet they exchange information and offer one another ideas and sensations: a piece of mint leaf, rubbed and held out to smell; the taste of apples; a wild, self-indulgent dance, arms tracing out what the heart feels. One of the women is ill and tells the other, "Everything about me is going to infect you." And the narrator sees that her friend is the wrong person to grow old with, but she is caught in her obsession. She becomes ill too, and for a long season the two women are in the hospital; they watch, they suffer, they talk of how they would like to live a healthy life.

Then one recovers and emerges into a new life. For the last time, her friend Kathleen comes through the door to visit her. She has been dead for sixty years.

Evelyn Schlag's beautiful story blends and dissolves the experience of the living writer and the dead Katherine Mansfield, using her letters and journals as inspiration. I find in her Mansfield's quick realism and touch of the surreal, her fine impatience with explanation, her immediacy. *Quotations of a Body* is both a tribute and an extension of the work of the brave modernist writer of the beginning of this century whose life was ravaged by gonorrhea and cut short by tuberculosis. As Mansfield's biographer I read it with particular interest and pleasure for its acute, wistful and haunting quality.

Claire Tomalin

1

Kathleen had been there with us all along, at least it seems that way to me now. One day she had slipped into the house, found a pillow and settled on the bed; cozy and with her back propped up she watched us, watched Jack and me, as our life together began to unravel. Whenever she was bored with us or knew all too well how things were and how they would turn out, she took her notebook and put down what we had said, put her day on record. Meanwhile we would leave the room, go about our chores in the yard, eat in the kitchen and shiver in the chill of autumn. The onset of autumn always seems to bring incisive events. But perhaps that is an impression left over from childhood, the end of summer, the beginning of school. Kathleen is a woman who writes stories and who dies of an illness. To say more would be to give away her life in a sentence or two.

Where to begin? Through windows that had not been cleaned in years, Jack and I can be seen looking into the interior of a house. On a small round table there is a botanical encyclopedia, its opened pages show a blue blossom surrounded by text. A glass with turbid brandy, perhaps tea. In a fruit bowl are pencils, matchboxes, little metal things. A notepad. An opened packet of tissues. Jack sees different things, the stove in the corner, its rounded ochre-brown tiles, the domed top. There are sheets draped over the furniture, the carpet has stains, in some places the edges are frayed. On the wall a farmer's calendar, a month with a short name, it might have been June or July when it was last used. Beside the stove is a stack of newspapers, from the ceiling a lightbulb pulls down on its cord as if it had hanged itself. My breath leaves patches of condensation on the windowpane, we move along with our faces. Jack's hand rests heavily on my shoulder, he leans forward. He is impatient, he wants to see everything all at once and then move on. Our curiosity is aroused, we will give it a try.

The house has been empty for a long time. Jack's grandmother was the last to live in it. Once it was burgled, drawers were opened and the doors of wardrobes left ajar, nobody really knew whether anything had been taken. Perhaps an old prayer book was missing, a cookbook, or some embroidered sheets. Jack says that his grandmother often made a show of taking out her earrings, pointing out to the children the marks where her earlobes had been pierced. She also accused her stepdaughter, Jack's mother, of hiding her rosary; ever more often she buttoned up her cardigan all askew, and whenever she did the dishes, the plates were still slippery with grease. The wooden cutlery handles never really dried. Jack's mother called her a pig, tough-minded and bigoted, the young had buried her without shedding a tear. That is what I am thinking when we get the key from Jack's mother. You must be crazy, she says. Who would want to live in such a house nowadays? Damp as it is.

It’s time for rubber boots. The farm women I've

come to know all wear canvas shoes, but I'm not up to that yet. I was raised in a small town where my father practiced law. As a child I was curious about cold water, sharp stones, banisters, window shutters, attics, about all that happens on the other side of the street, about unwashed fruit and musty smells: father well knew how to nip such curiosity in the bud. Father was the incriminating witness against the outside world, ever the nay-sayer who discredited everything around him. How irresponsible to allow the child to play so close to the railroad embankment, where she sits in the dry weeds, draws in the pungent smell of the stained crossties along with the summery air hovering over the tracks, until the train from Vienna announces itself with a ringing at the barriers and then with a noisy rush cuts through the brief silence! Wouldn't it be better to deny the child the rubber boots she wants for wading in the creek with other children of the neighborhood? The child, without boots, is ashamed as she stands at the little weir, in which the dammed-up water is already lukewarm.

Rubber boots are not bought in shoe stores, but at the farmers' cooperative. When I wear these boots, my stride gets longer; my skirt stretched taut around my thighs, I skim over so much ground, pace off the fields and fill the memory of my walking with the distance covered. In summer the corn grows up to my shoulders. I hear the boots slap against my calves. In the tall grass that no one cuts between the fence and the field I break into a run, lose my footing, recover from the fall, sprain my ankle. In the light of dawn I take a picture of the boots in front of the door, when they cast an oblique shadow and their edges clearly rest on the shaft. With a ballpoint pen I write my name on the lining. Who would think of taking them, says Jack.

Kathleen sits bundled up and with a cup by her side. She is writing, her gaze goes right through us whenever she looks up. The woman in her story is waking to the first morning in a new house. Kathleen is after the feeling of arriving and settling down but cannot place this woman in her new surroundings, nor does she really want to. On this first morning Kathleen writes; the room is filled with daylight. All the furniture had found a place. Even the photographs were on the mantlepiece and the medicine bottles on the shelf above the washstand. Looking at her clothes draped across a chair, she wished to leave this house. It all begins earlier, I say. What's important is the first evening. You have to begin with the evening before. How was it on that very first evening?

Exhausted from moving the many things, Jack turns the rented truck off the road and drives up to a farm house. A young woman whom he had met in the summer lives there. Just a quick hello, we're here, we're done with our apartment in Vienna. Would you believe such words? Forever... I can't believe that you're really here now, says the young woman and puts glasses on the table. She is a teacher and together with her mother also works the small farm on the side. This very night her sister is supposed to catch a train for Naples, leaving Leoben just before midnight, that's seventy kilometers. And there is a problem with the transmission in their car. The teacher makes big eyes. Jack can't very well turn her down. Just call her Rosie, says Kathleen. Rosie suits her well.

While Jack drives Rosie's sister to Leoben, I'm in the kitchen unpacking boxes of dishes. They are irregulars, sale items out of plastic bins that have accumulated over the years, everything and nothing, no particular style. Some things have to be washed first, others immediately find their place in the cupboard. I try out the meat grinder from Jack's mother by clamping it to the table, then I wipe the shelves with a damp cloth, put down some paper and brighten up the long-neglected house with the fuss of a housewife. Jack promised to make shelves for the jars filled with grains, they will be the centerpiece of the kitchen. I worry about Jack, he had driven off tired and irritated. I had asked him to take me along, but he had bluntly dismissed the idea. In four years, says Kathleen, we moved sixteen times.

The house stands on a rise, a five-minute walk from the next neighbors, an elderly couple. I wonder if they would hear me shout for help. Of course they would hear you, says Jack. Down by the road there is an old pub that has been abandoned for years. A rusty soft-drink sign on the front wall, next to it the weathered antlers of a stag. Now the grass and weeds of the meadow grow right up to the house, animals graze there, crush the grass into the ground, making holes in which water collects, stagnant little pools. They scratch their sides along the tables on posts rammed into the ground and against the long narrow benches where farm workers used to drink their cider. Jack shows me an abandoned beer depot across town. Once a laborer tried to hang himself in the cold-storage room, but workers cut him down in time and brought him to his wife; he went on living quite well. He didn't want a doctor, that was just fine with his wife, since the pangs of guilt could come all too easily, while it surely was a failing of God. How do you know about such stories, I ask Jack.

A farm without animals, that's like a wife without children, says the neighbor. There are two fingers missing on his right hand. When I try to talk with him about my work, he nods and smiles. Yeah, I see, he says, yeah, I see. Now and then he glances at Jack. A house needs a woman, he says with a few sweeping chops in the air. He laughs loudly. Anyway, that's what they say around here, he adds. Then the two men go to the stable to look at the horse stalls. The neighbor has two mares that he wants to pasture in the summer, but in winter they are to be kept in our stable.

After the neighbor has left, Jack asks whether I would mind our looking after the horses. We'd only have to put water out for them and hay from the loft, that's all. – But you have already decided, I say. It is you who wants the horses, right? – You'll see, you'll get to like them, Jack promises. – And if we both need to be away sometime? – Then Hans will look after them himself, he knows that. – Then we'll always have to tell him when we plan to be away? – Well? So? Is that a problem? – I would feel cramped, hemmed in, don't you understand that? – Look, in a few weeks all of us around these parts will have a phone. The digging is all done, yesterday they got as far as the gravel pit. Then everything will be quite simple. Right?

Jack is working on a book for his promotion. His research is on language acquisition by infants in farming communities. It seems to me that he has not enjoyed his work for some time and that he only persists at it because of his appointment in the Institute. His job brings in the money that we cannot do without. He had brought along the tape recordings and the completed transcriptions, but some of his research materials remain in Vienna. We rented our apartment to a student, but Jack will have the use of it on the two days a week that he teaches.

Something in me resists understanding certain events as they occur. It seems absurd to me, that as an adult I'm still not able to explain how electricity works. Somehow Jack's linguistic investigations remind me of my physics classes. Sometimes all I can do for him is to distract him into believing the story about being misunderstood. My own difficulties at writing are then betrayed in an obvious display of self-pity.

I have to gain distance from myself, I note. How can I best do that? By writing about myself. The strategy of interposing another person, giving her a name, hair of a particular color, a certain way of holding her cigarette or rolling the cigarette back and forth in an ashtray, smoothly brushing off the ashes – everybody would immediately see through this device. – Who do you think, Kathleen asks, should be reading your story? Do you feel embarrassed with people, with strangers? – No, I say. You know that there can be no shame except when you conceal something of importance. Do people tell each other the truth? No. Is that what bothers you so much, when they accuse you of lacking a sense of shame? – No reply from Kathleen, I hear the sound of her pen, nothing else.

How odd. Though there is so much to be done around the house, we take time to explore our new surroundings. Everywhere we find abandoned houses, their roofs leaky, shingle roofs with moss growing on the slats. We have a real villa by comparison, we agree with relief and yet again postpone needed repairs. The low-set windows of these houses are overgrown with hemlock, nettles and elders; looking closely one can still see the rusty brackets where the flower boxes used to be. The broken windowpanes look like someone had sneezed through them. Anything useful has been removed long ago, even the sign with the house number on it. For a moment the eaves trough turns into a withered, empty stalk of a primeval plant. The fence which had bordered the vegetable garden and flower beds sags forlornly between the posts. In every valley there is at least one inn that has closed its doors, sometimes there is a bowling alley with a blackboard, dusty and blank. The teacher used to bring the pieces of chalk. Since the enamel is peeling off, any writing on it would now look as if it had been done long ago, with a spidery hand. Some of the houses in these valleys have been renovated and are inhabited for at least a few months of the year. Here and there a forestry official who had opportunely acquired some property had built a log cabin for weekends, vacation and retirement. In between are the farmers, who have always been here and who are now waiting to see what their children will do.

Would you like to look at the collection, a farm woman asks and, her hands wet, extends her elbow in greeting. We don't know what she is getting at. What collection? An industrialist keeps a collection of deformed antlers here. She gets the key and takes us to the manor which had caught our eye as we had driven by. Well, says the farm woman. The owner inherited most of it from his forbears. – The curious collection is mentioned in an art guide. As we leave the cold house, a cat carries one of its young along the fence. The kitten is much too big to be carried around like that. – Do you want one, asks the farm woman. They are from this spring's litter. – We take along two kittens.

At home we give them milk. As they lap their milk out of the dish, they bump their heads, they don't see that they would only need to stand side by side. – They are stupid, I say. You've brought stupid cats into the house. What shall we call them? Gusti and Kovacs? – When Kathleen hears of the cats, she hurries down the stairs, dips her forefinger into the milk and tempts the animals to come closer. They frisk about, one of them climbs into the milk dish and hysterically shakes its wet paw.

How do you get close to a person who died sixty years ago, long before you were born? If she had had an exceptionally robust constitution, she could still be alive, even without any breakthrough in medicine. As a very old human being from an age long gone, she would be joined to you to face the contemporary world. You would probably try to reach her with a carefully thought-out letter, rather than attempting to get to know her acquaintances first and thus to approach her indirectly. You would want to write straight to her heart. For some time now you've been standing behind her chair, looking over her shoulder, how does she do it? How does she do it?

Now that we've moved in, are you getting to like the house? Oh yes, I do like it very much and its garden too. But it all seems so remote, so forsaken. I can't imagine people taking that dreadful bus to come and see us. And around here, who is going to come and call? – When she reads to me, Kathleen's voice sounds as if she were reciting someone else's text. I think of her death, a fatal illness closes off her future. Even a hope can be too long, collapses into the void or into what you imagine to be there. Always to live for the future is to postpone your life, is to get bogged down in life's preamble.

When Jack's grandmother died, there was no one who would have wanted to live in the house. One of the sons was a forest ranger and had married into another estate. The second son had been showing the symptoms of leukemia for some time and lay in a distant clinic as if engaged in a war, a condition beyond comprehension for the grandmother. Good neither for living nor for dying. For the farmers in the area such an ailment signified a failure to die properly, with the sick person at least partly to blame. The men, hunters all, counted on a dignified end, but it often happened that one or the other missed the smooth transition to a quick death.

Jack's father, who was employed by the farmer's cooperative, had one day packed up and disappeared with a salesgirl. Jack doesn't even know where his father could now be found. Presumably he is still alive. His grandfather did not reach old age. During the war he was assigned to the police force in the next town, thereafter he disappeared for a few months into a camp that the Russian occupation forces had set up. He returned embittered and true to the old slogans. He locked himself in his workshop, where he repaired boots, made handles for scythes, and cultivated his smell of linseed oil, wood and dust. He died eight years before Jack's grandmother. When Jack's mother was able to obtain a position as cook and housekeeper for a widowed dentist in the city, she moved with her son into an attic apartment.

We tell each other about ourselves, make guileless adjustments for a life together. Cultivated posturing – what would that be? To sift through one's memories and hear someone else tell the story. Step out of yourself and look on, as you casually make your appearance. All the details that are left out and remain unmentioned, do these produce in the reader a sense of their own? And does the story then replenish itself? – Admit to everything, says Kathleen. Lay yourself bare. Then no one else can betray you.

Listen to this, Kathleen says. In a dream last night my whole body shivered and seemed to break up. It disintegrated with a jolt, as if hit by an earthquake, it splintered like glass. The spinal cord and the bones and every part of me. In my ears there was a low rumbling sound, and there was the greenish brilliance of broken glass. As I woke up, all was still. It slowly dawned on me that I had died in that dream.

With both hands Kathleen holds onto the long lapels. And how about you, she asks. – I dreamed of a donkey, I say, his four legs in boots. He pursued me, overtook me, then again ran alongside of me, nudging me, baring his teeth. When we came to some stairs on the path, he stumbled and fell so that I could not get past him. There was no turning back. I high-stepped over him. At the foot of the stairs began a landscape with fruit trees in bloom. – Manuka trees, says Kathleen. All white with fluffy blossoms. – It was snow, I say. There were soft plastic sheets draped over the plantation, huge coverings made of soft plastic. Jack was wading along somewhere ahead of me, he was getting through, that was clear. It occurred to me that the farmers had forgotten to put up instructions, guidelines for proceeding safely in this curtainscape. Then the curtains pressed in on me, I tried to push through the folds, but it was too late. I had suffocated.

In the gusts of wind that are puffing up the sky, almost making it burst, there is a pigeon on its way. It risks entrusting itself to this power, obliquely sweeps through the air, quickly adjusts its flight before getting entangled in a tree. Its brown body with the black markings relaxes its controls, then with a twitch of the wings seizes them once more, as if inhaling danger and exhaling it again. Then the first drops fall, a rhythm is tried out, there is not much time, hailstones dot everything. In the house there is much running to close the windows, in one room there are already some hailstones on the floor, like an evil present from a fairy tale. The roof groans, Jack has not yet returned from shopping. Kathleen stands by the window, shaking her head, in a moment she will be shivering in the chill of the air. – Have you seen the horses, I ask her. I do hope that they are in the stable. – There is no reply. I know that Kathleen is of little use in such situations, but I ask nonetheless. When Jack returns after a while, he explains that in places the road had been impassable, thick carpets of water spread over the roadway, he had to detour across meadows and through the orchard, where the old road used to be. He had met Rosie, on the tractor, just before the storm broke. What an odd thought, he says, that these hailstones should strike just here and perish, for example on this patch of pavement, where one has just been standing. That here of all places the world must begin and the hailstones cease to exist.

All that happened, and indeed so much has happened, is irretrievably gone. It collapses into a meaningless hodgepodge. Jack has taken off his shirt and hung it up to dry. I get him a pullover. It occurs to me that I don't love his body, but then he is dressed again and continues with his story; a reprieve for us both.

One of the neighbors has a handicapped sister. She is well past fifty, with the haircut of a child, a shock of hair over a bony skull that is improperly filled. She bears no resemblance to Kathleen, although her hairstyle is so similar. She stands in the hallway on the dirty wooden floor, keeps on wiping across the boards with her thick socks until she catches a splinter and sits down with a howl. If she happens to be alone when visitors come, she calls for her sister-in-law; this other woman rummages around in one of the upper floors and pays no attention to the calls. She dangles her arms back and forth, jerks her shoulders – but these movements are not taken as they would be for normal human beings. Her life on earth is so restless. She is never still until she takes her place on the bench by the stove, looking as if all day long she had been contributing her part towards the cost of her keep. There is nothing dangerous about her eyes, nothing odd, they are the entirely ordinary eyes of an aging woman. She sits in the kitchen and cleans vegetables, uses her fingernail to scrape out a stubborn bit of dirt. Every once in a while one feels shivers of fright. She ties the garbage bags together with leftover ribbons from Christmas, as long as she finds any, tries to make loops, to tie the ribbons, but with little chance of success. She is afraid in the barn. With trembling step she flees up the stairs to her sister-in-law, stumbles across the room, garbling her words. She has almost no name.

A few days after the storm I notice a cobweb stretched from the gate to the small table outside. The wind now softly gives it breath. So far it has survived intact. Some of the vegetable seedlings that we had just planted are crushed. When we planted potatoes as late as June, they all laughed at us. Now the dark leaves of the plants already show through, on some days it almost seems as if there is something pushing them from underneath.

A pair of buzzards circle the yard, calling and searching. The bird call seems to approach and recede with one of the birds, the other apparently concentrating on its search. I would think that the calling bird is the female, trying to attract the lost fledgling with this sound, while the male intends to find it with the sharpness of its eyes.

The vegetable plot is at the far end of the large garden. Standing there and facing the slopes across the valley, one feels as if one had descended by parachute to this, the most beautiful place on earth. The parachute is still draped over a cherry tree. The broken twigs and branches that have been knocked down are waiting to be picked up. From there one's gaze always turns towards the west, even in the afternoon. The eye is always drawn back to the place where the sun will set. Places at which something withdraws from this world are also places that hold the eye. From where I stand I can easily hear Jack's car. A clump of trees blocks the view of the road, only the entrance to the yard is visible. The car trails a cloud of dust. Passing through the archway, the engine falls silent, the door slams shut. Then the whistling can be heard, interrupted by calls that search for me. I'm going to let Jack call a bit longer, if this is how he comes home.

When we then return to the house together, there is Kathleen sitting with her back against the wall.

Her head is tilted back, her white throat exposed for caressing, for grabbing and choking. She is wearing her brick-red frock, the one in which she was painted by a friend. She must feel the coarse masonry against her shoulders. Kathleen's body always evokes in me associations with touching. She says, I much prefer places that are too hot over those too cold. And I'd rather be with people who love me too little rather than being suffused with love.

Let's go buy some chickens, Jack says in the house. Where? I ask. I know of a farmer, he says. Should we see if she would like to come along? I ask. Let her stay, he says. I want to be alone with you. - Where did you get the address of the farmer? I ask. At the market, he says.

There are four chickens. We bring them home in a large box with air holes. We give them the names of Donald Duck's nephews. Huey, Louie, Dewey. And the fourth one? Jack asks. Phooey, I say.

For Jack this life on the farm is an adult's return to the images of childhood. Everything seems smaller, gives him a sense of greater strength. I'm afraid of the large opening through which the hay is thrown from the hayloft down into the stable. Jack leans on the bricked ledge of the stable and, standing on the tips of his toes, repairs the power line at the farthest reach of his hands. I try to do everything right, to pick up where I had left off with these stories of rural life. When I drive the tractor for the first time, I immediately hate the levers that are so hard to operate; when the meadow dips sharply, I'm afraid of rolling the tractor over. Clearly and as if he had just said them behind my back and not more than twenty years ago, the cautions of my father fill my mind. Children fall from tractors, their legs are cut off. Adults are crushed by overturning agricultural machinery. More than the tractor, heavy and unwieldy as it is, I hate my father and his fearfulness. I think of Chinese women who can only take little steps with their bound feet. My father, the hard taskmaster for the prison of my upbringing.

Have you ever seen your father cry, asks Kathleen. On the table she has the beginnings of a letter. Yes, I say. That was at the death of his father. He put down knife and fork and pressed the napkin with the monogram against his face. His face remained hidden behind the cloth for a long time, I began to think that he would suffocate and became frightened, but I could not say anything. His shoulders twitched. His clenched fingers were white. My grandmother, now a widow, had wrapped her handkerchief around her forefinger, as if it were injured. With this bandaged finger she kept dabbing at her eyes. My mother, as if guilty, looked down on the table. She always seemed to feel guilty for everything. – And your grandfather? asks Kathleen. What was he like? – I remember that when he took a break at noon he often had the angora tomcat on his belly. He sat in the armchair with his legs spread wide, wearing knickers and long stockings, his white-maned head supported on his broad, bulging neck, his face closed in at the mouth, hardened into a cynical pose, and on top of his belly, the white patriarch of a tomcat, lifted up and down by my grandfather's breathing. – Did you miss him? asks Kathleen. Actually, yes. The tomcat now sprawled in the empty armchair. A leftover attribute. He reminded everyone of grandfather.

I wrote a letter to my father, says Kathleen.

My dearest father, this morning I received a letter from you, in which you tell me you have instructed the bank to pay me all of 200 schillings a month instead of 150. I scarcely know how to express my deepest gratitude for his unparalleled generosity.

There is a fair in the village. A mass is read at the opening. Where shall I turn when I am stricken with grief and pain? Like the figurines on a music box, the faithful twist and turn to all sides until a beam of grace delivers them and releases them into the din and bustle of the fair. Now it is not the sinners who roast in hell, but only mass-produced chickens frying in oil, giving off obnoxious fumes. Rosie shoots and wins a flower made of crêpe paper, which she then stuffs into Jack's breast pocket. Jack asks me if I would like to go on the merry-go-round. He knows very well that I do not. Then he steps onto a swing with Rosie and pulls away, making a large arc across the sky with her. From one of the show tents can be heard the shouting of a clown, children screaming a reply, and much louder still the next question of the clown.

It's all going much too fast for me, I missed a cue somewhere, something important, perhaps right at the beginning. The thought of snuggling close to Jack's body, our limbs entwined, inhaling each other's breath, a confused jumble of desires, slowly the day slips away. I wish that this would go on forever. But wishes are loose and pervious, they readily tear open. We always seem to just happen upon things, there is no beginning. Rosie tells us how on certain occasions her aunt sneezes curtly, like a child, and to me that seems more important than anything I have ever written.

The only way to exist is to go on and to try to lose yourself, says Kathleen. I shake my head. I don't want to lose myself, I say. I want to find myself. And to stay there. – What I mean, says Kathleen, is that one should try to get as far away from this moment as possible. – She leans back, leans her thin body against the back of the chair, lets her arms hang loose.

Sometimes I think that I can get this story done in a week or two. I have carried this story around with me, as they say. But I am too heavy with it, too ripe. And the story contains too much of me as well. We have to part, and then each of us will continue with a new and separate form. In a few days, it seems to me, everything could be written down. But I know that it hasn't ever been this way. Who could possibly be interested in the uneven textures from which such a story evolves? The effort ought not to show; the smell of sweat, of the sweat of lethargy, of dogged sitting at a desk is repulsive. Who would care to know that? It is said that linden blossoms for tea should be picked no later than the fourth day after they open.

This year we missed the blooming of the linden tree. But there are varieties of mallows and wild thyme. My garden is cultivated with loving care, and the joy and praise magnify even the smallest result that it produces. Today I very consciously take in every smell and fragrance. Fine, finely layered weather is with us today, the herbs blaze in the sun. I read somewhere that the blue blossom of the borage can be candied. The weeds can easily be pulled up and slip out of the soil. I pull up the roots that hold the ground together, I can well imagine how the pain itches just a bit. On some days everything can be grasped with just the right touch, the soil arches up to meet my fingers. I feel the fine weather on my face, it feels so very good. To brush the rust from the iron fence, or to run barefoot in the crusted tracks of the tractor. A bluejay breaks into laughter, repeats itself, then its voice falls silent in the heat of the day. The heat of the day. One need only call everything by another name.

Brimming to the lips, to the eyelids with images that shift and slide and engage each other and yet hold the promise of solid ground, turn off all the small talk by people who can't help their talking, race up the stairs to the desk, put it all down on paper, if only it is caught right. Or excuse yourself and leave a room, the apron makes it credible, it looks like work, an abrupt departure. Or perhaps Kathleen finally appears in the late morning to brew some tea, her toes in her sandals are white with cold, she has forgotten to put on stockings, and in the house it is always cool. With her hand on the teakettle she waits for the water to boil, her head always turned away from us. She is in a story, the sentences freshly laid out in her mind. We must then be quiet and not stir, we must wait until she is gone with this festering intrusion in her mind. No questions. She would rather die of starvation than decide what to have for dinner. And people don't die of starvation in a day.

I met the man some weeks ago. He is so cautious when he backs his car out of the yard. Sometimes I despise him for that, he would risk nothing for me. He puts his hand on my hand, moves the skin back and forth around my wrist, turns my hand over, reads in silence what is yet to become of us.

Nobody wants to know about us. On one occasion his wife comes into the room, looks at us. Our hands jerk apart, that's exactly how it was meant. Later we press against each other and embrace, we are embarrassed, we can't think of anything else. When we have found a bed, we can hear hammering and pounding from a neighboring farm, something is being repaired. Farmers, it seems, can't work quietly; things are forever being struck. I don't think that I really understand the work of these people. The rooster that we've had a few days now crows behind the house. I'm reminded of the time when he wanted to fly down from the window of the hayloft to follow the chickens who all had already dared the plunge and were pecking at scraps from the dishwater. Several times the rooster got set to jump, flapped his wings and finally fell the few yards with a pathetic scuffle, landing with a screech on the back of a chicken that then tried to free itself. Pompously he then waddled off, looking as if he had amply soiled his trousers. We call him Hemingway. The man with whom I'm in bed notices my distractedness. The worst thing he could do now would be to get up and get dressed. On the next day I meet him while shopping. With tense arms I hold my basket in front of my knees, meet his eyes, my gaze firms up, I again know what I want. I can't afford to come home all confused, he says. – Don't make a witch of me, I say. – We avoid meeting again.

What do you think of when you hear this scream? Do you believe your language to have grace and beauty, its sounds to be so marvelous? Do you remember the wing of the dragonfly floating on the surface of the pond? It floats there as if it were in love with itself. That is what you don't really know about. To love yourself, to be tender to yourself. Not to transform your desires into tepid concessions. When you hear this scream, where do your legs take you? To get the wing of the dragonfly from the pond? Do you sometimes lie on your back with legs spread wide, soaking up the warmth of the sun? Can you write about it? Does your language have the necessary words? Can it tell you of your love for yourself?

My dear Victor, writes Kathleen. For several days now you have been on my mind, thank you for what you have done. I am in bed and not at all well. But despite the lingering pains, I can write, and write quickly. I long for a brief letter from you. Outside my window there is an ashen sky, the cold of winter. I hear my little maid moving about, and then in the quiet I listen to the wind. Such poverty! It makes me write about the warmth of summer, about happy love and cafés, all the things that make life to me. Today I had a lovely postcard from my concierge in Paris – hand-painted roses as big as cabbages – and so many of them they simply fall out of the vase! Always your friend, Kathleen.

Why do you write him these letters of December now, in summer? I ask her. Soon it will be August, rose petals will wilt, just before then we will collect them to be put in a large bowl, as they do in England. – I really don't care for England, says Kathleen, I'm a stranger there, a foreigner. We seem to grow apart, the wild colonial and these lackluster inhabitants. They lack the most important qualities, they are not ardent, warm, careless, lively, not spendthrifts of themselves. – You must be tired, I say. Why don't you go on back where you come from. To your rumpled bed. That's where you torment your dreams, lose a child. There on the wall hangs a pale little skeleton representing Christ. We are in France, they are trying to convert you. It is all in vain, it will come to nothing, you won't get to write your novel since you can hardly manage yourself. – You know almost nothing of me, says Kathleen. You confuse everything, the little that you do know. France, Switzerland and Italy, as I know them, these names of women and the fragments I write. You're wearing silk stockings with a butterfly worked in just above the heel, and it reminds you of something, you hesitate, you can't reply when questioned. That's how they always kept you in check. Certainly neither one of us has the right to lay blame, let's leave that aside. Let's always begin where something is about to meet us at full force. Your Achilles tendons, that's where the black butterfly hovers, borne by your every step.

One evening Jack and I go to the pub. There is a public talk on poisons in the household. The state official in charge of environmental matters makes an appearance, in a few weeks the local elections will be held. A few teachers are there, the director of the local farmers' cooperative, some young people, but the biology instructor did not come, people say that he had tickets for a musical this evening. The director of the bank, who is a member of the cooperative association, is hospitalized with an intestinal condition. The community physician briefly tells the pharmacist of the results of the intestinal endoscopy. At the next table some farmers break into laughter, one of them is drunk and is being teased. The waitress puts a pile of cutlery on the table, they all fish out what they need. They agree to eat a goulash soup, that would not disturb the speaker unduly. When the men suck the foamy head off the beer, they look as if they have no teeth. When things get to be too boring, one of them pushes his glass to the center of the table and sets it down hard. Important questions in the following discussion are met with jokes. The director of the local farmers' cooperative grandly motions with his arm across the table and claims the world for himself. When Jack tries to say something, no one listens to him. Besides me, Rosie is the only other woman at the table.

Don't you sometimes miss talking about literature, about writing? asks Kathleen. – But I have you, I say and know that at this moment she is beyond my reach. But I have you, I repeat. You are the only one to whom I can really tell things the way they are. – The way they really were, she corrects me. I touch her wrist, she withdraws her hand and puts it in the dark lap of her dress. If everything had to be tied into such strict relationship, she says, if the order of things were so important because it separates cause from effect, could you then still throw your arms up in the air? Could you forget what you want to forget? – I don't want to forget anything, I say. I want to know the measure of my hatred, my anguish. – There are many ways of killing someone, she says. I know some of them. But I'm still alive. I'm still alive and do sketches and write letters to my friends, all of them consigned to their compartments. There they sit and wait until Kathleen Beauchamp feels like tending to them. I delight in writing these letters, though I don't feel well and am getting older without accomplishing anything substantial. Or at least I sometimes have the feeling that my work is worthless, if indeed I can work at all! – She looks at me. Oh, I'm unfit, she says. I can't write. I can't write what will happen next. I can't write anything at all anymore, nothing, nothing, not a word, never again, it's all gone! – Her mouth falls open, she sobs and coughs, she's sitting on the floor and buries her head in her hands, she trembles all over, withdraws beneath her arched back. I kneel down to her, put my hands on her back, feel my warmth as it spreads through the palm of my hands. I want to comfort her, quiet her, restore her health. I want to restore her health. She must continue to write, to be able to breathe without fear. She has to forget Jack, her husband.

Is it a danse macabre? I ask her. Are you wearing your clothes? Are you showing them your body? The syphilis or gonorrhea that it all began with? The bangs of your bobbed hair, the smell of your bedridden body, of chamomile and long-faded desire. Saliva and blood, what else, I'm beginning to feel indifferent about you. But all the same I would still like to caress and comfort you.

We are taking a walk in the cemetery, Jack tries to remember what he once knew about the origins of family names. The cemetery sits on a rise, at the upper end there is a chapel in which the requiem mass is read, one can see the red sanctuary lamp. We walk up the hill, a man on a bicycle overtakes us, rides up the middle path towards the hilltop, doffs his hat, waves and calls out, hello there, Ludmilla, no time today, be back tomorrow, and without getting off he turns around and rides back down. That's old Weginger, says Jack. They've already told me about him; every day he visits the grave of his wife, he often talks to himself on his bicycle. – Jack, I'm afraid to be alone in the house, I say. Soon it will be fall, Jack will go to Vienna and I will be alone one night every week. I'm afraid of the older men who talk to themselves and have a lot of time on their hands, or have no time, I'm afraid of someone who has something to prove to himself. We'll have the telephone by then, Jack says, you can just call, you can get Hans if you're afraid. – Nobody mentions Kathleen, she is not present. Kathleen was the one with the dark dress, the illusion on the stairs, the imagined rustle at the end of the hallway. Aren't you afraid to be alone? they ask. Oh yes, I say. Very much. No, I'm not afraid. At night I see the red glow of a cigarette in the bushes, somebody is there lying in wait, I try to outwait him without moving, then I steal up the stairs, have another look, the light came from the neighboring farm. One can telephone of course, but how often, once every week? One does not want to waste one's credibility on a mistake, there is something to be lost; all too quickly they could say: she's always afraid, don't pay any attention.

In the evening there is a thunderstorm. We stand in the open and feel the wearied day's sweat. The thunderstorm calls out its signals and rambles about the skies. We feel apprehensive, dread to go to the bed we share, our bodies then withdraw to the bulwark of the nightwear. I read, Jack sets the alarm clock and with closed eyes keeps silent. The desire to fall asleep quickly as soon as it is dark, to take along to this edge of consciousness the characters from a story about others. In my dream I'm going into a pharmacy in white clothes, actually in shabby rags, looking seedy. Out of charity they give me some cellulose fabric, a mercy gift. At the entrance is a man in white, a doctor perhaps, I don't know him. He leaves with me and I ask him, do you think that I'm a vagrant? He nods. There you're wrong, I say. I'm really quite someone else. Surely he will recognize me, later on. I'm a beggar from Calcutta in white clothes, and then I embrace the man whom I don't even know, only his eyes seem familiar to me, an instructor from my student days had those eyes, and I'm a beggar who takes whatever comes her way. Skin on skin, with a cut the image stops.

Every season releases me anew, exposing all that I don't know, facing me into a headwind. Rosie is standing with Jack on the slope across the valley, they are putting up the sheep fence for the second summer pasture. I watch them, they are two little people carrying out some task together. With wide, sweeping blows Jack pounds the fence posts into the ground, Rosie holds the posts, her upper body bent back, she is not afraid, she lets Jack's strength come crashing down, holds on steadily, knows exactly what she wants. Jack buys two sheep from Rosie, but they stay in her flock. Now Jack and Rosie are sitting on the meadow, they are tired, they watch the sunset, I wave to them, they don't see me. Next day she shows us how to shear sheep. She presses the shears, which look like a gardening tool, into my hand, a swath of the animal's greasy hair bulges over my hand, folds over at the bevel. When the sheep kicks about, Rosie presses the sheep's front legs together and Jack holds it at the back and makes some calming sounds. At the wall of the barn is a rabbit hutch, little compartments, the rabbits pucker up their noses, they look as distraught as always. After a while I get a cramp in my hand. When I pass the shears on to Jack, my hand glistens with grease.

Kathleen says, let's quickly think of all that is important to us. I think I'll fall out of this world if I don't know that. You start, she says. Writing, I say. Men. Writing, men, illness. – Jack, says Kathleen. – Jack, I say. Illness. Writing. Why did you call him Jack? – She smiles wryly, all of a sudden I know her less than any other woman I have ever met. Her brown eyes, set a bit too far apart. Such eyes, this can never become my face. What's your hurry? she asks.

The greatest challenge has to do with the marvelous development of things, I say. To show how it all came to be. To be able to do that, you have to know yourself. Later, when Jack says, but we were so very happy together, he will have understood nothing. – And after you have told all that you know, says Kathleen, the story will close tight. You will then no longer be able to get into it.

I whisper the name of the cat, stroke it under the chin with one finger. The cat raises its head, shows its white throat, the thin line of its mouth. Her purring begins softly, only gradually does she let herself be won over. The irises of her eyes open and close like a kaleidoscope. She runs her tongue along her back, bites, grooms, shakes herself, throws up a matted hairy ball, continues to work its throat a little. Then everything is still, a quiet waiting. Listening with lips parted, a conspiracy everywhere. The birds have disappeared, have taken their song away from this land. The neighbors hold their breath, I seem to hear a distant stillness that is different from the stillness here. Finally a horse neighs, for some time keeps to a high pitch which makes the tension unbearable, unbearably beautiful, until the sound slides into the lower registers of the neck. Then there is thumping against the wooden walls of the shelter. Sometimes the horses race wildly across the fields, circle the farm buildings, noisily crash through the corn which is already waist high. They cause damage, which the farmer will more than recover from the insurance. Then, after calm returns, there is satisfied snorting, bathing their nostrils in the evening breeze.

If you could get into the habit of writing daily, says Kathleen, it would be more than I was ever able to do. I always tried it, again and again, but I could never keep it up for long. Whatever happens in the course of each day, seize it and put it down! Today a man looks at you with his eyes, eyes that pick you out among all the others and for a moment want to have you all to themselves. Then he drops back into his timidity, resignation, into the little farewell. You, however, have seen it and will take note, without shame or hesitation. You have seen it and won't forget it. Sometime or other you will remember this glance and you will be grateful to your shameless memory.

Do you love your life, Kathleen? I say. These thrusts at your heart that you are so proud of afterwards? Do you know the feeling of having a biography? The taste of apples, one's feet braced against the legs of the chair.

Not far away lives an artist. He makes a living from selling paintings to the few industrialists of the area; they make good Christmas presents for business associates. We meet him at a concert in a mansion an hour's drive away. He hasn't read my books, offers no excuse, I feel at ease with him. He invites us to visit him, perhaps I could write the text for his exhibition catalog. I say, I don't even know you, who knows whether I will like your work. He is wearing a pullover that his wife knitted for him before she left him. She now lives in Switzerland, he hardly ever hears from her.

I'm playing one of my favorite records, "Born in the U.S.A." by Bruce Springsteen. Kathleen stands in the doorway of her room and watches me dance to the music, which is turned up to full volume. I whoop and shout, working on the highway, working on the highway, and glory days, well, they'll pass you by. My body throbs, detaches itself with the beat, takes on a pulse of its own, my hands pluck at ecstasy somewhere above my head. During a slower song Kathleen takes a few tentative steps towards me, steps with indescribable gentleness out of the room in which she does her writing, the waiting room for her smaller and larger pains, finds the pulse of the music and glides into its beat. Her shoulders move, her arms trace out what she feels in her heart, there she is in this world, she's alive, I burn with desire for her. I got a bad desire, I'm on fire, we mouth these words with the music. I had something going, mister, in this world. After all, this is her language, the voices in her head. They now spread all over her body, she has this sensuous language in her whole body. Her face, her features that are usually a little severe are now the features of a stranger, yet so familiar, so much of the woman who loves life, this body moving to its inner beat, showing me what it is that I am doing, repeating for me and showing, showing and repeating.

Born in the U.S.A. she then says, we sit on the floor, sweaty and drained. I bring her a towel, she seems preoccupied as she dries herself, born in the U.S.A. – I sometimes long for America, I say and read off the names from the record cover. Roy Bittan, synthesizer, piano, background vocals. Clarence Clemons, saxophone, percussion, background vocals, Gary Tallent, bass, background vocals, Bruce Springsteen, lead vocals, guitar, Max Weinberg, drums. Do you understand that, Kathleen? She nods. She has such pallid shoulders. I can't keep the thought of her death out of this room. If she were alive, I would embrace her, link fingers with her, stroke my feet along hers, I would learn to accept her illness. Nonetheless, I would be afraid to get too close to her, and she would demand that I endure this fear. Not courage and resolve, not fearlessness, what she wants of me is to subdue the fear of fear. Come, she would say. I'm not going to spare you, I'm going to infect you, yes. Everything about me is going to infect you, my coughing and writing and waiting and the gaze that can see through a man. But I demand of you that you don't take it too lightly. You will not be able to leave out anything. In your story about me, which really is a story about you, both of us will blend and wholly merge. – Some of your stories were never completed, I say.

If only you had a clear head, says Kathleen. I'm exhausted, I'm being stretched over a wooden hanger by something inside me, I'm no longer in command of my body, I'm going to bed now. I hope I can sleep. I wish you a clear head for your story, which you will now write as night sets in. You will sit there and slice off the sentences. I will feel envy and kiss you on the forehead, as if I were older than you. While in fact I'm so much younger than you, having died almost sixty years ago. In four years you will have reached my age and endured the worst fear, you could then also be fatally ill. I'm exhausted, I'll talk a while longer, I'll postpone the darkness, turning over in bed, the search for a position where the burning pressure on my chest abates a little. I'm exhausted, I don't need you any longer, I feel far removed from you, as if we had never as much as shaken hands. Your hand, I quite know it, it touches the hand of the man you are pursuing, it moves up and down so deliberately and searches for the calm that it surely must be possible to find somewhere. You have a tender hand, for me as well, and when I lie awake at night I miss it. Your hand writes with its forlorn fingers, sad, thin, pale. I'm exhausted, I talk too much, I'm afraid of being alone, I won't beg you to come to me. You long for your artist, for Jack, as I longed for Jack when he did not come, when he did not come to Italy and France, which you always confuse and which you take for something other than what they were, simply two countries in the south, nothing more. Jack, my bad marriage, the stolen phrases, this damp evening in London, much of it seems inverted, backward. I'm afraid, I'm so exhausted, I'm afraid of death, I really would like you to know everything and then to give me courage with a good thought, which I won't forget when the door closes behind me. The closed doors, and the doors to the antechambers through which we must pass. Your dream and mine, your eyes puffed up from being alone and from a refusal to accept. I'm exhausted, I'm so very exhausted.

In his drawings Friederike, the wife of the artist, often wears laced-up boots, sometimes the kind of woolen stockings that ballet dancers wear, a paraphrase of the Lautrec women. He gives her large breasts, blobs without shape. Again and again the artist drew his wife this way, a shapeless body that insolently sits in an armchair, legs spread apart, muddled scribbling around her lap, a bunched-up skirt pushed high, belly folds, her upper body sometimes in a scoop-neck pullover, her arms at the side on the armrests. Sometimes she has the face of an old man, matted down hair parted in the middle, one eyebrow painted with a curl, a large nose with no make-up, a nose that is a lifelong burden. The artist stands next to me without saying a word, shrugs whenever I look at him. I have the impression that my visit means little to him. He didn't ask about the text for his catalog, and I don't want to raise this matter either. I try to conceal the fact that I find him attractive. He smokes, I have hunger pangs. I sit in an old upholstered chair and look on as he works, look at the drawings of his wife. If you need a great noise now, then let the noise burst out, says Kathleen. Write in this din, let it holler and shout!

The artist arouses my curiosity, pushes back my age and puts my dreams in between. On leaving I touch his wrist, we are alone as always, I'm inclined to agree with what the people in the village say about him. He looks at me, that look seems so calm, he can't be feeling a lot, but then I sense what he is trying to tell me. I stand at the car, leaning with my elbow on the open door, time retreats with such a heavy foot, perhaps there is someone waiting for me at home. Every minute drops heavily out of our shared cache of time. Sometimes it seems to me that he invented all this, the story about his wife in Switzerland, he was never married. It may occur to him that I'm after life stories that are compressed into such pithy events. He goes to the bedroom with me, shows me the lingerie, the clothes that she had not taken along. She ran off, an abrupt departure, there was no other way. No answer.

I am dreaming that I see myself in a mirror, my features have changed, my complexion is that of an old woman. With alarm I notice that the hair on top of my head is white, short and thinning. By degrees I fall into a new life, a life that can't go on much longer. I know the meaning of this hair, my scalp shows through everywhere. Someone says, you have aged. Who is speaking English here, I think angrily.

Aren't you afraid of the accusations afterward? Kathleen asks in the morning. I ponder this for a while. No, I then say. After all, it's all done. I have learned to cry about missed opportunities. I had neglected to breathe the air when it tumbled down from the mountain and could not yet do me any harm. – To give in to fear leads to the greatest concessions and failings, says Kathleen. One should never yield to fear. I watched you as you danced, you were beautiful, you were strong. I loved you, nothing could frighten you, you had no fear, not of me, not of your work. Keats wrote to his fiancée, not yet from Rome, not yet so ill as to be near his death, but ill nonetheless, he wrote, better to be imprudent and movable than prudent in rigidity.

Let's see, who are you now, the artist asks. Are you the writer who notes down the things she experiences? Or are you all yourself, are we both alone with you or is there someone who writes along in your head? It drives me crazy that I can't know this and never will. Will a character in your next book say what I'm now telling you? – Why don't you paint me? I ask him. Why don't you paint me in the nude? My face with my nude body, a nude with face, identifiable, a woman with a recognizable face. Don't you know that I would then cease to be the woman that you have painted? That I will then recede and lose myself in all the female bodies, all the nudes that have ever been painted and in all women who look at your painting, while I stand beside them? Do you have so little trust? I love the person who says, write everything about me, write down everything that you know and invent, do your work and stay with me. I would wish to meet such a man.

Look at the bird on the ridge of the roof, says Kathleen. When it flies away, when it suddenly plummets and gathers its momentum out of the fall and darts away – that's what it's like to write. I'm going down, down, down, down, she says. – Jack and I, we hesitate and postpone the winter. We would rather be cold a little longer and overestimate the late sun, we are not dressed for the cold, it takes a great deal of energy to look each other in the eye. It is damp in the room where the apples are pressed for the cider, the clay floor is firmly packed. Cobwebs and sawdust stick to the old cider press, a distinctive smell. You should put on a pullover, says Jack. Why don't you do something about the cold! Tomorrow I'm going to harrow the fields. The next morning I'm on the harrow as a live counterweight; while driving, Jack turns around on the tractor like a circus rider. He sees my contorted face, I'm supposed to balance the harrow as it bounces over the ground, I hang on with hands and feet and imagine losing my footing and stepping through the bars of the harrow as it moves on.

I write as never before. With the booming music of Springsteen in my head, in my foot a lingering feeling, a little forgotten already, I don't know, is it still there or not, a sense of the leg of the man who sat next to you recently, I was quite taken by him, that's who you need now, take him, or at least what he gives of himself. It is the artist I always visit when my head is empty, come, take me along. Writing as never before, I sense that I'm right in the middle, at the center where something important is taking shape. I write, I tremble, I lie on my bed with neither purpose nor future; no longer to wait, slowly to steal away from the way things are, to think nothing, not to think that I want to think of nothing. I fall asleep and wake up, in between a deep breath, I can go on writing until the next little end. To hold on to an emerging fondness, to accept what is offered of tender hands, of the give and take of desire, to seize, to know a fullness, to draw in the air and the smell of this man, the smell, the smell of this man; let it for once happen without words, wait to be touched.

Write yourself into a murderous pace, says Kathleen and sneezes. Her nose looks red. – Write yourself into a pace that leaves time for nothing else, that leaves you almost breathless, that leaves you just enough air for breathing, as much as you need for the next few moments. But then when you have it, when you are in this murderous pace, then admit no fear, surrender, write yourself into it, write as best you can, write for your life. Don't consent to pain, to the rope knotted around your chest, the stabs in your back, surrender to illness and be unaccountable, these thoughts alone must be put down on paper, that is life, that is strength, that is your work. Blaze and burn, play the relentless music of the American, working on the highway, and overtake him, overtake him, overtake him, write so you'll surge ahead, write through it all.

Now and then I rise early and take pictures of the morning as it emerges through the mist. The rose-lacquered window frames of the stable, the old circular saw that is no longer in use and that blocks one of the driveways like some giant spider, its serrated cutting blade like an arched dorsal armor preparing for attack. The horses, dipping out of the mist like some dark figures out of a movie, have already been about, they have the shorter sleep, the large legs whose knobby knees guide the movements, the hoofs that part the mist and dankly pound it to smithereens. The sense of walking over one's turf. I already feel at home here and when I leave the artist I say, I'm going home and mean my own home where I've settled, I now live here, want to stay here. I throw the firewood that Jack has cut into the storage room, pile it up against walls, think to myself that this will be our winter, that this will be our warmth in our first winter here. I count the seasons, I can well imagine living here for many years. I believe that I've arrived. I've always trusted myself to be able to deal with my emotions better than Jack. If Jack deceives me, everything will collapse.

Kathleen, how are you getting along in your

room? I ask. Should we put in different furniture? Do you feel at home there? – Oh yes, she says. – One never knows how she means things. Oh yes, she says again. It's a lovely room. In the morning I can look across the corn fields, and in the evening they are still there. That's rather nice, don't you think? – She bursts out laughing. Kathleen, you are hard to get along with. You are a silly woman, you have your tricks with men, sometimes your writing is superficial, I could read enough of it to you, and you contribute absolutely nothing to this household. – I can't be a housewife, she says. Both of you know that. You know that. Now if I had a home, my own perfect place to draw the curtains shut and shut the door, a fire with its sweet fragrance, where I could quietly walk around and watch the play of lights and shadows: that would be fine, but living as I do...Do you know what manuka are? White blossoms, manuka, as in your dream, remember? Perhaps you also saw the whares of the Maoris, and the broom blossoms, the toi-tois waving in the wind. – I shake my head. All this simply blends into an exotic impression, no childhood with cicadas, dark-skinned nurses whose stories can sustain one for a lifetime. – It is a chaos, I say. I have everything in my head all at the same time, Rosie and Jack, this cursed couple, and you, Kathleen, as you sit around in your black dress and long for your home country that is so far away that none of us can do anything for you. Yes, everything is in my head at the same time, you and the two others and the artist, and where the right expressions for this are to be found, everything crowds together. And then I don't even know how you fit into all this. There seems to be a plot or is it fear, chance, there is something that brings you together, all of them and you.

All's well? asks Jack. He's calling from Vienna. In the breaks when neither of us has anything to say I hear him exhaling the cigarette smoke. I think of his lips and try to imagine what he might be seeing just now. It's raining quite heavily, I say, it hasn't let up. One of the windows in the living room downstairs has a leak, the water runs along the wall on the inside, in a very short time the towels that I put down are soaking wet. – I miss Jack, I feel lonely this evening, even long for the other evenings when we sit together and leave unmentioned all that is important, we drink tea and praise the mints that grow so quickly in the garden. When there is a passably good film on television, the mutual silence is refined somewhat, we laugh together, offhandedly extemporize the remarks of an interviewed passerby, see through the language of commentators on talk shows discussing politics and the global questions, just as long as we don't have to consider our own failings in facing the truth, in thinking the truth about us. We make plans for a future with others, without mentioning their names. Rosie carries much more weight than the artist, Rosie is strong, her imagination dangerous, her knowledge lives in a strong body. I long for a good life together with Jack. – At thirteen, says Jack, I was angry with Lex Barker, because he once played the role of an insurance salesman in a gray suit.

My legs are draped over the shoulders of the artist, he kneels before me, grasps my thighs and with a start pulls me closer, gives me no time, he looks at me as I close and then again open my eyes, he watches my every response, he watches my unfaithfulness, which is no longer adulterous since it lacks the force of commitment that would reach Jack, he watches me, tells me what I feel, draws me into oblivious excitement, gives me no time, finally wedges his head between my knees, presses my knees together, there is not much happiness to be had for us. – Write your story quickly, he says, as quickly as you know how, because later there will be no time for it. Hurry, gather up all you can grasp, wrap your twine around the story from all sides. Later you will fall in love, your head will be turned by a different smell, then you won't be able to get the scent of this story back again, that's why you have to write now, hurry, nothing is to distract you.

The horses drink water out of the bucket that I bring them, they press down hard on the bucket, so that I have to bend with it. They know I won't forget them when Jack is in Vienna. One time the brown mare kicks the black one in the neck, leaving a tear that requires stitches. A rope around the animal's nose supposedly lessens the pain. The horse stands there, wide-eyed, wants to throw back its head, with all his strength Jack holds the animal in place. The veterinary sutures a cannula to the wound around which it is to heal. There is terror in the eyes of the animal that could at any moment break loose and rip up the railing, stampeding over collapsing logs, a fall, anything could happen. For ten days the horse's injury is to be treated with a blue disinfectant.

For some time I try to work as a tutor. Sometimes I take the train to the next town, which has a high school, grade the homework on the way. I'm permitted to use one of the classrooms, even though I'm not on the teaching staff. At two o'clock I meet with my first student, a restless boy who in the afternoon still has the previous night in the corners of his eyes. After him comes the senior who already has his own car, then a pudgy girl who blushes every time she meets the dashing senior. Together we reread the texts that they did not understand in class that morning because they were so bored; I wonder at the stories about housewives at home, office workers sitting in their office, practice irregular verbs with them, give them little memory aids which I secretly find embarrassing in their silliness, try to explain the use of conditional clauses by finding situations that might occur in the life of these human beings, as they sit there indifferently, with the smell of chewing gum or beer about them.

Don't listen to well-meaning advice, you should now listen only to the dictates of your heart. Later there will again be time to be receptive to everything else, but now you must write down without fail all that lashes out in you, that sweeps you along; run, race, fly along, let it drag you along even when you are knocked down, just those few words yet to catch, you already have the road on your lips, dust and blood, but that too is part of it, belongs here. – Take it easy, don't be so hard on yourself, says the artist. I don't want it to be tough on you: but I can't tell you that I love you, I'm still – so much in a turmoil. I lost my wife, that is something larger than you, I can't tell you what you want to hear from me.

Do you know what I love about men? I ask Kathleen. I love it when after two or three years or even later they at last can talk about themselves. When out of a merry and half-drunken mood they suddenly look at you differently, get up and sit next to you, a little apart from the others, and begin to talk with you earnestly, directly and courageously talk about themselves, when they say, I did not have the courage to face things then, I was afraid, and I lost you. Oh yes, that's what I love about a man. – Let's not pretend to ourselves, says Kathleen. We could care less about men, we are only ever interested in one certain man, and then we are crazy about him. And he doesn't even care. He would rather go back to Paris or to New York and we aren't supposed to write him too many letters, right? – No, I say, that was later. That with New York or La Paz was much later.

Sunday evening, writes Kathleen. I have meant to write to you immediately after you left me. For a long time I felt that our goodbye had been final, that I had left too much unsaid. Yes, my desire is to bring all that I see and feel into harmony with a rare vision of life; if I do not achieve this, then I feel that my life has been utterly wasted. Although I don't have the least idea of how to really live, life has never been a bore for me, that I do know.

In the morning the deer comes to the fence, its fleet legs still glistening wet from the tall grass, the crow makes its din in the tree, nobody cares about the deterioration of the old chapel in which we keep the gardening tools. Rendezvous in the doorway, I saw you coming, it takes very little and I promenade my desires out in front of me, without them pulling me. I have never felt so strong, I say. But it takes all my strength, at every moment.

Tell me when you've had enough, says the artist. I don't ever want to have enough, I say. I want to live fully. When he says, your eyes just make me crazy, when he says, your gaze, this gaze which – then I listen to him, let it all melt into my memory, I want to keep and recite it word for word, his face in mind all the while. With brush in hand, like a cigarette, he sits crosslegged, his head slightly tilted to the side, as if unable to ever quite free himself of his appraising glance, he looks at me, gives me the impression that I am a woman he finds attractive, and calmly expresses his thoughts – that in itself is worth a great deal. I want to be able to ask for everything I desire, and my desire grows larger every day. – What other characters do you still want to invent? asks Kathleen. – I say, you are right, it is best to get away from this moment as far as possible, not because of my failing to live here and now, but rather because of my desire for what is yet to come. And then there is a story to be written about this other woman. Who is this other woman if not you, Kathleen? And who was Kathleen if not I? How long until I no longer have to explain who we are. Those who think they know me will be filled with shame or bewilderment or disappointment, I like to play with them as they played with me and did not in the least know how to meet my eye, especially this. They could not be reached, they then simply turned around and continued with their work. On these days with capricious weather, when the clouds so quickly push past the sun and dull the luster of things, it sometimes seems to me as if only fate is at home, playing through its options. My restlessness returns to itself. As we part the artist touches my wrist.

Kathleen pursues her compulsion, it is difficult to speak about diseases. One day it will all come to an end, she says. One day I will write no more letters. I can't think of anything else, the pigeons are asleep in the hayloft. – No one can explain her affliction to her, she cannot even read, after a few pages she puts every book aside, the print obstructs what she sees, makes her impatient, blots out her own writing. For days she struggles with the texts, but she reads as if she were playing the flute with a bow. What makes sense for others does not come together in her head. With great effort she is able to suppress her aggressions. Her life has been shunted to a siding. It takes all her energy to convince herself that nonetheless this too is life. This too. She is breathing water.

When the sheep are called, they come closer, like a dingy cloud, push together their lumpy bodies with spindly legs poking out underneath. They crowd around me, eagerly grab for the bread that I hold out for them. If one of the animals gets too large a piece, it chews and labors over it, head askew, and misses out on the rest. Cheek to cheek the moist snouts rummage through the sack that I brought, there is just room for two heads, they stupidly look up. I grasp one by an ear, say something gentle, try to stroke the flat, bony forehead. Then I chase the animals away, free myself from their warm circle. In the evening the moon is broken down the middle, a part of it is gone.

Jack and I have known each other for six years. Our life together is without skin, without tongue, without lips. At some point our lives are welded together the wrong way around. We have always had a great deal of time. The smoke from Jack's cigarettes discolors the curtains; our friends aren't thinking of getting married, if one of them does nonetheless, we laugh at him and wonder what could be the matter with him. We forever worry and rack the brains of others, we don't need therapy, we're not yet thirty. Jack never asks whether there is something going on with the artist, sometimes I suspect that he would be glad to be rid of me, it would be a relief for him and a deliverance. Everything is so much simpler on days when I have a headache. I complain that I'm little more than the catalyst and target of Jack's ill humor. I wish I could close my eyes and for Jack's sake not know what season it is outside. Instead we skirt our obstacles, the old pains that we brought along have nicely found their place, my longing sometimes reaches over the mountain. Then again the walks that find the trace of pain, the prolonged walking, walking around the fields, postponing the return home. Only the neighbors seem to know how to live and make it last.

When I was five my parents went to America for a year, I say. I stayed with my grandparents. I can't remember the farewell, only the last walk with my father and my mother. My father went first, my mother then followed. We took this last walk on a muggy afternoon. I have no recollection of being left behind or of finding myself alone. My grandfather established the link with my mother, he yielded to my clamoring and taught me how to write. At first I wrote in a booklet which I had put together out of four sheets of paper. The covers were made of glossy red cardboard. Then I wrote cards to my mother. I wrote on the back of pictures that my grandfather had taken of me. Postage then was one Schilling and forty-five Groschen, the stamp showed a woman in folkish costume with a large hat, she looked like some kind of mushroom. My spelling mistakes were proudly and dotingly discussed in the letters of my grandfather and mother. I was praised at length. Actually I only wrote out of longing, and only to my mother, who, as I perhaps sensed, had been given no choice in the matter. – Every artist cuts off his ear, says Kathleen, and nails it to the door for others to shout into.

These evenings with Victor were something quite special for me, says Kathleen. He was so much more clever than I. I felt like – I don't know what. I suddenly checked my perfume, you know? He made me feel so uncertain, I didn't know whether I seemed – just ordinary to him. – In a dream I once came to know what constitutes the essence of an erotic encounter, I say. I was standing in a garden, in my hand I had blossoms which I had just collected, there were little beads of sweat in the palm of my hand, gently moistening the filmy skins of the petals. It felt so light and beautiful in my hand. That was it. – With one finger Kathleen softly dabs behind her ear and tests the fragrance. I still have the perfume, she says. I know what you mean. Everything changes, the tender slight touch, ever so disguised, fleeing from place to place, where you're finally alone, the pupils dark; to hold one hand is almost too much, the smell, always the smell, I always fall for the smell, hold my face between collar and neck and draw in the smell of this man. There is no escape, the desperate attempts to gain time, a borrowed handkerchief. – Don't forget the farewells, I say. – She gets up, stands by the window, whispers something. Hey, that's no way to say good-bye. Then she begins to hum the words. She has tears in her eyes, her throat works up and down. Hey, she says. She holds onto the long lapels of her collar. How long can you fall, she asks. Perhaps I wouldn't have made it if the cats hadn't cried so. How long can one really fall? And do you think that one notices when one hits bottom? What if there is no bottom? If that were death: to continue falling?

It is getting colder, we put on our yellow raincoats, take long strides in our boots, look for the leak in the rotted eaves trough where the rainwater splashes onto the house. When the rain abates, Rosie appears on her horse. Jack struggles to get the uninjured mare out of the stable. I have no idea where the old saddle and bridle appeared from so suddenly. Jack on his mount, I'm reminded of a story that someone told me recently. A horse had bolted and had almost decapitated both horse and rider in the mad dash from God knows what. Rosie's braid, heavy and dark, hangs down her back. Jack is best forgotten. As time passes, Jack no longer seems to know who he is and who I am. I look after his abandoned work, his caution, his plans of yesteryear. When he looks at me, his glance surfaces from deep in his story, heavy with things left unsaid. He doesn't tell me anything, he keeps the beginning and the end to himself, he drives the car diagonally across the meadow and loses all strength if only I remain. I love him, I can't imagine a life without him. In my mind I speak with Kathleen, as I look after the two of them riding off. Let me have what I am lacking, I say to her.

How is that supposed to work out? asks the artist. Jack deceives you, you are unhappy, but you deceive him, too, and that is not supposed to count? – And your wife, I ask. What about her? – He gets up and drinks a glass of water. His lips are cold and moist, he pins my arms to my sides, he's been thinking far too long. Then he says, I bought the record that you like so much. I'll play it for you now. The other day, when you casually said that you might go dancing with Jack, I spent all night looking for you in the discos. Born in the U.S.A., right?

It's raining, perhaps for the last time before the snows come. At the beginning of summer, in the summer rain I am writing of the last rain for the year. I'm frightened of the snow that will block the roads and weigh heavily on the roof. And so I let it rain some more, even though it is too cold. It rains diligently, the birds with the yellow bellies, crossbills and brown wings don't yet sit by the window. They fly and dive through the skies bearing the warmth of the sun on their little heads, they take no notice of the frayed cloak of the birches. When I whistle a song or two, my lips begin to ache. A friend, a woman artist, had once given me a little Christmas bell made of brass. The bell dangles at the window by my desk. I have not heard from this woman in years. One always had to call her, invite her, convince her, she never said anything of her own accord. The last I heard of her, she was doing restorations in a church out in the country somewhere. The church was damp, my friend had kidney pains, but she clenched her teeth and persevered. I have not seen her again, sometimes I think that she committed suicide.

Kathleen lights a cigarette. I knew a Frenchman, she says. He wrote articles for a French newspaper. We were together a few times. I liked him very much, he had esprit. One morning he came into my room, sat down on the bed, I asked how late it was, surely much too early. He said he wanted to be with me, he'd been awake for two hours, showered and with suitcase packed. He was to leave in an hour. I was still so tired. He said, God, how you cling to your sleep! I turned my head to the side, was glad that this man's departure meant so little to me. How nice not to have to endure the pains of parting. How easy to feel invulnerable. As in sleep. – She exhales the smoke of her cigarette with great pleasure. One of her feet taps out the beat of some inaudible music. – When Jack goes away, I say, it is as if he were never going to return. They must have comforted me with false promises long ago, when my mother went to America; that she would soon return, by next week, it was always next week. Perhaps I learned from the succession of days and weeks the meaning of eternity. Eternity, that's never.

Marvelous days, Kathleen! Hold out your nose, draw in this musty dampness of autumn, the smells, see the cold sweating of the grasses which had been left unmowed, feel the smooth imprints of your feet in the loam, step down hard, give the earth under you a good kick, so that she will notice it and turn a little faster! Set a good pace, raise your arms and sail away through the upper window. Just marvelous days. Down by the road we come across a busload of children, they are on an excursion in this rain, they dart around in the bus, point obscene fingers, spread their fingers and laugh. Kathleen shakes her head. We go on to the gravel pit where abandoned cars stand around like oversized toys. For a long time she looks down to the bottom of the pit, doesn't say a word. I stand behind her, take her wrist, hold her tight. I feel the tenseness of her body in which she seems scarcely to survive. So little remains of her, her voice conveys her thoughts; I will keep asking questions to provoke her contradiction. We must make an odd monument, she, the taller of the two, standing in front. But it's unlikely that anybody sees us. Nobody is looking for people around here at this time. I'm reminded of a postcard that Jack once sent me from Disneyland. Two Mickey Mouse figures in front of Neuschwanstein castle, which is dissolving in a reddish dusk, the black heads with the large ears are shown from behind, each with a hand in a white glove on the other's back.

I know so little about Jack, I say. – Yes, says Kathleen. I always wanted to ask him, what are you thinking about? Can one ever know? No. There is no point in asking. And yet if I did not ask, I could not be certain that he was not thinking of someone else, someone in particular. But if I did ask, how could I know whether he was telling the truth? She pulls her woolen blanket tighter. – I love Jack, I say. I can see him there, as we stand in a church where a friend plays the organ; Jack has his eyes closed, behind his eyelids he looks deep inside himself, he stands there like a blind person, his head raised to the light, absorbing the warm images which would vanish if he were to open his eyes. In the bareness of his face lies the answer to many questions, but all I can ever do is to surmise. – What do you want? asks Kathleen. – What do I want? I repeat. Oh, Kathleen, do you remember long ago, when you only wanted to write about your own country? The forming of recollections, the pleasure in arranging the biography. One takes vengeance on events by interpreting them.

One time Heinz pays a visit. Heinz is a biologist, a food specialist, who works for the Ministry for Health and Environmental Protection. He tests for cadmium content in grains of rye. For some time now he has been separated from his wife; together with a woman he writes articles for technical journals. Sometimes one of them is invited to participate on a television panel, then the other proudly calls to ask whether one has seen the show. At breakfast Heinz and his colleague laugh and casually mention that they had messed up the sheets, do we mind. For Jack that's fine. My answers are curt, I refuse to be drawn in. Heinz wants to know whether he might be able to get the cooperative to stock phosphate-free detergents. Jack says that on the way to the village they could stop off at Rosie's, there's a relevant article in the newspaper of the farmers' association. After breakfast Lena insists on taking the bread, marmalade and milk into the pantry. You've got ants in there, she says. They can make life difficult.

Heinz likes to take pictures. There I am in front of the bookshelves, at my desk, holding my hand to my chin, my forehead, I sense the power of a full gaze. Lena says, you look so pale, you're working too hard in this place, you are just not used to that. – The artist calls, he has cut his finger. Kathleen seems to be the only one who knows what she wants. In the evening Jack drives our guests back to Vienna.

Later on, when I see the artist, the music makes me sad. He begins to tell me about his trip to Prague. I was there with a woman, he says. We had to wait a long time at the border, it was August, we opened the doors, chased out the flies, walked around the car. On the horizon a tractor plodded across the field. The restroom of the last service station in Austria was filthy. The entrance went through a shed in which tires were piled high. Bright-colored children's clothing hung on a line, the clothespins were much too big. The key to the toilet door jammed. The border guards stood at some distance and checked the papers of an Italian couple. Their car was red and old, a Fiat. An older man and a young woman who could be his daughter. When we finally arrived in Prague, we were accosted on the street by a woman who had a room for rent. Twenty minutes from downtown. We preferred a hotel. We then lay in a large double bed, the sheets smelled fresh, we felt quite elated. Prague, Prague! We loved this city, even before we had a closer look at it. I hadn't been to the East Bloc in years; the woman, her name was Brigitte, had never been. We visited the old Jewish cemetery, the synagogue, the memorial to Theresienstadt, the exhibition of drawings done by children at the concentration camp. We fell silent. That was Prague. – He lights a cigarette. I feel as if I'm ill and somebody caringly and a little helplessly is paring my nails.

I dream that I am caught in a conflict. A young man, who was still at school, had been unjustly treated. He had been identified from a newspaper picture as a participant in a demonstration. The principal of the school had the picture copied and distributed to all teachers. I, a tutor, confronted the others and screamed. I screamed at them. On the photo the boy's face could be clearly recognized, the hair style, the glasses, he wore a striped shirt. He stood among others, looked vulnerably and in good faith straight into the camera. Diagonally in front of him there was an older man who was just giving a speech. He wore a scarf around his neck, a watch could be seen on his wrist, his hand partly in his trouser pocket. In the other hand he held a book from which he seemed to quote without actually looking at it. I stood in the hallway of a school where I did not belong to the staff and screamed, screamed against the misuse of this picture, against the stupidity, the fear, against the false submissiveness and conformity, against my fear of losing my love if I should withhold my submissiveness. – Submissiveness to whom? Kathleen asks.

It is such strange delight to observe people and to try to understand them, Kathleen writes. Yet, when I am overcome by despair, all this turns to ashes and becomes so intolerably bitter that I feel it never can be sweet again. But it is and then you explore these things and detach yourself from them and after the ferment has subsided you write about them.

2

Winter will no longer be denied. How long is she going to stay, asks Jack and motions with his head toward the ceiling. She is going to stay as long as you keep seeing Rosie, I think to myself. Before dropping off to sleep, a few sentences occur to me, which I should write down. Is there any importance to what we do, is it important? asks Kathleen from her room. Her hands are beautiful, I love her hands, a difficult question to answer. Yes, I say, the last words, these important last words before nightfall, that's when you should tell Jack that you love him and that your love's witness will come with the break of dawn. – She shakes her head. Go to bed, I say, you need your sleep for the journey, you are so overwrought today, you moved ahead a few days and now you lie awake to fill in the time, without sleep, without writing, your eyelids tick off the seconds. Every few seconds your eyes fall shut. – In her winter coat and with her two suitcases Kathleen is off to the south.

Everything ought to be permitted, I think, while Jack types his word lists. I reproached him for looking after the farm and nothing else, for neglecting the students, for doing little research, for doing no research at all. – And you, he says. And I, I say, I'll be finished with my story one day, and not before. – Who is going to earn our keep? asks Jack. Why don't you get a teaching job? Why do I have to teach classes that don't in the least interest me? – Everything ought to be permitted, I think to myself.

When winter arrives at last, it snows for days, filling up the hollows, making bridges where there are none, softening edges, slowly and without end the snow keeps falling. The sky has drawn in close, we are often alone, I wait for Jack, as always, and I miss Kathleen. In winter one manages, but the transitional seasons, autumn, spring, they bring on festering sores, infections, the threat of collapse. In winter our writing holds the world at bay, gives strength to our friends.

Jack borrowed Rosie's tractor; with the heavy, dark-red snowplow he pushes the snow to the side until he gets stuck and has to back up, then takes a renewed run at this second landscape draped over the old. He waves to me, dances, hops around on the seat, shouts something which I don't understand, he shakes his head, it was not important. I shovel the paths to the barn and the chicken coop. The air is vigorous, smells fresh and as yet has no story of its own. I sometimes bruise the ground with my shovel. The chickens poke crazy messages into the snow. When the telephone rings, I don't get to it in time, the last tingle lingers in the hallway. Glory days.

What we have known for some time now unavoidably confronts us: in January and February Jack has to report for military duty. Because of his appointment at the university, the term of service is reduced from eight months to two. We arrange for Hans, our neighbor, to look after the snow removal. His sons will take the hay down from the loft as needed, all I have to do is feed the horses and give them water. We plan to celebrate Jack's farewell with a New Year's Eve party.

For the first time in years I go to a hairdresser to have my hair cut shorter, I gaze at my slender face and a little helplessly meet my eyes. Deep shadows underneath. Whenever I looked into a hairdresser's mirror, I always glimpsed this face, withdrawing to my large eyes and the lines around the mouth that were getting more noticeable and along which my courage for life seems to have drained away and disappeared. My lips pursed, never a broad smile. And above my pale face there was always a professional mirror-gazer, all made up and trying to persuade me to change my hair style, to convince me that I now really did look so very attractive, while I still saw myself with the same eyes, the same expression around the mouth. Tentative, helpless, and relieved to be able to get up and leave.

I have taken a simple little villa for the winter, perhaps for longer, writes Kathleen. It is on the slope of a hill. There are olive and fig trees, tall yellow flowers, and an overgrown garden. Down below is the sea, almost an ocean as it thunders and breaks over the rocks all day long. On one side there is a big veranda, if only the mosquitoes weren't such roaring lions. Nonetheless I am working. My birthday is on the 14th. It would make me happy to receive a letter from you on that day. Love, Kathleen. – Kathleen's birthday is in October, it is now the week before Christmas. I look at the letterhead, Kathleen has sent me an old letter.

Sometimes I walk aimlessly about the house, wait for Jack, imagine what it will be like when he will soon be gone for two months, how I will deal with the dread of night when it has gotten dark. Dusk now sets in at four already, the days are short and filled with the sun, with light, the snow crystals make everything sparkle, but it does not last long. The day exhausts itself too quickly, sinks back into an old long sleep. I bake cookies, sheet after sheet, Christmas pastry, and prepare tins in which Jack will take them along. Once a neighbor comes by who has never done so before; he asks whether he might borrow the snowplow, which Jack had not yet returned to Rosie. He declines to try the cookies, he doesn't care for pastry. His rubber boots leave dirty puddles in the kitchen.

Each sentence seems to bring an end with it, the impression that the story has come to an end. Facing what is so resistant to my pen, facing the ever larger context looming beyond me, I think of the few people for whom I do this work, for whom it is important to know that I am persevering. I think of Kathleen, I get older with her, live with her towards an age that even as a child seemed to me unattainable, as when a forty-year-old man in his bulky suit stood in the doorway, completely filling it. Kathleen in her villa, paid for with her father's meager contributions and her occasional royalties and fees. The wrong person to get old with. She sits there quietly for a while, then ponderously joins the conversation and with firm, unmistakable language tells us about herself, her moves, a debacle.

The comparisons shift a little, traces of dialect intrude. The bottles filled with cider are kept in the former laundry room, some of it is in kegs. I often think of the advice for handling a runaway horse: it is best to go towards it calmly with palm raised, then it will stop. On the shortest day of the year the sun is caught in the branches of the pine tree, blazing with a redness that is much too bright. A red spot, not black. I have not seen the artist in weeks. His wife is back, so they say.

I walk about, get dressed, eat, write, but all along I am breathing you, writes Kathleen. I want you, I want you. – Jack holds the letter in his hand, we read it and shake our heads, we both feel touched, neither of us could deal with it. – There is another dream to tell, I say. I dreamed that I was sitting in a café, two women were with me, one of them I knew, the other not. I knew one of them without knowing who she is. She asked me to lend her friend my coat, I consented readily. When I added that I would need the coat by seven-thirty the next morning since I would be leaving on a trip at that time, they laughed at me, reproached me for my pettiness, laughed and laughed. I asked again for the return of the coat by that time, and was jeered. I got up, grabbed the stranger by her hair, pulled and came away with a handful of it. Shamed by this, I awoke.

On New Year's Eve almost all our invited friends show up. In the afternoon with the help of several women I roast a large turkey and prepare many side dishes. The wife of the veterinary pays a visit with her son. When she sees the crowded kitchen, she says, my, you have a lot of visitors today! So many people, it's going to be a wonderful New Year's Eve for you! – Meanwhile her son takes the poker and bangs away at the stove top. Have you seen Friederike, she says. Lena is making apple strudel and draws out the dough. I'm chopping nuts and apples. The kitchen is overheated, sweat runs down the window panes, posteriors keep bumping into things, one laughs and wipes her dripping nose on her sleeve before the drops fall into the food. Nobody pays any attention to the men, who must be there somewhere. One woman is counting the bottles of champagne, I help myself to some brandy. Tears in our eyes, we plan to form a women's group, but we will soon be leaving again, someone says. Nobody minds the dirty dishes, the cats snuggle against our legs, play piano on the carpet that covers the hideous floor of the kitchen. Ah, Chekhov! why are you dead?

Jack is not there when the food is served. With misgivings I go to the stable, I wish the horses all the best, touch a rusty chain and then smell my fingers. Outside it is snowing, not a star to be seen. Our car is not there, just the vehicles of our guests. Drive off, follow him. Look to see if there is a key in the ignition in one of the cars. Go back into the house, to the others, who are waiting and wondering. Drive off, look for Jack. Go back into the house. Huge tides must be reversed with every thought.

Rosie had not been invited. You could write a whole novel without mentioning that you love a particular man, Kathleen would say. If you write as I do, you can't hide anything. Poison that is slowly infused in letters, drop by drop, diagnoses that are suppressed to spare one's vacillating partner, the laughter that truly leads to yourself, only to release the fear of what you find. - I stand in front of Rosie's house, in the dark, and inside someone else's life takes a course that touches mine; what if it is already too late, if Jack and I don't have a place that is our own, if it does not quit snowing, the season resurrecting my childhood, if, if only the year would come to an end at last...Doors slam, louder voices, the voices of Rosie's sisters, I imagine that there is a smell of incense. I pinch folds into the pockets of my winter jacket, hold on to myself. When we, the host couple, finally get home, Lena says that the turkey had to be put back into the oven, it was still pink on the inside and only lukewarm.

Amid the popping of the champagne corks nobody noticed the arrival of more guests. The artist and his wife had come, Friederike stands in the room, she is wearing a wide woolen dress of undyed material.

Icy blood seems to circulate under the pale skin of the redhead. The artist grasps me around my waist, performs an exaggerated hug, a fatherly gesture to dispel any suspicion once and for all. Friederike seems to be tipsy already; after the embracing and wishing well all around, she suggests a game. But first we listen for the bells from the village, somebody turns on the radio and dances to the Blue Danube waltz, Friederike clings to me. When I open my eyes for a moment, I see her broadly laughing, silently laughing face, she seems to be a confidante of Rosie. It has stopped snowing when we go outside. The night is black, the sky stippled with the injection marks of light.

For Friederike's game we sit in a circle, with two of us in the middle. The circle constitutes an audience, nothing more. The two in the middle invent dialogues. Friederike says, I broke your favorite vase. The artist replies, that doesn't matter, I already hated you anyway. Friederike says, I wish I had a Spanish farewell. The artist says, for that you resemble yourself too much. No one wants to continue the game when they finish. What's the point of it? someone asks. Then somebody asks for disco music, the chairs are pushed against the wall, Jack gets a red lightbulb from the toolshed. Among the guests is Hanna, a paraplegic; in the afternoon she had peeled carrots in her wheelchair, balancing a bowl on her knees. Now she imitates our dancing with the movements of her upper body, she dances from the waist up.

Somebody suggests that couples tell how they first met. I suspect that this is easier than the games yet to follow and therefore volunteer. It was in London, I say. He came in just as I was making tea. I went to the door and there he was in the hallway. Hello! Would you like some tea? He came in. We drank tea and talked and smoked and told our lives. Leaning against the window we saw the expanse of the sea and a ship under sail. Friederike gives a nervous little laugh. Oh God, she says. Of course, I'm not a writer. We met on the roadside, I had run out of gas, really.

A little encounter in the kitchen, the artist drinks a glass of water, it is difficult to take up the sweet gestures of affection once again, to speak of things that, beyond their charmed meanings, lie around empty. Surrendered terrain, so gray. Certain mannerisms are taken far too seriously, to have laughed unduly about something, to have betrayed oneself. I miss you, he says. I see that his mustache is growing over his lips. One ought to watch out for wind, chill cold, draft, for all that one is exposed to in passing, the idea for a story.

Next morning Jack says that he needs to talk with me. It's all over with Rosie, he says. Yesterday we talked about everything. – I feel like after a headache, images dissolve on my tongue, a feeling of elation, with numbed limbs. I ask no questions, let him talk, the little that he does say. I'm afraid that the wrong question might reverse his decision. When he is finished I go to the bathroom, turn on the faucet and begin to cry.

Don't you yet know, writes Kathleen, that the more you fill your life with your own thoughts and deeds, the more it appeals to him? For him the lack of privacy is like living in plain view, on exhibit under a vacuum jar. You cling to him, you want to please him, but he would just as soon see you go. Don't you understand that you have had enough closeness to last for years, that renewal is possible only if you go your separate ways? It is up to you to take this step. You don't seem to have learned anything, that is the reason why you find it so hard to write.

The school custodian sweeps the snow from the roof of the gymnasium. In his sweatsuit he stands on the flat roof and does a few warm-up exercises. When his cap falls down to the street, a passing grandmother puts it on a fencepost. Except for the shoveling figure on the roof, not a dab of color brightens the concrete building, and even he looks dark from a distance. Sometimes the custodian plays with his son on the P.A. system. They make announcements that can be heard clear across town, it sounds like an emergency. In winter the gymnasium is used for soccer games, bazaars by the Lions Club take place there, regional gymnastics competitions, or an auto show which is advertised on posters in the town mall.

On the second day that Jack is gone a cold front moves through. In the morning the thermometer reads minus eighteen degrees Fahrenheit, I hope that the water pipes won't burst. The municipality donates two portable heating units to a traveling circus in its winter quarters not far away. A number of people from town volunteer to help with the care of the animals. Kathleen writes that she dreamed the cats had died of anti-pneumonia. I put a log on the chopping block, take a big swing with both hands on the ax, exhale with the blow, the ax is stuck. To lift it again, now with the wedged log, and to bring it down again is almost beyond my strength. The impact, my strength splits the world in half, I can't split more than a basketful of firewood, it is enough to make me proud and exhausted. Meanwhile Kathleen spends her days in a hell; unable to do anything, she drinks brandy, she is determined not to weep, and then weeps. All night long she hears drowned souls sing in the sea.

In the evenings when I go to the chicken coop, I hope that all the fowl are there, so that I won't have to go a second time along this dimly lit path. I count the chickens on the roost, one is missing. At some point this evening I have to decide when to close the door. I get the last two buckets of coal for the stove in the hallway, I have a feeling of foreboding in my neck. On the bedside table there is the car key, a flashlight which I check every day, the telephone. First thing in the morning I hurry to the tiled stove and try to catch the glowing embers before they die, try to make a roaring fire. At breakfast the news reports that there are record low temperatures in Finland, temperatures as low as minus sixty degrees Fahrenheit were recorded. There are long delays in train travel, the Chopin Express from Moscow was eleven hours late by the time it arrived in Vienna. Switches on the tracks freeze up, the automatic doors of the carriages stick. At least twenty people have already frozen to death in Europe.

I clean out the stove in Jack's workroom, where we usually put up guests. There are rusty nails in the ashes. Next to the stove there is a pile of tissues and pieces of cardboard. When I look for some glue on the desk, I notice a slip of paper. In Jack's handwriting I read: You allow certain people to smoke in your room, you put their coats on hangers, blow dandruff from their coat collar so that they won't be embarrassed, which they wouldn't have been in any case. I resent these concessions of essential qualities which you had committed to me. Committed, when? Somebody must not have heard quite right.

Two students come for a few days, Jack has sent them. They start to cook at once, noodles, vegetables out of the deep freeze, onions are peeled and chopped, a cassette recorder is set up in the kitchen. While eating, one of them wraps the noodles so slowly as if waiting for some metamorphosis. They play guitar and sing along, they play table tennis and direct the ball towards each other's genitals, they grab each other around their waist and by the shoulder. For this night at least I don't have to worry about burglars, rapists or madmen.

Later I sit with Paul for a long time in front of the stove. His friend has gone to bed. We drape blankets around our legs, sit in the dark, opposite each other, sometimes when we are taken by an unexpected turn of phrase our toes touch. I refrain from asking whether Paul and his friend are gay. Paul tells me of his tai-chi course, of the encounter group that for the past five years has provided an outlet for his problems, he doesn't say which. He quotes Bhagwan, his breathing audible in the silence, in the darkness. I try to control my impulse to laugh, I'd like to draw my foot along his, but I'm too unsure of myself. Some time ago I read a book about transcendental meditation. That's what I talk about. When we take turns adding wood to the fire, an intense light flickers up, what we can see then fades away again. I can't imagine how this night is going to end. I nervously expect his friend to knock at the door, an indignant question. In the darkness I try to imagine Paul's face, it looks as if severed along one side. I push back my weariness, I feel a suppressed yawn rising in my nose. Then we separate.

Next morning Josef, his friend, has already prepared breakfast, an American breakfast. I try to figure what his sleep had brought him, he looks at me with amusement, with exaggerated gestures shakes pepper on his omelet. Later he chops several baskets of firewood, straightens up the closet in which the wood is kept. Paul writes a letter, asks how to spell cardiomyopathy.

Josef brought a cassette with Gurdjieff's sacred hymns, played by Keith Jarrett. Paul grins when Josef asks if there is any millet in the house. I should certainly stock up on it, and also rock salt for the toilets, so that they won't freeze up. Is it too cold for anybody? Since Kathleen left, heating has been less of a problem. I tell them how she just never managed to adjust things to the right temperature. Her room was either freezing cold or overheated, her life was all wrong. – Both of them listen to me, are surprised that Kathleen supposedly had been here, they do not quite take me seriously. I wish that I would finally receive a new letter from her. I lapse so easily into into a feeling of betrayal. Some thoughts just won't leave my head. Thoughts about minor heart attacks, a green finch in the rose bush who looks at you as if he were thinking about you, that was in summer. All these thoughts that won't fit together, I quickly change the topic. I miss Kathleen, I bid both of them a goodnight.

As I lie in the dark, the door opens. I try to remember Paul's face by day. He says nothing, holds back my question. Chaos, the legs of another person, his smell. He bends forward, pulls a feather out of the pillow. I feel his warmth, another night alone is averted. Minor aches of the heart, I think. And that Kathleen often was afraid that she would die of her heart condition. Not my lung, she says, my heart. Paul caresses the inside of my thighs, talk to me, he says.

I wish I were a crocodile, Kathleen writes. It is supposed to be the only creature which doesn't cough. I dare not talk for fear of bringing on an attack of coughing. I feel I can't bear this silence today. I am constantly haunted by thoughts of Jack. Cold, exhausted, cold. It is depressing to be able to concentrate just on breathing alone. I am impractical, no housewife, no gardener, I envied you the way you walk about and carry tools back and forth, the way you close the heavy garden gate...all I can ever do is lie here, breathe, take care that I don't stop breathing. It drives me to madness, I can't write any longer, what is there left to write about? I can't write about myself, it would destroy me. I can barely endure it, I wouldn't be able to read it. No, I am no housewife, no marriage partner, no healthy strong woman who prepares dinner. But that is just what Jack needs. I have destroyed his life. Shall I send this letter? Or write a happier one instead? No, you'll understand. I see a little boat out there, it moves along, inevitable and deadly silent – a little black spot, like the spot on a lung.

To write every day, I think to myself, that means to include my experiences of the day. And it would mean to write a story that develops parallel to these experiences. My story about Kathleen's life, as it draws to a close, would be written according to my own encounters and farewells, according to what is in store for me after I get up each morning. To write daily, since otherwise your gift may go to waste through neglect, don't forget your fear of this, says Kathleen, it is one of your largest fears. To sit for hours in front of the typewriter, to turn it on and off, hoping that the hum of the machine will sweep you along into the text, and then in the silence not to be able to think of anything. To yawn, as after prolonged work, to wait, to concentrate is to work, meanwhile a fly crawls under the slightly raised cover of a book about Kathleen. The fly sits under the cover as if to wait out a thunderstorm. I slowly press down on the cover.

I take Paul and Josef to the train station, they no longer belong here. At about this time I sense an old man behind me at the checkout counter at the supermarket; it is said that as a farmhand long ago he liked to take his shirt off for work, especially if there were girls around. They consider him to be a harmless old fool, but how does one know? The cashier with her broad face glibly interjects a few remarks between working the register and moving the milk cartons along. How do I manage up there, all alone? She would go to pieces out of fear, she says and laughs. Am I afraid to be all alone in the house like that? Looking straight ahead, showing no sign of life, I leave the supermarket and take refuge in the car, drive out to the other end of the village and make a big detour to cover all traces, I just really don't exist. After a while I notice that I've lost the chain on one of the tires. It's not far to the artists's house, I leave the car and walk there. The air feels good. The artist opens the door and says, Friederike has been gone for some hours now, I worry about her. – We go into his studio, there are new paintings of Friederike propped up everywhere, Friederike in a dance pose, a tango, her belly a shapeless globe; she struggles to hold a small umbrella in one hand. Two short lines mark the point of contact of her toes which bear the heavy load of her body. The laws of physics make the buttocks bulge out. – I worry about her, the artist says. It's too cold.

For a time as a student I wrote by twisting my hand inwards in a cramped arch. I wrote into my own hand, as it were. It seemed impossible to bend this hand outwards, as if I thereby would have to change the direction of my life. That's what I think of, as I look at the paintings. The artist tells me about their quarrel. I kissed her, he says. Her cheek felt cold and lifeless, like that of a mannequin. That's what I told her, she then started to cry hysterically, and accused me of wanting to kill her. It was awful, I had no sympathy, I'm less than a human being. – Standing in the middle of the room in his overalls, he looks like a pilot who has crash-landed and now apologizes for the damage that he has caused. I try to get a sense of his fear. I wish that Jack would be as concerned about me.

We wait for hours for Friederike. Should we call the police? She should be back by dusk. No acquaintances whom he hasn't already asked about her.

I delay my leaving, hoping that Jack would call and miss me, wondering why I'm not at home. In the days since New Year's there must have been some unpleasant confrontations in the artist's house. – I don't know why she came back at all, says the artist, why she didn't stay in Switzerland. She is forever looking for pretexts to quarrel with me. I'm left behind in the kitchen, with a bad conscience, I hear her close the bedroom door. She doesn't answer, next morning she comes into the kitchen as if she were blind, drinks black coffee, takes some pills for her migraine headache, eats nothing, just drinks this coffee. She has eaten hardly anything since coming back. – I ask him whether it might not be better for Friederike not to find me here. Probably, he says. But what am I to do until then? Do you know what I keep imagining? I imagine that she's sitting right here and I'm feeding her semolina by the spoon. – He bites his lips, looks toward the ground, points downward with an outstretched finger. I'm reminded that the limbs of those who freeze to death have to be broken, so they'll fit into the casket.

When I get home, I can see a light in the kitchen. I try to remember whether I had turned on the light before leaving, cannot say with certainty. Meanwhile it has turned dark, I go to check on the chickens, they are all there. I peer into the kitchen from the outside, search for evidence that somebody has been there, has left a used plate or a glass on the table. If only I could laugh. What is it like to freeze to death? What could be worse than the fear just now? My thoughts blur at the edges, drift away a pace and then become stiff and rigid. I unlock the front door, check out all the rooms. Then I remember that I have forgotten to feed the horses. In the stable I try to keep an eye on the front door. The horses throw back their heads with a jerk, they try to ward off a bad mood with their nodding.

Jack has not written. I wish there were a postal strike, but there are two other letters. – Do I have a home, writes Kathleen, cats, a man's affection? Jack never tells me anything, all I ever get are those completely self-absorbed letters. He wants me to believe that he loves me, that I should not give up on him. But as if expecting it all the same. He wants to be free, no less. Why am I haunted every single day of my life by the nearness of death and its inevitability? I'm obsessed with the thought, yet can't speak of it. Jack is unhappy to hear of it, he leaves me alone to struggle against it. I'm tired of this struggle. No one knows how tired. – I wish that she were here, Kathleen, the third person. The artist calls. All is well, he says. She's back. I have to hang up now. – To know the place where the phone rings, that's part of such affairs, I muse.

I try to write to Kathleen. One can't be certain, she may be long dead. Tell me exactly how it was. Start again at the beginning. Don't I understand anything? Have I now turned simple-minded? The quick confessions one sometimes receives from a glove, a cigarette or a hat. One provides this dreadful report, for weeks one writes daily letters to a man. Then the fear, too much deception. On your observation post everything is to be permitted. Kathleen, this invalid of a writer who got herself dropped into my story. No, not dropped, but rather gently set down, hands busy with her cup of tea, her pen and her notebook. Shallow breathing on the way; months later I find an abandoned bird's nest in one of her shoes. Now in winter one can actually still feel the warmth of the sunny walls.

Next evening we have a meeting, a few women from town, they bring along home-baked cake. Anita tells us of a pen-pal in the GDR, the contact had been established through a church, they've been writing to each other for twelve years. Chocolate and pantyhose cross the border, not all parcels reach their destination. Maria explains that much has changed since she had her first child. Then her husband didn't have the courage to push the baby carriage. Now with the straggler he is of course too old for a baby carrier, but nonetheless. Burgi and Gerda have spent countless weekends helping their husbands build their houses. Now at last they again have some time for reading. The worst is over, for the children as well. Perhaps after the worst is passed, old age is waiting in the wings. We don't really get any closer in our meeting. The way we dressed for this evening shouldn't matter. The men, well yes. All of them are married. You are just more of a free spirit, they say. The next morning I meet Gerda in the supermarket. A little flustered she rearranges her things in the shopping cart, it's enough to make me weep.

When Jack comes home for two days, he is immediately back in charge. He looks for some tools in the closet, corrects what I have done on my own. His new short haircut makes him look oddly fashionable, his head asks to be touched. His whistling fills the house, I accept his paying a courtesy visit to Rosie. Meanwhile I look after his things, find the letters that I have written to him in the past two weeks, it needn't have taken so little time, moved so fast. They look like a used present that can now be put away. He returns with a box of fresh cookies from Rosie, that's too much for me. To ask again, better not to ask. We sit together; when our eyes meet, they come from afar but seem nonetheless to be preoccupied with matters of shared concern. That makes everything even worse.

The cats are playing with a bat which is hopping in the snow like a night watchman. They strike it in the neck, in its tiny face, they raise it up a little when the claws are caught, shake it off. I go into the house to get a hammer, strike dead the animal that would not survive its injuries. The cats turn around and disappear. Next morning the bat lies in the yard, at the same place where I had killed it, stiff and stretched out, one elbow jutting out, the body a prune. I hear the horses pawing the ground. Look at these birches, Kathleen would say.

Is this the way it was? Just look at the birches again, try to remember a sentence that you once wrote. Don't they now seem to you like a very civilized audience? – After I've put more wood in the stove, I sit on the carpet; with a guide to the birds of Europe in my lap, I watch the birds that come to the window. For a friend in America I write down the Latin names of those birds that I can identify. Sitta europaea, that's the nuthatch. Using an ash scoop, I add sunflower seeds from a large sack to the tray in the birdhouse.

Down in the village I meet Rosie. Two widows, I think. She doesn't say much, seems to wait to see what I will say, and I, diffident and apprehensive, talk far too long, betray something. She prefers to besiege my mind, with her I take everything as intended. What is it really that I'm waiting for? She gives an embarrassed laugh, but she knows exactly what she wants. Come and see me tonight, I think. Let's work things out. I can't bear this rivalry and what's more, I'm afraid to be alone. Now of all the people she is the one to remain. The postman interrupts our silence, gives me a letter, one to Rosie. Mine is from Kathleen. I find refuge in my car, Kathleen's letter is reflected in the window. On the way it occurs to me that I have not yet done the shopping. In the yard the chickens peck listlessly in the snow. The horses are thirstier than usual, I lug a few buckets of water from the house, consider whether they might have fever.

I feel thin and ill, writes Kathleen, but that is the

real me! I am not an ox, my hold on life is weak. And I don't have such bovine eyes as in the photograph that Jack sent to the newspaper, I have always detested this photograph. He knows how much I detested it. I'm not his healthy wife. – No salutation. I look at her face again, the smooth bangs, the part of her hair severely light, the signal in the corners of her mouth, lips narrow, slighty parted, a wet, dark curl pressed on each cheek. I can feel the pain whenever the comb bumps her ears.

Everything is quiet in the house. The fire is occupied with itself, in the pantry there are provisions and emergency supplies. In the afternoon I could drive down to the village again, perhaps risk a short visit to the artist. I resolve to finish a book that I started to read a few days ago. Have I ever loved a woman? How do I feel about Kathleen? I long to touch her, her hands, which will never blotch with age, this woman with a few years more than I. Her stories hardly interest me, that's how most people feel about her. Diffuse, hesitant, open – does that describe you? I long for spring, the sky is freshly laid out today, all that needs to be done is to bring out the landscape underneath. Plenty of time, Jack is far away again, Rosie can already write her replies, she has to hide whatever she gets to know sooner than I do. To go through a certain pain many times without getting to the bottom of it. Jack lives with Rosie in his mind, that can no longer be denied. What I feel can no longer be rendered in thought; what I think puts bars around me.

In a dream I lead the American president by the arm down a wooden staircase. The president is pale, taller than I, he wants to move quickly. Slowly, Mister President, slowly, I say. When we arrive at the bottom of the stairs he disappears into a limousine, I must still get something that I had forgotten in the hotel room, hear the President sound the horn. Unable to decide which of the things to leave behind – hair dryer, curler, slippers – I sit on the rug beside the bed and feel my historical moment slip away.

Nothing of all that is put down on paper, it is written in my face. When I visit the artist, his wife has already left him again. He says, do you understand what she wanted here? I have the impression that she only came by to freeze up a little, that is now done; people have been worrying about her, her hale and hearty return has been duly celebrated, now she can continue again with her other life elsewhere. What is one to say? I'm no longer afraid for her, I have no visions of her death, she has gone to live across the border. It's just as well, or perhaps too bad that we don't have any children, I don't know. – Then he shows me a painting – Friederike's return. She is returning from a war, her face aglow, it must have been hot there, her limbs are clay-colored, there is snow. Barefoot, showing no coldness and having been on the road for a long time, Friederike looks at me. I don't understand anything anymore, the artist remains silent, the quiet of the room dampens my thoughts. I put my hand on the artist's back, a hesitant glance, it's not going to work out for us. We lie down on the couch, climb into the hollows of our arms and legs, our breathing works up a sweat, we are hinged with our heartbeats. I feel a trickle of sweat form under my pullover. I can only bear the closeness of his face by closing my eyes.

A few days before Jack's return warm winds set in. The entrance to the yard is blocked by a mass of snow that had slid from the roof. Wherever the snow had not yet broken loose and crashed down, there are thick folds threatening to fall. This wind does not fit the white season. The branches of the trees point here and there, perhaps they are coding strange signs that give directions, one should not lose sight of the whole. Down by the road the ice is being broken up, one can hear the splitting apart of the ice, the crashing impact of metal on pavement. The gate to the hayloft is ripped open, a few boards are broken on the right half of the gate, it hangs askew. It won't budge when I try to move it. The snow lies heavy and wet on the ground, shoveling it only seems to firm up what lies underneath. The horses give a long-winded neigh. It is of course enough to make one laugh. I have not yet seen all the cats, the phone doesn't ring all morning.

Jack never asks if I'm being unfaithful. I would be afraid to tell him that I sleep with men. It would be the needed evidence for concluding that we are not suited for each other. One can look at the objects on the desk again and again, they always remain the same, the only thing that would make a difference – the story about them – remains unwritten. – They say that I smell like a civet cat that roams the streets, Kathleen writes. What does a civet cat smell like, I think and bend towards her in my mind. She remains dead or abroad, bundled off to the south with her notebooks and her Chekhov. In her private heaven she has already reserved a place for him. Don't talk out of your story, writes Kathleen. Be careful, if our story tears open, it will crash into the sea. I don't intend to go under with you.

3

Do I know what time frame I'm in? I don't always have the facts of Kathleen's life at hand, it sometimes happens that I put her year of birth ahead by as much as ten years. Nothing much occurs to me, she simply filled in her little more than thirty years. On gloomy afternoons she asks herself whether she has lost her spirit. Illness can be taken as the hybrid of life and anticipated death. Falling ill from the afflictions of society is not what is happening, that would be too easy an explanation, the underlying coherence would be lost. I forget the names of places and of her doctors, the day she saw soldiers kicking something around on the beach, a dead dog perhaps or a cat. Times change, only these few people live on as if they had nothing to gain. Kathleen will soon return; in preparation I have been airing her room for days. Again these conversations, the counting off of mint leaves for the tea, the renewed writing. In what time frame? From which injustice do we withhold our attention, while the wheels are set spinning?

Do you sometimes think of the time we danced together? Kathleen asks when I meet her at the train station. Her pale face, her eyes draw me close, for a while we embrace across the car seats. I don't think it possible to repeat anything, she says. I can't spend a second summer with you, everything has been said, I haven't been able to finish our story in France, yet I can't think of a second summer. You have become a stranger, or an intimate, or a stranger – who are you for me? – Do you take up this matter in your story? I ask. – Why don't you read with my breath, she says and kisses me on the cheek. My thoughts linger on this touch, my hands are already on the steering wheel. I am not to be found in her life, I did not torment her, I am not to blame. It is only this heightened sensibility that I'm after.

Behind our chicken coop stands the rusty cab of a truck, the plastic of the seats is brittle and faded. Kathleen can't resist climbing into it. Since the cab is tilted, she sits hunched forward, trying to hang on. I take a position in front of the cab, wave for her to advance, while I stop the traffic from side streets. Go ahead, I call, go ahead, stop, now turn left, and Kathleen steers and laughs and laughs, she is not such a good actress. I forget that she is hardly able to walk, that she spends the larger part of the day in bed, but nobody wants to change her here. It is spring. Hairs from horse's tails are tangled in the barbs of the fence, their galloping has left behind a message.

Traveling is terrible, she says later. Everything is so dingy, and the train bumps and shakes. Old women sit in the compartment with you and talk about illnesses that you have yourself. It's dreadful, after some time I then begin to talk as I do in the letters I write. – We go down into the cellar, climb down the narrow stairs on our heels, back up again on our toes. This year we intend to plant potatoes, more vegetables. Jack is using old windows to construct a seedbed. In the evening we design a layout for the plants. A gardening book tells us which are best put close together, and which not. Onions and savory keep away pests.

In the morning Kathleen tells us her dream. The red geraniums act as if they owned the garden. They are firmly established, with every leaf and flower in place, and they are determined to stay. That did not bother her. But why do they make a stranger of her? Their arrogance and pride. If she comes near them, they ask, and what are you doing in this garden?

A superb sentence out of someone else's book can ruin my working mood, I say. It is no longer at my disposal, since to have written it myself is what would matter most. – You are immodest, Kathleen says. Let me have my sentences, why don't you just leave me in peace. – I didn't mean you, I say. There's not one sentence that you have written that I would wish to have written. You are a butterfly made of lead. – Butterfly is Psyche, she says. Psyche is breath. That is why you have to get on with your story, without regard for any harm it may cause you. The only means for you to find your way home. – Home, from where, I ask. – From the waiting rooms, she says. From the rooms whose doors Jack has always just closed. If he does not tell you what is happening, you have to tell him. If he does not ask questions, then one of these days you have to put the longest answer on the table, all finished and done. You can't choose the people to be with, that is a fallacy. Who stands guard over your imagination? Do you have sufficient imagination? A visible body seemingly near death, so that nothing will distract you, so that the words will fall into place, your connection with us? Meanwhile I'll tell you the names of my cats.

When I cradle Jack's head in my hands, there is little love for it. A heavy head whose thoughts cannot be turned around, a head with the wrong polarity, the bones so close to the skin, a casing that is complete and finished. I skid off his glance, off the green pond of these pupils, the frozen green pond. He has angled the pupils of his eyes so that I can't help but slide off. To hide my annoyance I talk about other things that have always irritated me in the past; that makes it easy for Jack to accuse me of being ill-tempered. I always do react to this particular reproach with a bad mood. Angrily I say that I'm not in a bad mood. Jack says that he once noticed his mother hiding easter eggs. He was then four or five. Ignoring his disbelief, his mother insisted that it was the easter bunny and not she who had hidden the eggs. – I ask, why haven't you ever told me this story? – He had only recently been reminded of it, he says. – I really don't want to ask by whom. He now sits there without saying a word, his foot is keeping time to some thoughts, no doubt about a little utopia down the road. Then he pulls a packet of cigarettes out of his shirt pocket, lights a cigarette, laughs at me with his eyes. I have such desire for the feeling of desire. I would so very much like to be available for something that I don't yet know.

Burgi, one of the women from town, invites me for coffee. I wonder whether I should tell her that someone else would be along, but then I decide to leave Kathleen at home. Burgi shows me the varieties of herbal vinegar that she is starting in bottles, vinegars refined with rosemary and apple slices. How do you ever get the apple slices back out, I ask her. For a moment she is deadpan, her lips pursed, then she says, I don't, they stay, and we both laugh. A little later the question whether I'm writing about something. Yes, I say. She doesn't know how to go on with her question, I feel sorry for her. I want to show her that I am as normal as can be, betray myself with all kinds of concessions. I feel guilty of denying her the ability to take me as I am. I sense that she is now treating me as she would a man, putting down her own work as unimportant and cute. Jack is often in the pastry shop, she says finally. Oh, yes, I say. We look at each other. I'll have to be getting along, I say. Our stove needs stoking. Yes, she says. You still have to heat, that's going to go on like that for some weeks. – I thank her for the coffee.

The waters of spring form pools in the hoof imprints of the horses . On the soft ground the animals trot their rounds, roll over and wallow in the dirt, alternately stretching their legs up, trotting in the sky. Their nostrils itch, the gums show. When I look over to the trees, it is not long before a bird flies off, makes a loop and ties its flight to another tree. The pulse beats closer under the skin. A little farther away a boy rides his motorcycle along the path, adeptly steering back and forth between the ruts and stones. He doesn't look over to me, there is something tied down on the rack. Jack comes, speaks with a playful voice as we have not used in months. I have to laugh. Are you going somewhere, I ask with this voice. Just for a little while, he says. Just for a little while, I taunt him. The voice is thin and delicate, making it endurable. Jack checks the money in his wallet, he is going to buy some lumber. They told me at the sawmill that the boards wouldn't be ready until the afternoon, he explains. That's where I'm going now.

It cannot be denied that Kathleen has severe pains in her back, on some days she can barely get along, if indeed she is able to get up at all, however late. She then sits with us at the table, remains silent, because she knows that I speak for her. Her fear of the wind hadn't always been the same, windows, cars, public transport, the sultry evenings by a river, on the deck of a ship – the fear could quite simply be transformed into a fear of closed spaces. One must be inventive, one must attach a certain pain to a character in a narrative while one can still remember the structure of this pain. Kathleen shows with what difficulty such matters yield to writing. She has grown to be less demanding; if someone maintains that she just expects too much, he hasn't understood her even for a minute. One begins to accept in one's mind what would bring one's grandmother to tears, namely, that one has to face the illness, to give it time. There are now expectations for which, as part of the bargain, one is willing to have quarrels, some words keep getting tripped up. I make every effort to continue with my work on the story, to put down what is happening to me, while Kathleen is rehearsing her departure. I hesitate to interrupt her attempts at maintaining order, she lapses into empty staring, the staring at the hands of the incurably ill. To move a word to its proper place becomes a large exertion. She reads to herself her few new texts, listens to the rise and fall, polishes here and there. She is not in the least touched with madness or in some way special, not fragile, deathly ill, not diffuse or numbed, she sits by the window and reads her fragments out loud. When the first thunderstorm breaks over our house, I sit in her room. What about the lightning rod, she asks.

Through my part-time tutoring I come to know several teachers. One rarely gets to meet their wives, either they are also grading written assignments or just keeping out of sight. I don't tell anyone about Kathleen, I'm afraid to lose the little trust we share. Comments about the unencumbered life, the life of the uncommitted, which they mean partially in seriousness, I meet by defending family values. We humble ourselves to show the pictures on the driver's license, that is about as personal as it gets. Cautious questions about Rosie lead nowhere. Quickly it is evening, tennis lessons have their fixed time slot, the cafés close too early. I give some thought to names, I search for the tone that would go with certain noises from the outside. The cashier among them, buses driving off, sometimes the screaming and yelling of children which disheartens me. Once found, the name sets imagination in motion. Vocation: teacher; location: small town. Excursions, flights of fancy, mostly it has to go quickly, so that one thing leads to another, something is left behind for later, without certainty and agreement.

The man could be Victor. He tells me that Charon, the ferryman of Hades, accepts the coin under the tongue of the dead. The last taste of the earth, I can feel it. The entry fee. I leaf through his historical school atlas, find a map which shows the occupation zones of Austria after 1945. The sector occupied by the French is colored purple, that's lavender, a perfume, how appropriate. We play word games, I gladly have things explained to me. It happens softly, with an open end; in passing I think of my father, who could only give explanations in a command voice, as if speaking to himself, slowly, with stresses and in High German. My father's traps still lie about, I touch Victor's hand and allow myself to be distracted, fall in love a little. No excuses, the evening's silence now has new substance.

When I come into her room later on, Kathleen

says that she thought it possible to write an entire novel about a liar. A man who was devoted to his wife, but who lied. But she couldn't. She couldn't write a novel about anything. Stories perhaps. There seemed to be a barrier between her and her world. Everything she thought of seemed false.

Next morning I read Kathleen some poems with some striking images that express touching and tracing. The thoughts seem to embrace what they signify. On Kathleen's table there is an empty bottle of cider; drying up, the residue of the foam shows the level to which it had been filled. She doesn't say anything, just listens attentively. Behind this closed mouth lies her life, I think. I have stopped reading, look into her eyes. You are the illness, I think to myself. You ended up here as in a dead bay, waiting, waiting. The whole house smells of our talk, old houses are containers that can be filled up endlessly. On the surface Jack's ways are so coarse, the noise of the car leaving the yard, I had imagined so much to be different. My failing is fear, the unthinkable end.

Victor is taken aback by my desire. He strokes his beard with his hand, closes his eyes for long pauses. Some sentences are too simple, roundabout ways lead to quite different places. We secure our defenses by reading together, he has his freedom to lose. I have always been afraid of getting involved with such a man. He says, you transform reality in your thoughts. He tells me of a friend who hated her husband's favorite author since in these books only broken marriages occurred. I remember that in our bathroom my pullover and Jack's hang with heavy arms over chairs and drip dry. We lose ourselves in the feelings of strangers – that dulls our sensibilities. Victor was unsociable, says Kathleen. He liked it best to live without social contact. We wrote each other often. He did not have the money to visit me when I was in Italy. My greatest wish was once more to have a long talk with him, he wrote of wanting to go to Russia, oh God, Russia, I would never have seen him again. – Did you ever meet again, I ask. – It isn't Victor, she says. The way you describe him, it can't be him. We wished someday to publish a book with both of our names on it.

When in mid-May, on a day known in folklore as Cold Sophie, it snows once more, Hans, the farmer, smirks about the malice of this woman. He rubs the lever of the gearshift on his tractor and cheerfully nods his defeat. I am amazed how quickly the hand movements of these men always seem to end in the ritual of spearing, splitting, lifting and plugging. As if to excite the genitals of the landscape, the machines, the weather, and to keep them under control.

Kathleen is hardly to be heard. When I think of her, while I put out the first plants in the garden, I feel her ingenuous warmth. She takes care of her place as well as she can, does not retreat a single step. Clings to her resolve to write daily; for me the disappointment and humiliation of failing to do so counts as much as the actual work. She is not sparing with her judgment, she can't escape herself. Sometimes she can't remember the English term for an herb, she then asks me whether I think that her command of English is deteriorating. Je ne parle pas français, I say. Yours are open secrets, she says. – When it gets warmer by the day, she lies on a blanket in the sun. My hands tremble as I touch her skin, working in rosemary oil. Her hands are always lying there with the palms up, at the crook of her arm the pulse of the artery can be seen. With my forefinger I trace along her face, touch her behind the ear. You want to be a writer, she says with emphasis, as if otherwise the words would tumble down her throat. But you don't write anything. As soon as you don't write, you don't know what to do with your arms and legs. There you are, you stumble around and distract others in work you don't understand, you have yourself sent for tools and get cold feet. Then you describe the pain of destruction. Isn't that just too funny?

When Jack comes with a sack of wool from Rosie's sheep, I'm supposed to already know something about natural dyes. Jack lists them: the bark of the ash, the elderberry bush, apple, pear and cherry trees, the leaves of the common privet, the skins of onions not yet too bleached by the sun, the blossoms of marsh marigolds, the leaves of the lily of the valley: all of these dye yellow. Wild marjoram produces purple. The capsule of the spindle tree red. – Down by the apple trees there is a spindle tree, I say, and about all that remains is for me to raise my hand obediently as if in school. It is at such times, when I try to work up an interest, that Jack finds my efforts to be pointless.

The evenings are taboo, Jack stays at home. We sit in front of the television set, the motorcycle of a policeman rears up, streaks along and disappears in a gap in the horizon. The next shot shows a curve, the extended leg of the uniformed rider, sliding and slipping, circles as on artificial ice, a body in the uniform of a police officer, still and supine, a spinning wheel. Then a matter-of-fact announcement about a bomb attack, on a stretcher a man is carried away, one of his hands holds a parcel that he managed to save. Alongside lie the dead. Somewhere a state of emergency wipes out the last vestige of human dignity.

Jack wants to lead a double life, everything goes so quickly now. And it seems as if summer is having its fun. The meadows around our yard, and the meadows around Rosie's yard, a thunderstorm brewing farther towards the west, the cold front veers off just in time, sultry days as we haven't had in a long while. Then the dammed-up anticipation breaks lose and everywhere farmers begin to mow. Erect and proud Rosie drives past on her tractor, I notice her straight back. The hay rake stirs up dust behind her. Jack repairs the prongs of the tedder as if he had been doing this sort of thing all his life. For the night the hay is gathered up in rows in order to keep the surface as small as possible. – Kathleen too keeps her arms close to her body when she takes a walk through the garden in the evening and watches me water the plants. The evening rolls towards us down the mountain, the cool waves end gently, almost imperceptibly on our skin, and Kathleen listens inwardly, so as not to miss the moment when the yet harmless coolness begins to turn damp. Next morning the hay rakes are out again, spreading and turning the hay, then in the afternoon the swaths are gulped up by the hayloader until belts and bars cut in deeply.

Victor wants to spend a day with me in Vienna. I lean against him in his car and wait for him to reciprocate with his arm. Victor drives on silently and safely, he hardly ever passes, but when he does, he strikes down on the turn signal lever sharply with his finger. He wants to have all of the morning to himself, we agree to meet in a café. The feeling that I'm a burden for him until noon rests heavily on me. I feel abandoned in this city that I know so well and that nonetheless can leave the impression of not knowing me at all. I feel the urge to buy something, without knowing what. If he should ask me how I spent the morning, I will think up some lie. In a record shop I get my head filled up, I'm afraid on the escalators, it feels as if the city is lashing out at me. Finally I end up in an art exhibition showing nude photography, I buy the catalog for the artist. The few men who are depicted all look like gymnasts to me. I think of

Kathleen's bare chest when the doctors examine her, her hunched shoulders when they listen to her disease from the back, the discouraged pulling down of her nightgown or the lonely dressing, numb with hope. On one of the pictures a woman is confronting a tiger, its claw the size of a chest. I observe a man who goes up close to the pictures, readjusts his genitals and then moves on. I escape to the street, a girl with a greyhound is waiting at the traffic light. The greyhound leans its slender cheek against her thigh, closes its telltale eyes. I am going to buy a dog, I think to myself.

For a long time we then sit at our lunch, listen to other people talk, as if the sentence for a beginning could be found there. It seems that the world has nothing to do with us any more. I have to tell you something, Victor then says. I'm going to Bolivia for a year. When, I ask. I'm leaving in mid-August, he says. – I touch my forehead with my hand, rush through this separation, I wish I felt strong in my body. I feel tears welling up in my eyes, my face should be bandaged, only leaving air for breathing, I can't cry quietly. I never could. Stop it, my father would then say. Stop it. Come here. Stop it. Eat now.

Kathleen and I take our story out into the sun. I've been looking forever for the right climate, she says. – On some days she is incomprehensible to me, talks about yesterday, has suddenly broken off with Jack. – He ought to ask me to be the godmother for his children, she says. That would be the only thing I would want to do for him. Otherwise – but enough of this. – Whose children, I ask. She is lying diagonally across the blanket in the meadow. I long for a lover, she says. I'm cold, cover me. Close me off from the world. Say that you love these games, don't go to Victor anymore. As long as you can't imagine yourself screaming in front of strangers, turning everything around, clamping shut your open eyes and tearing open your closed lips, out with your tongue, as long as you are in the thrall of shame and want to appear beautiful, as long as your body merely totters along behind your thoughts and your features are composed, you will not be able to write. – The world is all awry, I say. You have to describe it from the opposite tilt, then it becomes recognizable. – And do you do that? asks Kathleen. – I say, sometimes I confuse gymnastics with Germanistics. – Kathleen laughs. We are the blending of paths that matters, I say. The disastrous meeting of two women who are akin through profession and illness, one and the other within me. – I don't understand you, she says. – We look into the sky. Rearrangements of huge proportions are being enacted there. What has just taken the shape of a continent now drifts apart. That's how it should be, is there something to be lost? Is it possible to live with another person if you are not in their skin? – Kathleen, I say. I write with your hand. And then I sit sealed in my work room, all but forgotten.

In the morning I awake from dreams that seem to be much too large for me. I can't remember any story or location. A history of the world went through my head, yet I have no recollection of it. I start to run, try to gain speed, a longer breath; love as a question of competencies, barefoot eroticism and the avoidance of the word 'eroticism.' Jack reads a newspaper article to me. Donald Duck's voice mysteriously taken ill. – A few days ago Clarence Nash, known to millions as the voice of Donald Duck, was admitted to a hospital in Burbank, California. To date, the doctors have refused to give details about the condition of the eighty-year-old Nash. Dreadful, says Jack with his puppet voice and makes a sad face. Oh God, how very sad, I say. We look at each other with grief.

One time I bundle up Kathleen in the car and we go for a drive in the neighborhood. If Kathleen were not so tall, she would look like one of the old farm women who on Sundays are driven by their sons to the cemetery and the inn, the rest of the family accommodated in the back seat. I again wish I had a dog who would have his place on the back seat and who would attentively look at the road go by. We come to a valley where I have not been before, we venture to drive on. At the side of the road some mullein are in bloom, and mints. I stop, pick a mint leaf, rub it and hold it for Kathleen to smell. The road gets steeper, finally we come to a plateau, a large area covered with gravel, a shed, a ski lift. In summer everything is abandoned here. The slopes are destroyed, the posts of the lift poke out like toothpicks. The cables hang slack and heavy, like a monstrous toy. Everything looks like it's been used up in play and discarded. I sense how things that once were familiar threaten to grow together into a different world that is more and more difficult to explain and that puts distance between me and the people with whom I live. Even with Kathleen I fall silent. I try to understand what has become of it all, but refuse all understanding. Stop it, I think to myself. I don't even manage this phrase that is just waiting to be turned into a scream, not to anyone. The world ends on my lips. One thus presents a comical spectacle for others. Piqued, Kathleen's voice curtly announces, I'm still around. – Visitors like her cease to be visitors after a few days. Close your eyes, I tell her. Isn't it surprising how the thin tissue of your eyelids sustains you as a whole person, when you are already burst apart? – On the way home she sees a jacket on a balcony, hung out to air. She fights off tears.

The woman in the room next to mine has the same illness as I, says Kathleen in the morning. At night I hear her turning, then she coughs. And I cough. And after a while I cough, and she coughs again. This continues until we are like two roosters on some distant farms, calling to each other at false dawn. That's right, I say. Farmers admit to nothing. They intend to spend the rest of their life in their place. Confessions don't give release. Dreadful events are always thought to happen to someone else. Sure, sure, they say and protect their peace of mind from anything that could threaten them, with their hands they push down any anxiety welling up. They flush away the dung from their cows with an automatic water-jet unit, and they have the baker deliver bread and pastry to their house. At the offices in the next larger town, where the walls are painted in one color up to hip-level and in a different color beyond, they speak High German, and it sounds as if they are reciting a poem on mother's day. At home the television set has its place in the corner with the crucifix above, the early programs overlap with the work that still needs to be done in the stables in the evening. Plastic accumulates in the kitchens, the attics have long since been cleared out by antique dealers. – So who comes out ahead? asks Kathleen.

I couldn't have known that I would meet you, says Victor. – I sense that that is more than he intends to say, and he realizes from my expression that I've caught him in his betrayal. I feel ill, ill in my desire, in my loneliness in facing this departure, this running away from me. With a finger Victor traces along my hand. His silence mutes my demands, once again we can sensibly deal with the farewell. His sadness easily fits into the plans, by evening he is back at his Spanish lessons again. For dreadful moments I stand in the departures lounge, the indicator scrolls to his flight.

The features of a face leave their impression, to no avail. – I am not likely to write, he says. I never was much of a letter writer. – I listen to him, as he removes himself piece by piece. Again he traces along my body with his finger, I think to myself: he is younger than I am, but by how much?

Severe thunderstorms and rain squalls press down on us, submerge us beneath sea-level. The birds have become fishes. This design flaw giving the water the wrong direction will be corrected at some time. – You forget that under water there are no drops, Kathleen says. – She then says, except for you, Victor was for the longest time my most intimate literary advisor. I have already told you of our names wedded on a book cover. A gross wish, you will say. Not any more gross than your separation now. – I make no comparisons, I say. Victor and I, we lie down on a bed with a book and read together. While I read, I sometimes think, how can he possibly read when he holds the book at this height? It causes me difficulty, but I don't say anything. I have the feeling that one should begin with everything all over again. Then I ask him whether he likes dogs. Yes, he says, I do. I say, can you imagine a life without books? No, he says. I say, look into the eyes of a dog, it is a life without books. He laughs, I laugh with him a little. – Victor and Spanish, says Kathleen and shakes her head.

In the middle of this summer, while it rains with such virtuosity, a longing for the artist suddenly overcomes me. My longing, it seems, strikes out blindly. In the newspaper I read of heavy seas on the Côte d'Azur, of tidal waves and a vacation village that was swept away. I feel with certainty that the artist was among the victims. My feelings and I would believe any story. I call the artist, he answers after the first ring, how did you know that I'm back? – I say, can I come see you.

His house still retains the heat of the previous weeks. He shows me sketches that he made in France. And how are things with you, he asks. You still live with Jack, your curious friend mediates between the two of you, you are writing a story with all the names mentioned in it? – Are the names that important? I ask. They can be found in every index, it is all documented, the names of the cats, nicknames and terms of endearment, the landlords. I'm just trying to close my doors on these evenings that are a little shaky already. Kathleen could be negligent. I was always afraid that she might forget to turn off the gas and blow us all to smithereens with a cigarette, all for nothing. – Don't speak of her as if she were dead, says the artist. That only alienates you. – I would like to paint you, he says after a while. But to my regret the picture that I would want to paint of you already exists. – What do you mean by that, I ask. – I would have painted you in terms of your heart cavity. This chamber would be a library with a large fireplace, in front of the fireplace Jack sits in an armchair and thinks of someone else.

Your friend is a thin bronze statuette, which could be placed anywhere. Her shadow divides the floor into domains. The chamber would be recognizable as the muscle that pumps you in between your contemporaries. I can imagine holding your heart in my hands. I would be careful not to drop it. It all seems very simple to me now. I can begin to understand your life. – But nowadays one does not paint such pictures anymore, he says after a pause.

The rain has caused damage, in our garden the potato plants are down on the ground like a flat jungle; the fennel, which I had transplanted shortly before the sudden weather break, is plastered to the ground like seaweed. The currants have held up well. In a few hours the moisture, just beaten into the ground as if there weren't ever to be other kinds of weather, climbs back up into the clouds, the sky heats up in its blueness. – For months the story has been fitted into suitable words, says Kathleen. What happens now sounds immensely loud. – Don't exaggerate, I say. I'd like to be a little crazy with someone, a trifling hurrah on my lips, but you make it so difficult. I can't look at your face any longer, nor at mine. Your field of force consists of paleness, of back pain, anxiety about your heart. Why don't you recover in the summer? they ask me. I say, all's well, and then forget everything. – Kathleen shields her eyes with her flat hand, the sun glares down. I look into the light, close my eyes. A green footprint throbs on my retina. That is the keeper of my dreams, whom I haven't ever seen yet.

More and more often Jack drives off to do some shopping, goes a second time. When he returns, he repairs the typewriter, a task that he doesn't mind doing. Every day I turn into a phantom in the tree, promise never to come down again. Every day Jack's whistling in front of the door brings me back, without him knowing it. Jack betrays me and he doesn't betray me. I betray him and I don't betray him. As soon as the truth threatens to weigh too much on one side, it tips to the other. Crows are lined up on the fences, they can be chased away. They then lumber about on the fields, old and tired, peck at the stubble on the fields. When in flight, they scream their dark commentaries to each other. Victor fades out of my immediate life, but first he still holds on to me, weeps without a sound, trembles, defenseless against the emotion that shakes him. I try to imagine that his pain is larger than mine.

The narrative trail is only faintly marked, I say to the artist. I must not deviate a single step from it; if I hold my head in the wrong light, then Kathleen is gone and will not ever return. Then I won't know how to deal with myself, I know it least of all, but sometimes you too want to usher me out. You feel ashamed of me. Then you notice that I correct you on some historical detail. For you it hadn't been so important when you once mentioned it to me, only I filled up my memory with it, retained it for tempting you later. There is nothing worse than favors rendered out of love and received with indifference. I dream of my grandmother, she stands in the kitchen, I say, I'm going to marry Jack. To my back my grandmother says, and what will you eat? – Pity and compassion play a large role, says the artist. Out of pity we stay with people whom we have met by chance. Why don't the two of you put your cards on the table?

In the last week of August Jack goes away on a trip with Rosie. One thought recurs over and over again: You can't do that to me. But it remains voiceless, the tongue shapes it against the palate, it ends as an empty sound and loses all meaning. – Kathleen collects rose petals, asks where Jack is, I lie to her. The thorn, this drop that so exactly drains away, I say. – Don't search for excuses, she says and with rose petals lays out the pattern of a bird on the tablecloth. Let's take the case of Kathleen Beauchamp, she says. As long as she can remember, she has led a very false life. Yet, there have been moments when she sensed the possibility of something quite different.

Every day I write to Victor at the German School, La Paz. A finch comes right up to my feet, hops away a bit, stops, runs again, stops. The sun is high in the sky, the shadow of the beak points to the throat of the bird like a dagger. I write that these letters are my work as writer, the daily work that I expect of myself. I add that these letters constitute my journal which he now has for safekeeping. I shake my hand as if to cast dice. I can well imagine that it could be oppressive for Victor if I were to let go of the last hope like that. Both of our names on one book, I repeat. What should the book be about? I still can rethink again and again what bound us together. – He would have been capable, Kathleen says, of throwing you into the Seine after having relieved you of watch and purse, only then to extend a helping hand. The amusing thing was that, scarcely saved, one felt the need to thank him. – Whom, I ask. – Gurdjieff, she says.

The morning bathes for hours at a time in the mist of these last days of summer, I say to Kathleen and lead her onto the balcony. Is the morning bathing? she asks. Is the mist sleeping, does the cattle gate lean against the wall of the barn? – We laugh. Still sputtering from the laughter, Kathleen says the most notable thing about Monsieur Gurdjieff was his gaze. From the first meeting one felt that he could look right through you. They all simply called him Monsieur. He had a room that was reserved for special talks, it had the quiet of a library. It left the impression that there were books, but there were only shelves full of jars in which onions, leaves and roots of spices from around the world were kept. – When was that, I ask her. She shrugs her shoulders. I always feel ashamed of being ill, of pleading illness. Better to be dead, in fact, it is a kind of death. And one is ashamed, as a corpse would be ashamed to be unburied. Write that to Victor, he will understand.

Sometimes it happens that I forget my friends. I live alone, quite alone, I put single words at the unfinished end of the story. I have no idea how it is to continue. In the village I meet people, I ask myself what they could possibly think about this crazy person, I know that everybody knows, I walk through the town as if branded, as if laughed at behind my back. Once a farmer calls after me using Rosie's name. On this day my hair is braided similar to hers, I wear a similar skirt, it had just turned out that way, but for a few hours it takes away my identity. Perhaps I am mistaking this short recurrent pain in my chest with what Kathleen feels. She says it is as if a hot iron presses on her. She does not associate a human being with it. I, on the other hand, and I have got to get back to this, I can feel someone reaching for me, somebody grasping me with a firm feverish hand, with a sweaty grip.

When the mailbox again contains nothing but the advertising brochures of the farmers' cooperative, the local papers with club announcements, Kathleen and I surmise a strike, misplaced mail, conspiracy and intention and we think of Victor's new life. Obsessed with mail, with the envelopes bearing the airmail border. I see myself as letter writer, lose strength, sit and wait. Rosie leans towards Jack, holds her face up to him. In my thoughts I conceive a narrative plot.

Dr. Sorapure's approach to medicine seems very sound to me, says Kathleen. I would gladly have him remove my head, dissect its contents and then attach it once again, if he thought that it would benefit future generations. – I wouldn't want to know anybody who wrote a story with the memories in your head, I say. I would really prefer to glue all your letters together along the edges, one on top of the other, and then drop them in the sea. I feel sorry for you, but I love you nonetheless. Even the summer does not end that quickly. – When I die, I would want to have Dr. Sorapure at my bedside, Kathleen continues. He would arouse my interest, I would think of the process of dying and want to take notes about it.

I am so very afraid of what I will be doing soon, Kathleen says. – What are you going to do? I ask her. – There is no more Chekhov, she says. Illness has swallowed him. But perhaps this makes no sense to people who are not themselves ill. He has always considered it odd, Chekhov writes, when people whose death was at hand talked, smiled, or wept in his presence. When this blind woman on the veranda laughs, jokes, or hears stories read to her, what begins to seem strange is not that she is dying, but that we do not feel our own death and write stories as though we were never going to die. – She looks at me. Chekhov mistakenly thought that with more time he would have written more fully. But in fact, every story is a compromise. It's always a kind of race to get in as much as one knows before it disappears.

Behind every velvet curtain there is a broken

bicycle, says Kathleen after a while. One could also call it the biographical moment of a physical disease. I feel that I have hardly any time left. Wherever you are sparing with resistance, the story will hurt. Do you notice how we yawn in turn, everything dissipates into tiredness. The night is knocking at the window, luckily one does not hear it. We are unjust, we have a romantic disease, an illness with imagination.

Jack is scarcely gone, and the waiting begins. The front door slams shut, the starting of the car, backing out in reverse gear through the entrance to the yard, down the road, that's how Jack removes himself from the world for me. I wait for hours, listen in dazed faithfulness to the one noise, check everything that comes to my ear with this possibility of mistaking the noise, the returning car. In my head the blood follows its course, I can almost hear it scrape along, the body gets as loud as a child that tests its voice in an empty house. Stepping in front of the mirror shows me how pointless it is to recognize oneself; after all, what are eyes, my gaze sends me away. I sit on the sofa, the telephone that I had put down next to me, slides against my thigh. As if to show its great trust. The receiver now rests askew in its cradle.

I'm going now, Jack says. – But don't stay long, I ask of him. – I'm going now, Jack says every day. His fear is the secret for his return. He is afraid that one late afternoon before the chickens are herded into the coop, he will have to search for me in the dusky drowsiness of the evening, that he will have to go into the empty rooms, the attic, the closet with the electric meter and the fuse box, that he will have to search the garden, the grounds past the trees, that his calls will have to become louder so that they will reach the edge of the forest, up and down the slopes as far as the next farm, not to forget the garage, something obvious, to go to all the places where his secret flourishes. It is no secret, I know about his fear.

While I'm sitting at the artist's and watching him as he paints me, I hope for a decision. At some point there has to be an end to my waiting for hours and taking walks, taking walks and delaying my return home, only to have to wait for the whistling, for the whistled greeting on Jack's return. The voices in my skull, to which I always listen, exclude me more and more. My interjections are disregarded, the old arguments are continued without pause. The artist doesn't say anything, I suspect that he is afraid of the truth of his speculation.

Gurdjieff looks like a desert chief, Kathleen says. And he forever mixes up expressions from different languages. All those present form a queue from the kitchen to the dining room, in the kitchen Gurdjieff cuts up the meat that he himself has prepared, puts a soup bowl upside down over each plate, the plates are then handed on. – You think that I am like other people, I mean, normal, she says after a while. But I'm not. I don't know which is the sick me and which the healthy. I simply play one role after the other. Only now I recognize it. I believe that Gurdjieff is the only one who can still help me. – Do you think that there is such a thing, that there can be only one person who can still help you? – Your suspicion grows with every ring of the telephone, she says. How does Jack ward off his fear about you? He gets new strength with Rosie, then searches for you with the renewed, fresh strength.

In the artist's picture I sit on a chair in an empty room with open window in a fur jacket with wide shoulders; dangling from one ear there is some triangular fashion jewelry, my lips are sightly parted, the air going through this body can be felt, the head slightly tilted, Kathleen's fear in my eyes, the mood of departure. In my hands, which rest on my lap, I hold a small pump, from the pump a tube goes down to a mouse sitting on the floor. – If you work the pump, says the artist, the mouse jumps up a ways and screeches. Without fail.

I don't believe that you read my letters, Victor. I can't imagine that you simply disregard everything. All week long I waited for your letter, which did not come and now no longer can come. That made it impossible for me to work. I fully acknowledge that all your extra energy is directed to finding an apartment. It is discouraging to write letters. If you were here, we could talk or keep silent as we pleased. There is no reason why one should pay attention to some things, while wholly neglecting others, why one should give orders to some, while obeying those of others. Inside me there is chaos. Jack has had his beard trimmed. Yesterday he dug in the garden as though he were exhuming a hated body or making a hole for a loved one. I feel ill.

I'm tempted to write fantastic stories, I say. About grand staircases, hidden passages, about soulless catastrophes far away. To invent a border official in his late night drunken stupor, formulating petitions, with one foot in no-man's-land. Then I would give a name to the no-man's-land. – The more you want to take in the world, the more lonely you will feel, Kathleen says. I've always felt in disharmony. This, my secret sorrow for years, has now come to the fore. I really can't go on any longer pretending to be one person and being another. – What are you then in reality? I ask. – I only know what I would like to be, she says. I want to be all that I am capable of becoming. I want to be part of this world, to live in it, to learn from it, and to lose all that is superficial and acquired in me. I don't really know what I am. When I say that I am ill, there is still something else hidden underneath. But I don't know what it is. – I reserve the right, I say, to visit later all these people of whose existence I sometimes dream. My dream still excludes the names, it spares me certain details, but it preserves my stories for later. – More than I can possibly say, I understand your wish to escape your autobiography, Kathleen says. If one could remain oneself all the time, like some writers can, it would be a bit less exhausting. She folds the quilt, holds it in her arms like a small child. I would like to ask you for something, she says. And don't laugh at me. Gurdjieff thinks that I should spend several hours every day in a barn with animals. I could have a little couch of carpets and blankets in the hayloft. The animals' breath is supposed to do me some good.

It shocks me, I say to the artist, that Victor doesn't even ask how I'm doing. Yet another childish letter and entirely impersonal. Of course, he is always glad to receive mail. But only because he is alone. Do I just imagine this? Is there not relief in every line? Nothing seems to hold him any longer. Then let it be. – The artist is silent. Side by side we walk to the gravel pit. – The summer is almost gone, he then says. I have given some thought to the misuses of desire. And about punishment for desire, the desire of living. It is the worst thing that can happen to you. But we can't get this Catholic formula out of our head. I am all for exempting desire from punishment in our world, he says and laughs. When I look at my paintings, I would like to scrape the colors off again. – I don't know what I could ask of him. I'm afraid that it might be important now to prove with a question that I take him seriously. – Don't look so desperate, he says. I don't want to ask too much of you, given my circumstance just now. I don't yet know myself well enough that I could give advice to anyone else.

I haven't written a word since October and now

I won't until spring. – I don't see her, I only hear her voice from the hayloft. – But it's only September, I say. – We steal from other people their bitter pains, she says. They then die almost without a word. We, however, we survive because doctors now listen to our talk. – The cat has had kittens, I say. She has revealed her hiding place. I'll bring the young cats up to you. – Of the five little creatures, four thrive at their mother's belly, one is pushed aside and must be bottle-fed. The face of this little cat looks as if being born a cat is the worst possible fate on earth. It shivers, its head is damp, no one knows why, it just won't get dry; we blow on it, warm it in our hands, with a hair drier, give it chamomille tea, only a few swallows, then the water runs across its face, the animal refuses all help. We bury it. – Dead like a sheep, Kathleen says and weeps.

Listening when there is silence, when Jack isn't here, when Kathleen rests in the hayloft, surely there still must be something in this world. Whatever I start seems to turn away from me with revulsion, as if I had the evil touch. Crying, a melodic crying to lay down a trail in the air. At some time Jack is back again, as a matter of course no questions are asked, returning together to the shared evening. To love you forever, your terrible precept and commandment. Who could that be? In my thoughts I step on kitchen chairs, tie my estranged body to the beam, step down again, wipe off the traces of my boots, for it has started to rain once again. Much as the shadows in lungs afflicted with some disease, patches of condensation form between the windows and vanish again the following day. – The continent Gurdjieff, Kathleen says.

You can't force me to leave this place, I say. Then I'll go, Jack says. And you won't be able to live here alone. – Then I won't be able to live here alone, I repeat. But I'm not going to leave. – Kathleen looks up from her reading. The female figures of Miss Beauchamp are all immature, so to speak, she says with a mocking voice. They are afraid of their bodies, repelled by sexuality and birth and male aggression. The vulnerable child that is intimidated by the brutality of the adult world always speaks out of Miss Beauchamp's stories. The child in every one of her female figures has no possibility of escaping. In this sense Miss Beauchamp has never achieved artistic maturity. – What is one to say to that? I ask. – Mr. Gurdjieff strides into the kitchen, picks up a handful of shredded cabbage and eats it, Kathleen says.

Someone, something has followed a decree and slaughtered the life that Jack and I had shared. The clutching hand that I've felt for some time now raises me up, I seem to lose weight, under me the surroundings are quickly exchanged as in a set for a play. Another place is put forcibly under my body. The closeness of women, waiting for the mail, all that is a reminder of the past, of yesterday. The black notebook is a sharp contrast. Predictability, that is what separates me from Kathleen. We can't agree on a final word. – Prey still, but already beginning to act the predator, Kathleen says.

4

Once the diagnosis is made, Jack takes me to Vienna. I am supposed to report at the hospital at seven thirty next morning. We spend the night in our apartment. Jack is asleep next to me, while I quietly cry and consider how I might leave the room, get out to the hallway. The apartment is on the fifth floor, surely that should do it. The fear of waking Jack grows and swells up, lulls me into a semblance of sleep. It is a lonely morning, washing in the bathroom, everything resists my leaving this apartment. Jack takes the most direct route to the hospital. We have to wait for some time in the respiratory department. Almost all of the custodians and nursing aids are dark-skinned. An old man in an open hospital gown is pushed into the elevator, he sits hunched over in his wheelchair, the cold air on his exposed chest. We meet once again in the x-ray unit on the first floor, a woman doctor joins us and tells me that she had applied for a position as director of a clinic but had been turned down. Now she is glad about it, she probably lacks sufficient experience and training for the position anyway. We have an hour to wait until the x-rays are read. Jack and I go to an espresso, a quiet place at this time of day. A German shepherd lies down on the bench next to me and lets me pet him. Jack buys some cigarettes, we talk about the atmosphere at the hospital, I say that I can't possibly stay there. We pick up the x-ray report, I explain to the doctor that I would prefer to be admitted to a different hospital, she accepts this. But then I think that I might be better off to stay after all. I trust her as a woman. On the way back we stop for lunch at one of the restaurants along the highway. Everything seems so normal, we are just on a short journey. The car keys there on the table, the thirst can be quenched. The waitress wears a dirndl dress, its colors matching the table cloth and the curtains. I am envious of her for her work, her serving tray, the crude remarks by the cook. I envy her for her heels that peek out of her working shoes and may give her some discomfort.

Jack and I spend another night together, I am to be admitted to the hospital in Linz. Linz is closeby. The next morning, as we leave, we meet one of our neighbors. Jack stops, I roll down the window. I say: I've got tuberculosis. Not contagious, I add. The neighbor shakes her head, wishes me well. In the rearview mirror I see her standing and waving, she already is part of this meadow on a hillside on which some chore will claim her attentions, the trees of the orchard, however old they may be, that is where she belongs and where she will remain for the time being.

Any children? asks the admitting doctor who is taking the patient's medical history. None, I say. Last gynecological exam? A year ago. The chart at my bedside gets a red nametag. I share the room with Mrs. Koschitz, who looks like Miss Marple. The doctor has hardly left when she sits up and asks, what I'm in for. I've already been here a week, she says. Asthma. Are you married? – No, I say. Yes, says Kathleen. But I've been living with a man for seven years. – I have two grown-up sons, says Mrs. Koschitz. One of them lives in Linz, he is a tax consultant. They have three children. The oldest, my favorite, is in high school, she will be graduating next year. She gets straight A's. The boy is a little rascal, but smart. He knows all about computers! He keeps trying to explain to me how they work and then laughs and laughs. And the youngest, she's a problem child, she often gets ill, mostly with her throat, her ears, she always has a cold. Almost every week my daughter-in-law has to take her to the doctor. I was the godmother at the confirmation of the oldest. We drove to Krems, she had really wanted that. Most people in Linz get confirmed in Linz, that's how it is. We then returned by ship on the Danube, that is when my brooch fell into the water, the one my husband had given to me for our twenty-fifth wedding anniversary. – And the other son? I ask. – Oh, him, says Mrs. Koschitz. Him. He lives in Vienna. I only hear from him every once in a while. And even then you can't be sure he's telling the truth. You wonder where he got it from. Decent parents, we always had work, there was never anything like that with us, not like that. – What do you mean, I ask. – That someone would do such a thing, says Mrs. Koschitz. That's no profession! Everybody knows that. Often enough you can read in the newspapers about yet another incident, with such people. At the casino, that's where he is! As a – I don't know what it is called, but it isn't right. That is my big worry. My really big worry.

Only the first few days are really difficult, says Kathleen. Once you've gotten over them you can already look back, you've already accomplished something and done your part. The first days, they're the worst. You think, a week of hell, you won't be able to endure it. But there comes a time when you proudly count the weeks that you've been here already. And then sometime later on you'll be discharged and you leave for home and it is all in the past.

Mrs. Koschitz sits heavily on her bed. Her head wobbles a little when she gets excited. She used to own a riding school. When both of us have gotten well again, she will teach me how to ride, she says. Even the bishop has taken lessons at her stables! – Towards evening she finds the mugginess unbearable, with nail-scissors she cuts the collar and the sleeves off her nightgown. Now you look like a famous dancer, a celebrity out of the Golden Twenties, I say. She lifts the gown a little, takes a few dance steps, the shuffling sound of the slippers is just right. She prances in front of the doctor on evening rounds. Mrs. Koschitz has made herself pretty for you, I say. Just have a close look. – The doctor doesn't notice a thing. The neckline, I say. He laughs, asks whether on top of everything else we are going mad. That we already are, Mrs. Koschitz says and tilts her head and with a finger traces along the serrated edge left by the nail-scissors. She places her dentures in a glass of water and asks whether I mind if she continues to talk without them. I shake my head. If the Pope really does come to Vienna, then I simply must go see him, she says.

The confirmation, says Kathleen. Or is it: grandmother Koschitz. In Mrs. Koschitz' riding school. My greatest fault is not working up and writing out my ideas. The old woman who goes to Vienna to see the Pope. She can't stop herself from going to the street with the casino. She stands at the entrance, looks at the people who go in, always a little unsure of what she would do if her son should be among them. With indignation she sometimes thumps on the ground with her umbrella. Every time the door opens, she strains to have a peek inside. She tries to imagine what it must look like in there. Red plush, but no, it isn't a brothel. Mirrors, the gaming tables, what does a gaming table look like? Oh God, she has no idea. Today she saw the Pope. And for an instant his gaze lingered on her face, as if to say: don't worry about your son, Mrs. Koschitz. In heaven there is more joy over a lost son who returns than over...she had forgotten how it went on...than over a hundred...And she thought that it had to do with the bishop, that must have been the reason why the Pope had looked for so long at her of all people...

I think of home. I love the place in which I live. One could say that I'm attached to this house with all my heart. I close the doors behind me, forget the fears that tormented me there, now I just wish to be there, I long for it across these few kilometers, so far away, so near, so irrelevant is the distance between the hospital in town and the farmhouse.

The hospital is run by an order of nuns. I can't bear these women meekly putting up with their role, nor the soft chanting in the mornings. In the glossy brochure I can read how efficiently this hospital is operated, in one picture I recognize the nun from the EKG unit whose fingers I had found so repulsive, I look at the pictures of the student nurses and novitiates. They are recruited from the farms north of the city, close to the border. I'm thrilled by the notion of a community of women working autonomously, but then I see the picture taken during the bishop's visit. Loudspeakers spread the morning mass from the chapel along all the hallways, dragging the patients into a new day. I wait a few minutes longer, then I disappear into the bathroom. I try to be the first to use the bathtub.

The diagnostic work on the X-ray table. With his ballpoint pen the intern draws a cross on my chest where the inflammation is concentrated. Each time he says: now I have to make a mark. Each time I reply: That's all right. Make a mark, that's all right. Hold still, that's all right. Under the table he inserts and removes the plates; between the exposures, while waiting for the developing, he covers me with a cotton sheet. I hear his voice next door, he discusses something with a nurse, doors open, unfamiliar voices, curt exchanges, they seem to get along with few words. Time seems endless to me until he finally comes in again and continues with the procedure.

The danger of exaggerating my importance has never been greater. And yet, it has never before been more important to give myself precedence. I have some difficulty in finding the right balance. Like a wave, I break over me, in the very next instant who I am will be absorbed in the story which someone next to me is telling. The need to reconcile. To leave behind the wild battles, but not in exchange for the leaden peace and quiet which the calcium injections bring. The panic-stricken, heavy quiet, a deep and slow coursing in the orbit of my blood that disorients my head, renewed alienation, my familiar world taken away once again, to begin all over once again. I ask the attending doctor to discontinue the calcium treatment.

I miss going over sentences for faultlines and uneven textures, lovingly examining what has just been created. I long for my work, for what I know how to do. At the hospital there are incessant encounters between those who are competent, and those who do something very poorly. Every patient demonstrates an incompetence, a lack of control over the body. The patient wants to do one thing, but the body does something quite different. They no longer fit together.

In late afternoon, after five, I have access to the

typewriter in the doctor's office. I type a poem, over and over. The letters of the machine are very upright and tall, my language lies sinewy, unfamiliarly masculine on the page in front of me. I write: I feel weak. After having written a few lines, I feel that I am perspiring. Steps outside the door make me feel insecure, I shrink from explanations that may not be believed. I look around me, colored binders, a calendar, blue books, I touch the paper and the typewriter, nothing else. I sit in my robe on the swivel chair, try to block out the surroundings, to find to myself in this place. It seems that I have brought along all the insecurities, the things unresolved, all that depressed me, but where is my true self in its strength, my persona as a whole?

Back once again in the darkness of my room, I bare my teeth, cry while raging within, until my ears ring; my head is heavy with blood, I feel impaled by an unmistakable pain – which pain? I have an intense longing to be back home, I don't belong here. When I was a child, I could never imagine leaving home. To lose what was close and dear to me was the most horrible thought. Every separation cuts straight through me and I fall apart. – I went out into the garden just now, says Kathleen. The stars are out and there was a little bell ringing. I heard the evening meal being prepared. Dishes clattered, there was a soft movement on the stairs and in the passages and doorways. I imagined little children already asleep. Sometimes I feel that the stars are not at all solemn, but secretly full of joy. I thought of Jack, within call, in the house, at home...

I sense the professional curiosity of the doctors on their rounds, but also their reluctance to get too close to the patient. Perhaps some of them may wish to have a little more time with me. Most of the patients are asthmatics. In the morning they are hooked up to the cortisone IV, at eleven there is a meal, the visitors between one and three-thirty unwrap the fresh nightgown, sometimes there is crying. During the visiting hours the asthma inhalers are mentioned, their use is prohibited, like little children the patients are ashamed and hide the spray. The same happens with sleeping pills, which the family physician had always prescribed as a matter of course. So much is taken away and tainted with guilt. One curses one's weakness which draws one into this humiliating ritual. – When my medication has no effect, I'm switched over to an infusion. No one ever asks me what I might possibly need this disease for.

Kathleen sits in her bed, her head resting against a pillow. She sips sage tea, hesitates and then swallows. In the morning she had one of her wisdom teeth pulled. Yet another day gone, she says. A wasted day. All there to be written, but I just couldn't do it. – Why of all times do you want to write when you feel so weak? I ask her. – I'm an invalid, she says. I spend my life in bed. The whole day long I try to write but yet do not succeed. This is my reality, bed, medicine vial, tea-stained glass, tablespoons. Can you tell me, how I am to recover my self-confidence? I always had so much of it; Jack resented it, he considered it a coarse thing – my belief that couldn't be shaken.

Soon I will write this story, it runs through my head. I will invent two women, I was one of them, the other Kathleen. They shared a room, they wept over one man, they both wanted to write. One of them never knew the other. One of them was dead, the other ill. One of them lived, the other had been dead for sixty years. The one always kept appearing in the head of the other. The head of the other was confused, and then grew calm and quietly lay on a pillow. Someone had brought her a butterfly made of lacquered paper; she attached it to the tubing of the oxygen bottle which she never used. That is Psyche, she said to the doctors. One of them was treated, the other died. The one was sometimes the other, sometimes she herself.

As on thin ice, my thoughts are breaking through. In my head all manner of things are adrift. I say to myself: here I will be cured. It is the certainty that Kathleen will recover from this disease with me – how, I do not know. I won't let her go. I say: come with me to the ophthalmologist. And she comes along. His office is on the ground floor. There are some patients waiting in front of the door, complaining that these examinations are always scheduled during the visiting hours. One girl stares at us with dilated dark pupils. She is on atropin. Googoo-eyes, whispers Kathleen. Such a word you must be willing to accept, googoo-eyes, children's words or whatever you imagine, googoo-eyes, exactly that! My stupid eyes, a little too far apart, eyes to be annoyed at, googoo-eyes, there you have it! – Mrs. Koschitz, says the doctor at the door and Kathleen gets up.

Jack pays a visit, brings underwear, takes underwear away, brings books. I try to read in his face what he and Rosie had talked about on the way here. We don't mention her name to each other. I'm afraid that it might annoy him, and also I'm afraid of making him feel guilty, I know that guilt feelings would further weaken his love. As for our love, I can't expect anything of him, that much I sense. Nonetheless I keep on calling it love. – What remains of all those years together? asks Kathleen. It is difficult to say. If they were so important, how could they have come to nothing. Who gave up and why? Haven't I been saying, all along, that the fault lies in trying to cure the body and paying no heed whatever to the sick soul?

Every morning a student nurse cleans the bedframes, the window ledge, the crucifix on the wall, the tubing on the oxygen bottle. What are you reading, my dear, asks Mrs. Koschitz. – "Conversations with the Starving," says the girl. "Conversations with Stalin?" Mrs. Koschitz asks horrified. – I can't read anything. No stories about diseases, no stories about healthy people. There are no others. People are either healthy or sick.

Last night I had a dream, I say. I could choose between you, Kathleen, and a woman with whom I was acquainted from the Helenen Valley in Lower Austria. You know me from the Helenen Valley, said this woman. She stood on the lawn, pale, her eyebrows drawn up diffidently, as if she were about to be photographed, her closed lips slid back and forth over her teeth, she wore a wide-brimmed hat and her hair was still long, one strand of her hair, which was tied in back, dangled in front of her ear, she had her hands clasped behind her back, a habit left over from the long hikes, her legs stiff in thin stockings, large shoes. She says, all summer long I was driven to madness, but I was not mad. Nobody believes me. – You, Kathleen, were sitting in a wicker chair, legs crossed, with the long lapels on your chest, you were perspiring under your arms, on your upper lip there also were beads of moisture, you were smoking, jiggling a foot, your fingers spread wide, your dress taut over your thighs. Is it my turn now? you asked with a glance towards a group of doctors, who only now came into view. One of them gestured and you put away your cigarette. Everything in life, all that we really accept, changes on us, you said. – I looked at the woman and back to you again. Then I heard my daughter playing the piano in the house.

Are you married? asks one of the sisters. I say, no, I'm not married. – That's good, she says. Then it's easier for you, the time you spend here. – I dread self-pity, it keeps me captive, a stranger in my bed, it puts me in Kathleen's clothes. I see Kathleen sitting in her rented rooms, teacup, notepad, the doll Ribni on the bed. I search for her friends, again and again I try to come close to her. Later, in the doctor's office, I imagine that these hands do not belong to me, that they are her hands, the hands of a letter writer, of an unhappy guest in a hotel in the south. For what purpose?

The next morning Mrs. Koschitz is discharged. She demonstrates how her dog will greet her. But she will have to air out the house. Her husband always forgets to do so. I'll visit you, she says. As soon as I can, I'll visit you. – Kathleen lies in her clothes on the bed that has been vacated. I always try to do things too quickly, to think that everything can be changed in an instant. It is terribly difficult for me not to be intense. And whenever I am intense, I am a little bit false, to my regret, that is the truth. That and my inexcusable idleness. Look at the stories crowding at the doorstep. I should let them in. Their place would be taken by others who are waiting just beyond, waiting for their chance. The neat little garden which makes you feel sure a widow lives there. Mignonette, pansies, star of Bethlehem grow there. A narrow asphalt path leads to the door. But there is something about the windows – something quenched, expressionless. And there is something about the bell that suggests that your ringing at the door will not be answered at once. Or the farmer woman who comes into the room with a little overnight bag, looks around, greets you quietly, finally undoes the laces on her shoes and keeps rearranging them. She cannot know that the woman who shares the room with her has permission to take walks, and therefore believes her not to be quite right in the head as she now gets dressed.

I put on my clothes as I would another life, then quickly leave the room, worrying that I will be detained at the nurse's station. I walk past the sister at the reception desk and out; visiting hours. I am my visitor, taking myself for a walk. I come to a windy corner, hug myself in my coat; if only I don't catch a cold...Across the street is the showroom of a car dealer. The display window features a life-sized stuffed horse, its head seems too small to me. A store that sells lights, a boutique, a store for devotional artifacts, a religious bookshop. In a side street there is the Israeli prayer house, a policeman paces up and down in the garden. The man who sells roasted chestnuts in the pedestrian zone, the French fries hawker, Indian scarves. I imagine that I am short of breath, lying in bed has weakened me. After half an hour I turn around in the middle of the main street, go back the way I came, I don't dare to deviate. Exhausted, I walk up the steps to the third floor, greet a laboratory assistant, I knock on the door to my room before I enter. The farmer woman is asleep, in the bathroom I resume my masquerade as patient.

I hardly ever tell the doctors here what I'm really thinking. I'm amiable, show them a little of my determination, but then revert to the nice young woman, their sweet daughter. The sweet daughter of the chief of staff, the sweet daughter of the doctor on his rounds. It is fun, it makes me quite sad. I feel feverish in every reaction, I perspire while I phone, I perspire while I write, I lie on my belly and adjust the bed to be flat, I put my arms around the metal bed frame and move the palms of my hands to the next cool place. I spread my legs far apart, feel my knees pressing against the sheets, feel my body supported, leaving the odor of my body in this bed which is not mine, but which they insist on calling my bed, the sheets which practiced hands change every week. Once one of the patients wanted to take her dog into bed with her, says the nurse. I can understand that. – No need to cry. You just have to be patient, it takes time, it's not as bad as you think. And then – everything will once again be. And then – everything will be fine again. Do I trust medicine alone? No, certainly not, says Kathleen. The sciences? No, never. It seems a little silly to believe in a bovine cure when one is not a cow.

I admire the head nurse for her independence, for the warmth that she has managed to retain next to her almighty God. I have never liked to approach people via the detour of God. To love the crucified and abused Christ in every human being – that has never seemed plausible to me. One does not have to love God, what a waste. The head nurse asks me whether I might write an intercession for the next mass. You have an education, she says. No immediately relevant theme occurs to me. I try to explain to the sister what my priorities are. I don't know whether she attributes the heated words to my medical condition. Questions relating to the church have always provoked me. But perhaps that was only my imagination. I get enraged when I think that my rage can always be attributed to my disease. In my mind I hear the buzzing "Lordhearourprayer."

For a time as a child I went to Sunday mass at the municipal hospital. I avoided going to the larger, more splendid parish church, where everybody could observe me and the path to the communion was long and agonizing. I was also repulsed by a certain stained glass window depicting the Holy Hemma of Gurk, partly because of the female figure, which I did not like, and partly because of the name, which I thought very ugly. I felt close to the convent sisters in the hospital and trusted them. I was usually the only child at mass, and sometimes they took me along to their common room. Their names - Veronia, Silvana, Equina, Miktonia - were closely linked with their plain faces, which apart from their hands were all that testified to their corporeality. These faces and hands strolled about, like quotations of a body, the way they walked under the ample habits no longer had anything in common with the way a woman moves her body, they waddled along in their sandals and laced shoes, and the white cord about their waist meant nothing. The patients who sat behind me during mass gave off the odors of their medications, I was afraid of getting infected. Even the air they breathed could make one sick. I sat in the first row, so I could get to communion before the priest's fingers holding the host had touched the lips of the sick.

My exposed upper body, being turned, moved closer to the X-ray machine; somebody holds me firmly by the arm, pulls me closer, I shrink from the screen between us, I'm being pulled closer, gazing into the grayness, grayish grayness and lighter grayness, islands that dissolve in each other, intent on reading this landscape, my secret cache, which I won't reveal, my hidden sorrow, an emerged island, a little Atlantis, my hidden corner of an island. Doing battle with its shape, being compared, I as the mainland carry this island around with me. In their X-ray aprons the doctors look like butchers.

Kathleen, I say. Do you feel that someone loves your body tenderly? She is standing by the window, her arms stretched out, in this black dress that covers her body, a piece of material carelessly thrown over the thin, neglected body. Love? she says. This body? How can you love a sick body? What man wants a woman who is sick? I am only the Kathleen-who-is-going-to-be-better-some-day. But you, she says. You, and she turns around, now her face is in the dark, only the voice of this woman, with you it will do some good. Everything will be taken care of, just give it time.

The autogenics sessions are on Wednesdays. One of the men falls asleep, stirs, excuses himself with bewilderment. Someone else says that he just can't relax. It is twilight, late afternoon. The traffic outside on the street seems far away. I see myself sitting in a circle with these people, harnessed in this communal listening to the doctor who wears a different pullover at every session. She is very attractive. An older woman says: you are a beauty. A beauty, that's what you are. – It sounds almost obscene, the way she thereby gives the younger woman the power over everything.

Franz lies behind the curtain on the next bed in the massage room. He has been in the hospital twelve times already, he is missing one of the lobes of his lungs. He tries to tell me that he is his father's nephew, his father is also his uncle, his uncle his father, the son at once also the nephew, he, that is: Franz. After a few sentences he has to gasp for air, he looks like a parody of an opera singer. Some sentences he produces very softly, he can't articulate properly, then the shape of the sounds is lost. The uncle and the mother. His mother is strict with Franz, his uncle gives him money. Not much, and the health insurance is not working out very well. – The other side, Franz says to the new masseuse. No need to massage here, there is nothing underneath there! – The tapping of the masseuse falls silent, this gentle drumming is supposed to loosen up the mucosa. The women wear white face masks. Franz is eighteen and works in a special shop for the handicapped. Maybe I'll get pensioned soon, he says.

Franz is always on the move, he takes care of the medical floor from dawn until the radio stations go off the air at night. He brings newspapers and postage stamps, he mails letters, takes an old woman in a wheelchair to the X-ray unit, in between he goes to do his inhalations, can't stand it for very long and again pokes his head in the door, do you want to play twenty questions? When he first meets Jack, it takes some time before he leaves us alone. Jack has hardly gone when he comes into the room again and asks, is that your husband? – All this time no news from Rosie. Not a word from her. She remains loyal to herself. I admire her resolve. I would behave differently, I would visit her, perhaps once again talk myself into a comfortable deception. I know that I can't endure much. Don't make everything so difficult, they say. Sometimes the former contented life wells up in me: when I'm able to put something down on paper, when during visits I can make people laugh for a few minutes. Carefully take everything in, I think. The only way of getting through this trying experience, in this room, always exposed to the endless presence of others. How much I needed these hours at home, when I was all alone. To be able to take a walk, to be alone.

I struggle with my images, always knowing that it could be worse, much, much worse.

It is as if she's always watching me, never dropping off to sleep, says Kathleen. My sigh lifts her head, her concerned eyes asking why I had sighed. – Whom do you mean, I ask. Kathleen says: If I turn, she is ready with a cushion. If I turn again, then it must be my back. A back-rub surely would help? There is no escaping her. – Do you mean me? I ask. All night, the slightest rustle, says Kathleen, the hint of a cough, and her soft voice asks, can I do anything? – Who, I say. And if I do nothing at all, then she is sure to detect some fatigue under my eyes.

One evening there is a public lecture on Nicaragua. A development aid worker who had been there for five years speaks and shows slides. One of the sisters plays a recording of Sandino music. The aid worker describes how she taught the women how to weave, a skill that had been prohibited some fifty years. The women in the slides are all laughing. From the respiratory department only the school principal has come to the event, I saw him yesterday for the first time. He has a silk scarf around his robe, he nods to me. Afterwards he enlightens me, tells me how things really are in this world. For the first time in a long while I think of Victor.

We are going to change over to streptomycin, says the attending doctor. First you have to check for balance problems, a little walk to the E.N.T.

department at the Hospital of the Good Samaritans. But if you like you can take the ambulance. – No, I say. Why should I. – The old wing of the Hospital of the Good Samaritans has a certain grandiose decadence about it that no one would deny. The cables lying on the floor pretend to be in a film studio, high ceilings in the wide halls, I try to spot the cameras. The E.N.T. specialist doesn't show up for an hour, I imagine the nurse saying to me, I have time, time, I have endless time. I remember what I dreamed at night. I was in the basement of a house, a man bent towards me, he did not have the strength to endure his feelings, and then a woman came along, not as tall as I, a more delicate frame than I, blonde, I embraced her with both arms, pulled her to me and held her tight. She gave me great pleasure. How much do others get out of their life, I ask myself. Victor in Bolivia, I hope that he will be aware of the sun, the slums, and the children without a future. Some people rush about the world, schedule every free day, while I remain shut-in and pale in my room. The sense of having missed out on something. The feeling that there will be a time when I will not be able to turn around. And in front of me there is – nothing. Fear of death, yes, to be sure. The doctor establishes that there is nothing wrong with my balance.

If only every drop of the viscous, red fluid which slides into the vein on my forearm would be a word. After two hours, at the end of the infusion, I would be pumped up with a story and could spend the afternoon extracting it again with my writing, word by word. A circulation that makes good sense, squeezed into a vein, drawn out with my fingers. Writing is exhaling, casting off. My fingers produce odd pantomimes to accompany this process, one has to get used to this.

What does it mean when men hum? I ask. First they sing out loud, then they suddenly reduce the volume of their voices so that the sounds rise softly into their head. Whom do they quiet with their humming? And have you also noticed how the weight of a man no longer seems a burden which almost makes you suffocate; but rather that this weight is confirmation that you exist and the world with you, you could not believe it in any other way? And the much smaller weight of a child that fell asleep on you in its weariness, as if it had at long last come to rest in the cove of your arms, quiet and bliss? Kathleen says: Now I am – Anna Bichler. I am thirty-four years old, married, and have four children. – Any miscarriages? I ask. Yes, one, says Kathleen. I lifted a heavy suitcase onto the wardrobe, that's when it happened. – Children's diseases? Measles, she says. Mumps. Smallpox. What pills are you taking for asthma? Just a moment, she says, it will come to me in a minute, they are purple.

Anna has some difficulty tying her handkerchief around her forearm. She is supposed to keep the spot dry where she has been tested for tuberculosis. She tries to pull the handkerchief together with her teeth. Then she asks me to help her. When I touch the corner of the handkerchief it feels damp. She perspires, she doesn't wash often enough, the nurse tells her that she should shower every day. In the morning Anna winks at me, points at her forehead, motions to the hallway where the showers are. I don't know my way around these contraptions, she says. I'm not going to do that. - With prim fingers I touch the faucet in our bathroom, carry my towels back and forth, look suspiciously for telltale residues in the basin. In the evening she looks like a tent as she sits in her bed, legs stretched out, an equilateral triangle in all directions. Her head is turned toward me, I'm of great interest to her. I'm writing a letter, I say and hope that she will realize that her curiosity is disturbing me. She nods and smiles sweetly. I could slap her face. Why can't I say: Look away, turn around, leave me alone! She doesn't say a word, keeps looking at me, she is magnificent, I hate her.

I lie there with closed eyes, trying to breathe evenly and calmly but always forgetting to do so. Kathleen adjusts her pillow, I can hear her turning pages in her book. For her sake I cough a little. She gets up, gets dressed, asks me how she would look with short hair. Something like this, she says and and holds her hair away from her face. Should we get our hair cut? I ask. All at once I would like to do something together with her. Oh, she says, I don't know. It is so far. – I have a friend, a woman, I say, with whom I often talked about children. We decided to get pregnant together. For a long time she didn't know the right man. – And now? asks Kathleen. Now she has a daughter, I say. As you do sometimes, Kathleen says. She goes to the wardrobe, drapes her nightgown, which she had taken off before, on a coat hanger.

Facing Kathleen in a dream tonight, I say: I would like to shave the back of your head. I really no longer want to see your hair in a bun in which you shelter your delicate equilibrium. Something in Kathleen's face is not quite right, as I say this. Suddenly there are other people in the room as well. I sense that Kathleen is keeping something from me and only for that reason she has listened to me so patiently. Then several surgeons with quick strokes of the scalpels expose my chest cavity, pry ribs apart, murmur. I ask what might be the matter. They say nothing. Then they turn me over and shake me, and brown, wilted maple leaves fall out of me, but more than could possibly fit into me.

How are we ever to be disentangled? Kathleen has the doll along, as if she wants to settle in here for a longer time. Can't you stay here? I ask. – Now? she asks back. When at last things are getting better for me? Isn't that asking a bit too much? – Kathleen and Jack and I, we are the loops in a glass marble. Gently tapped, and everything begins to turn, overtaking itself and ending at the beginning.

Again the attending doctor fills up a new page with my results, that's enough for ten days. Sundays are red. I would like to be at home now, not just outside in my clothes, I would like to be at home, in the barn, with Jack, without the Jack who keeps me waiting. I would like to be somebody else and at home and don't dare to ask how much longer my stay may take. Why does one so readily give up one's accountability for oneself? And nonetheless is ready to have guilt feelings for being sick. I try to read, take out Canetti's autobiography. When as a yet undiscovered writer he is a guest at a doctor's home in Strasbourg and is lodged in the room in which Herder had received Goethe, he feels treated, as he might "perhaps later deserve." A comedy of vanity. Back to the shelf with the book.

After Anna is picked up by her husband, I pull open the windows, lie down on the bed, inhale deeply, wish never again to be disturbed, no meals, no X-rays, no faces. No voice, no body odor. Just the quietness of the city outside that chatters along without relevance for me.

After two weeks on streptomycin, the attending doctor asks whether I notice any color disorder. I say: Yes, I see nothing but green. He slowly turns to the wall, which is papered green. I'll ask you one more time, he says. Nothing out of the ordinary, I answer. – I suddenly realize that I have become used to his ways, that even the nervous scribbling of his black ballpoint pen on my temperature chart produces in me something like a soothing reassurance; I can imagine him as an artist who gets rid of his enormous restlessness by drawing on large sheets of paper, who stands at my bedside, sends me on foot to his colleague in the other hospital, and leaves me at least a hint of myself. Sit next to me on the fence, Kathleen, I think, hold on to my belt, play a little with your balance, feel the shock in your spine, catch yourself and tell me a story from your first marriage, or about your schooldays on the beach, or of your last night. In the meantime a specialist examines the secretary in the bed next to mine, trying to find the cause for her allergies.

A secretary who always eats a cheese sandwich for lunch, says Kathleen. And who can't resist buying green garments. Once again it turned out to be a green dress, while this time she really had intended to be careful...but when she stood in front of the mirror, which the salesgirl had moved a little in the wrong direction so that the rays of the sun sparkled and glittered in it, she had, right where she stood, seen another woman, an elegant, different woman who was just taking her leave, since she had to go to a rendezvous. A woman in a green dress. The sun made her nose itch, she had to sneeze, and again, she excused herself, and then she once again saw herself, the end of her nose slightly red, and she wondered why it could not be she whom someone was waiting for with a bunch of lilacs.

Once I climb up the hill to the castle and go into the museum. There is an exhibit about animals and plants of the native marshes. It's all the same to me. I am all alone in the museum, it would be the ideal place for getting to know someone, if only someone were there. I imagine seeing a man, about forty, who enters the museum halls after me, I adjust my pace to his, flirt a little with him as soon as I notice that he is interested in me. He has a short scarf, an open coat, horn-rimmed glasses, thick hair, his hands in his trouser pockets. Without speaking we go outside into the park, to the stone wall where the landscape drops precipitously down to the river. Mine is an aesthetic disease, oh yes, one can say that – it does not disfigure me, it allows me to take walks, it sharpens my sensibilities and all too quickly tires me out, no temperature or fever, it leaves me pale, as I always have been; the streptomycin, however, does have its effect on my hair. There is no need to have fantasies about death, the consideration given is tolerable, I only need to live for this indefinite period in an unaccustomed rhythm, to begin the day at six with a Hail Mary, temperature taking, ending the day with a "Good Night" to one of the four night nurses. Only after this "Good Night" does my day begin – the treasured letter-writing without being interrupted by doctor, infusion, laboratory appointments, the time when my body belongs to me and gradually my body and mind come together. A disease with a sense for intact appearances, no shortness of breath, no prolonged coughing, no vomiting and catching one's rasping breath, things are going quite well for me. Kathleen, with the searing iron in your chest, I think of what you told me so excitedly in the dream: H. came. He tells me that my right lung has almost recovered. Dare I believe such words? And the other is much improved. Tuberculosis no longer seems a scourge to him. One recovers more often than not. Isn't that fantastic?

Why you? Yes, why you of all people? Not my question, it is the question posed by others. Why you? Yes, why you of all people? Fear puts distance in one's eyes, the anger dissipates, then returns. I try to explain to my visitors what my illness might be good for. They look at me as if I had just joined some exotic cult. – In a dream I button up a little girl's winter-coat. She stands quite still, I crouch down in front of her, but she isn't my daughter. I can still feel her cheeks...then the dream ends.

On the second of December Jack brings an Advent calendar. I hang it up on my wardrobe with adhesive bandages. Every day someone different may open one of its windows. The head nurse takes her turn, fumbles with it, finally jabs the little door open with a syringe. When it is the turn of the attending doctor, a donkey awaits him. A horse, he says. I say: It looks more like a donkey. Finally he accepts my suggestion of a compromise, a dapple-gray horse.

There is construction in front of the window, that's where the new dialysis facility is to be built. The workers cast quick glances into the room, they are glad to be on the other side of these windows. In the morning, when I have breakfast, it is still dark outside, but one can already hear boards being unloaded. Mrs. Koschitz comes for a visit, I'm startled, she looks much worse. Perhaps it's only the tawdry coat, which I hadn't noticed when she had gone home from the hospital. She asks about all the doctors and nurses, about Franz, whom she had gotten to know before. She waters the plants, plucks off wilted leaves, looks around the room and stands there, but there is nothing that needs doing. The secretary looks on over the rims of her glasses, she again has blotches in her face. Mrs. Koschitz asks whether she is running a fever. The secretary takes off her glasses and explains that she may be allergic to synthetics. Too bad, but no contact lenses for her.

The staff spoils me. Every day I receive a new IV reservoir; the procedure can then be interrupted and the IV disconnected; I can get up. The other patients keep theirs for several days. You are the most expensive patient on this floor, says the attending doctor. – The little crucifix on the wall looks like a slender ski-jumper, or like a white bat. He inhales a thin stream of air, he does not like the air in hospitals, he is afraid of getting infected and having to waste his special reason for dying. Later a young man comes into the room, he is a Jesuit and as part of his training he works as an orderly. When he is supposed to remove the IV from my arm, he perspires while I look on. I ask him how he likes it here. He doesn't reply, he has to concentrate on his work. Then he says that lifting and washing the woman in 204, who weighs well over two hundred pounds, is not exactly the kind of work he had expected.

Once, when we are sure that no one will come into the room, Kathleen and I hold hands, dance quietly and solemnly around the two beds. We hear a melody in our head. Kathleen has such desire in her eyes. I press my palms on her buttocks, press her against me, as she presses me against her, we have everything in our head like a story that is thought out, a story for which nothing remains but the labor, in which not a word is missing, regardless of who may write it. I feel her limbs against mine, her flat belly, softly filling the palms of my hands. She closes her eyes, cheek to cheek we look into the world in different directions, that is how you let go of yourself in the outside world, not here. Her gentle fingers restore my body's dignity.

One afternoon the door opens and the artist is there. There you are, he says. There you are, I say. He has brought a bouquet – that shows me how uneasy he must feel. He moves a chair to the bed, puts the flowers on the bedspread, keeps readjusting his chair.

He is wearing sneakers. It's been a while, he says. Nothing much is happening at home, it's all the same, nothing has changed, you haven't missed a thing. – What about Friederike, I ask. Has she been back again? – No, she wrote me a letter. She apologizes, "for everything," she writes, I don't know what she could mean by that, it sounds as if she were apologizing for her very existence. I can't make it out, somehow it just doesn't interest me, I don't know, I don't know...let's talk about you! Tell me what they are doing to you! No, don't tell me about it, it depresses me, I really don't want to hear about your disease. I'm sorry. But I can't deal with it, I feel ill just coming here, I'm sorry, I'm impossible, I know, but I can't deal with it. I'm really a loser. I should be cheering you up, giving you strength, encouraging you, and what do I do? I'm hightailing it. Oh, God, you, I'm really confused, it really distresses me that you are here. I suppressed it, went away for a while, wanted to see you first, then something came up, but probably it was just that I simply couldn't get myself to come, I just couldn't do it. I just wasn't far enough along.

While you were gone for a walk, says my new neighbor Franziska, a woman came by. At first I thought she wanted to visit you and I told her that you would be back in an hour, but she didn't even listen to me. She went into the bathroom, flushed the toilet several times, then came to your bed and wanted to get into it. Hello, I say, what are you doing? Then she took your X-rays and disappeared with them. And, oh yes, on her finger she had a swab, she must have come from blood analysis. I think, her nightgown was – pigeon-blue. – Pigeon-blue? I ask. Pigeon-blue. – On his rounds the doctor has heard the story already. The disturbed woman was found in the visitor's lounge. That's the physician, says the doctor. Franziska says, no, she was a patient. Yes, says the doctor. The patient is a physician.

This looks like a story, says Kathleen later, but I wouldn't buy it. – What's wrong with it? I ask. What's wrong, she says, is that Franziska is no longer taken seriously by her neighbors in the village, ever since she became sick. In her village only those who can work hard matter. It is this feeling of exclusion, which is so difficult for an ordinary woman to understand, that should be described. She no longer understands the world. Her husband and the children are as considerate as they can be, but the people in the village, and especially the women, her former allies in the many small confrontations – they are no longer there for her. As if she had the plague.

I want to get away from here, I say, away from this room without a key, in which I am trapped behind a door that can open at any time. What is the point of taking a walk, if you have to come back. I want to go back to my house and lean against the wall, inhale and wait for the command for execution. And say, not now. But thank you for the beautiful life that has been returned to me. Out of the room, the air is cool, but it doesn't matter, a few cars pass by, somebody parks laboriously, a woman? Everything is happening at the same time, we are all alive at the same time and don't comprehend this, we irritate each other with "Leave me alone!" and "Can't stand to see you!" But you I do want to see, I want to see and touch you and go dancing with you, look at our feet, back and forth, hopping and with our hands clapping the beat and applauding and defeating boredom. You are wearing your sneakers, under your arms the black wings of your jacket flap and flutter, and there is nothing to remind us of times gone by. For the first time everything is so that it lifts me up, all of me, caught up in movement and gaze and a brief charged contact.

At night I have two kinds of dreams. In one dream looms a place, a building, an institutional building, a hospital perhaps, with old hallways, brick walls, hallways that are dank, long hallways, rooms in which faces look up with indifference, the building of an institution that holds me against my will. In the other dream I find myself running with leaden legs, this exertion of lifting my legs, the ground beneath me remains fixed, without pain I dive down against a stronger weight, but no one is pursuing me, I just fail to reach a destination, miss an engagement.

It takes me almost twenty minutes to get to the cathedral – it is cold inside. I listen to the stillness, a woman crosses the nave, kneels, leaves by the other door. I think of the artist. Hello, I say to him in my mind. I'm well again. – In the hospital I have just removed my masquerade, when Jack arrives. A hello from the artist, he says. I met him today. On Jack's sleeve there are some wood shavings. What have you been doing? I want to know. One of the sheds, he says, the one to the left in the front yard, you know the one, I put on a new bolt. – After Jack is gone, I estimate when he might be home again. I wait another quarter of an hour, then I call him. Then I think that he must be at Rosie's. After a half hour I call again, I'm afraid that something may have happened to him. The coins get warm in my hand, my hand smells of metal. Other callers all speak into the receiver, I now keep trying until Jack answers. In between I call people who are at home, wait and listen to the busy signal, as if that could suddenly change. At last Jack is there. I went straight to the barn, he says. The wind had damaged the entrance door. There's a snowstorm out here. – I am grateful, relieved, I postpone my anger, postpone everything which could terminate this waiting.

I know that I shall soon die, says Kathleen. But not because of my lungs. How one is flung up, held, and then plunged back, part of the ebb and flow. I feel that meditation would cure my overly sensitive mind. – She falls silent. Outside it is snowing lightly, snow on the verge of turning to water. Thus it takes a great amount for patches to form. In my mind I hear the cars driving through the slush, their windows smudged.

This wet snow plummeting to its death, I almost feel sorry for it.

If only I could go to an art gallery, white walls with great paintings, only one on every wall. Paintings in yellow, red, brown, clay-colors, warm landscapes assembled on a few square yards of canvas. Shall we visit Victor in Bolivia, once we are healthy again, asks Kathleen. Oh, there is something so lovable about him – his eagerness, his passionate eagerness for life. – And the terrible postcard that he wrote you? I ask. It's true, she says, he did write that he despises me. That I repulse him, as I lie here steaming in my consumption. But one has to understand that. He is full of agony. – Let's go for a walk, I suggest. I have to get out, fresh air. Fresh air and an art gallery. – I haven't been to an exhibit in years, says Kathleen.

Do you know the painting with the sunflowers? she then asks me. That picture revealed something to me that I did not know before, these yellow flowers brimming with sun are still with me. This picture taught me something about writing, a release into a kind of freedom, a shaking free. In time, as one works, one's vision narrows and contracts. Only when something breaks through, such a picture, then one is released again. I can then smell the picture as I write.

Facing the paintings in the gallery, I have the urge to thrust my hands into cans of paint, to paint over a wall, to press my forehead against a painting that is still wet, to show that I am alive and not the way some people think. The red, oily medication that I take every morning mixes with my blood and with the color found on the paintings. The second pulse to which I am connected and which I can speed up until my head throbs and fear seeps in nonetheless. The pulse that one can slow down until it feels as if one is sliding into a deathlike sleep. I struggle for knowledge about myself, for the person who accepts accountability, the person I had been and that I am. On the staircase leading to the ground floor of the gallery I stop and check my face in front of the large mirrors. My face is in hiding from me, I know it all too well, it has nothing to tell me anymore. Eyes, cheeks, mouth, nose, forehead, lines and wrinkles, blemishes all gathered for this face that carries my name. And otherwise? The longer I look at myself, the more familiar and stranger at the same time do I become, my eyes turn into generic eyes, my mouth turns into just a mouth, my story draws together into a pain in the back of my head. – Back once again in my bed, I think that the artist should paint my face. A nude painting of my face, nude in the distortion of the brush strokes, reaching nudity through colors which I do not have, by making it unfamiliar, which would then reveal its true reality, the essence of my face.

Greta is twenty. One senses that at some time a terrible fright must have swept over her childlike features, injuring the corners of her mouth. At sixteen she had a child and got asthma. She works in the warehouse of a large department store – the forklifts are all operated by men. The child is in the care of her grandmother. Greta sometimes looks at me as if I were taking her picture and she had to pose. In the first night she has an attack, she coughs, clings to her bedside table, she tugs, shakes, coughs, says: Don't ring for the nurse! She rages with the bedside table, beats on the table top, wants to conquer the rasping noise in her by beating on the table top. I don't know which is worse for her – to suffocate in this coughing, or to have to see the doctor. I get the night nurse, Greta slumps back on her pillow, her nightgown drenched. Then the doctor comes, asks if she would like some cortisone, Greta says that perhaps she is pregnant. Would you like some cortisone? he asks again. I don't know, says Greta. She nods between her coughing fits, strikes the sheets with her hand, quiets herself with her beating, weeps in her fury with whatever breath remains. Soon the noise has abated, she asks me whether that had been the Persian doctor? I say: yes, I think so, at least he looked Persian. How does she know that there is a Persian doctor. That is the kind of sly cleverness I remember from school days, bad students sometimes tossed me a few snatches of information while copying the homework from my notebooks. Greta, I say. Will you be able to sleep now? Yes, she says, I'm all right again, quite all right. After Greta has fallen asleep, I remain awake for a long time. These are hardly stories, says Kathleen. Life is taking a new breath, nothing else matters.

During the day Greta dispels her ghosts. Her radio by the bed is on at full volume, hard, loud, and fast. There's too much talking, too fast, I can't ignore it, I wish I were deaf. Reports, commentaries, music, breaking news, music, jokes, everything that I would rather not listen to, clutters up my mind. My memories torment me, I don't want to have to understand anything anymore, just let there be peace and quiet. At what point should I have said, please turn it down a little, or: Turn it off, and still have been able to do so with a calm voice? You and all your noise – !! Later she turns it off by herself, says: Hey, I hope you don't mind this music! She plays with the rabbit-ear antenna of the TV that she has brought along, tries to focus the test pattern. When I first came in here, she says, I thought that you were a teacher, you looked so strict. Intimidating. But actually, you are really sweet, so – sweet. Could you bring me some cigarettes, please? Please.

If I had a child, says Kathleen, I'd play with it and kiss it and make it laugh. It would be my guard against the most troubling feelings. I think that's true for all women; with their child in their arms they feel secure and safe.

The head nurse was horrified when I told her that I might be pregnant again, says Greta. I hope that the pills work. You haven't learned a thing, she told me. – How often have you been here, I ask. Three times, she says. She is coughing again, her anger clumps across her tongue, it noisily thrusts along, a sing-and-throw-up language.

Franz looks in the door, how is everything. I may be discharged next week, he says. After each third sentence he inhales deeply and then the coughing releases him from this exertion. What's your girl friend up to, asks Greta. Which one do you mean? asks Franz. The night nurse on the surgery floor, she says. The redhead. Oh, her! She won't be on duty again until tomorrow. Franz is sitting on my bed and jiggles and moves his feet back and forth. He grabs at my foot under the sheets, Greta cries out, Franz brings his hand to his mouth, I kick at him, he laughs and coughs, spits saliva on his sleeve and gasps for air. I've already been to mass today, he says. Did you hear me sing? – Later on we watch a ski race on television. Once a doctor comes in, ah, here you are, he says and gives Franz his injection. Franz holds his arm out as if it didn't belong to him, gets excited about an Austrian skier. Hold still, says the doctor, I might hurt you! If you get tired of your admirer, just throw him out!

I once wanted to write a story about a young woman who every morning walks along the beach to do her shopping, says Kathleen. She sees the men, the way they mend their nets, she is annoyed about the ugly oil barrels, which some boys on horseback are using as obstacles. She always wears a thin scarf that is crossed in front and tied in a knot. And once she sees soldiers bending over to strip, their hair blowing in the wind. This gives them such a defenseless, innocent appearance. – And then? I ask. Kathleen shrugs. Then she feels this enormous anger, I say. And on this morning the grocer, with whom she usually has a nice chat, wonders why the young woman is so sullen, disregarding the dates that he so attentively had offered to her.

The artist has come for a visit. He has baked and brought along some whole wheat rolls. As he bites into one, he chips a tooth. He sits there with a crooked mouth, one can see how his tongue keeps working at the sharp edge of the tooth. I have to laugh, I give him a hug. You smell of soap, I say. You smell so fresh. I miss you, I say tenderly. He brushes my hair behind my ears and from my forehead. Then he says, I'm sad about your illness. I feel sad, I miss you. You are always just here. You don't walk through my rooms with the paintings, I miss you. I feel sad, I cry, I drink a bottle of red wine all alone and don't feel like inviting anybody. – I want to ask him about Jack, but I don't. I feel love for you, says the artist.

I lie in my bed and in my mind travel up my spine, feel my shoulder blades, my elbows resting on the sheets, the back of my knees, the calves, heels, slowly turn my head to the side, feel the tension in my neck abate, feel how my head rolls loosely in an arc, press the back of my hands against the sheets, feel every single knuckle, feel my buttocks, my head slowly rolls back to the other side, time passes but I don't think of time, I am at peace and lie in my body on this earth, on this arc of the earth, in this hospital bed. My eyes are closed, I see yellow inscriptions on a red background, a peaceful painting. I am happy to be alive, to be in my skin, I forget the seat of the disorder, the smoldering, occupied tissue. – Now in winter Ribni wears boots, says Kathleen. She can keep them on when she sits with me on the bed. – The woman that you are for me does not exist, I say. For example, I would like to watch you as you walk across a stage. You are wearing tight jeans, a loose white shirt, your hair is loosely gathered up with a few barrettes. The soles of your feet caress the floor. Right up to your neck you feel the pleasure of every step, you nod, with your fingers you snap the rhythm to your enormous desire. Everybody laughs and applauds and perspires and knows, that's it. That's what it is all about.

In the coffeehouse I observe the men at the chess tables. I feel closer to them in age than to the students who toss their book bags into the corner, light a cigarette and stick their heads together until they move apart with thundering laughter. I leaf through a magazine, decide to bring something along for Greta, but not the cigarettes she asked for. I sit on the cushion like a pensioner who is afraid of her apartment. The waiter brings coffee and an open-face sandwich, which I eat with knife and fork. Strong coffee that takes a hold of my body from within. The lobes of my brain keep order for me, make sure that I don't pay with foreign currency or push my leg against the man next to me, a pursuit under the table, left, right.

On the seventh floor they all have the flu, says Franz. I don't go there anymore. That would be just what I need, to get the flu from those old hags, nothankyou! I put the newspaper in front of the door, let the Jesuit take it in, that little shit! – Franz laughs. I can go home Monday, he says. You'll see, come Monday and I'll be gone.

Greta has gotten to know a patient in the visitor's lounge. He is on the sixth floor, kidney problems. When she comes into the room, she brings along the smell of smokers. Sometimes she smokes secretly, but then brushes her teeth for a long time out of fear of the doctor. If you smoke, you are tossed out. I ask her whether that has ever happened. Don't know, she says, but I'm sure it's true. – Then she says, guess what I just did. Had a beer? I say. She shakes her head. Kissed your new friend? No. Well, OK, she says. I went to confession. Since it worked out again, since I'm not pregnant after all. – I try to imagine what it would be like if I went to confession. Haven't believed in God in years, felt much anger, even more fear. Restlessly tried out the years between twenty and thirty. I'll be celebrating my thirtieth birthday in this hospital.

The attending doctor draws a bouquet on the temperature chart, Franz brings herbal candy and kisses my hand, runs out, comes back to say good-bye. The artist brings a kaleidoscope. We take turns looking around the room, Greta makes faces when I see her multiplied as if coming out of an unfolding crystal. She then looks through it, without closing the other eye, her eyes stare out birdlike. The artist says: It's a miracle that I never meet Jack here. Would you mind very much? I ask. I think he wants to fix me up with you. Today, of course, the chances are quite good that we should meet.

Once Greta is asleep, I say, well then Kathleen, what is a healthy life to you? – Work. I want to live in such a way that I work with my hands and my feelings and my brain. And then I want a small house with a garden and lawn, animals, books, pictures, music. And out of all this I want to write.

I want to speak with my voice, yet cannot find it. Once it presents itself as confident and self-assured, but that is not how I am, another time it is too thin and small. A kindly man speaks with me on the stairs. I have often seen him on our floor, I know his brown dressing-gown. He says: Now the head doctor is angry with me because I refuse chemotherapy. I'm now trying something quite different, I'm not going to let them take my hair and have myself totally and slowly destroyed. I've been kicked out! – The thought that every day countless people are being told that they have only a few months to live frightens me. I listen for this fear in my head, to see whether a curiosity that

I thought I had long lost was hiding in it.

I dreamed that you worked in road construction, I tell the artist. You drove along the street with a paving machine, the street along which I went to school. The road was dug up along the way. Boards led over the trenches to the doors of the houses. The danger of collapse was very real. You very calmly drove back and forth on your machine, there was not a sound, nobody spoke. – The cat had a butterfly in its mouth today, he says. For weeks the butterfly had been dangling in the tool shed and was passing the winter there. The cat sat in front of the door to the shed and munched and had colored dust around her chin. After that she softly gasped for air. I gave her some milk. Then the telephone rang, I ran up from the basement, when I answered, there was nobody there. I thought of Friederike. A few minutes later a friend called and told me that an acquaintance had caused the death of her child. He was very upset, it was just too much. There was nothing that I could tell him, I was silent. After that we only said: Well then. And hung up. I felt surrounded by an incomprehensible world. I thought of you, that you would get well again, that I need you. Reassuring words simply deceive you past the fear, they slip away once fear begins to grow bigger – He remains silent for awhile. I think that I should be careful, he is not at the center of everything. I can't go on with the same old mistakes; there would be so much to talk about with Jack, but Jack has no words, Jack can only leave without a word and return whistling, his inner life remains inaccessible to me, I slip off on the pupil of his eye, he doesn't let me in. – By the way, last night I went to the pub for the first time in a long while, says the artist. And do you know who was there? The Edelweiss princess. – Who might that be, I ask. – You don't know her? The Edelweiss princess is about sixty, she wears a red folksy costume with full sleeves, almost like wings, she usually sits alone at a table and loudly talks to herself and to others, she is terribly tall and skinny, a scarecrow. When she walks, she flails these long limbs. Years ago she used to dance on the tables. For a while she sold souvenirs at the parish fair. She lives with her brother. – And why Edelweiss princess? – Because of her white panties. Which could be seen when she danced.

I've been thinking of you for days, says the artist. That way we are together in my head. My thoughts end with a "you" marker, that is, they are sentences that are addressed to you. Don't ask me whether I love you. I couldn't tell you anything about that. For days I talk with you, that's all. That's a great deal.

Do you want to know how I'm doing, asks Kathleen. Yesterday, upstairs in my room, I suddenly wanted to take a little leap, a jump-for-joy. I hesitated, held on to the window sill for safety. Then I went into the middle of the room and did jump. And this seemed almost like a miracle, I needed to tell somebody. But there was nobody there. So I went over to the mirror. And when I saw my excited face, I had to laugh. It was a marvelous experience.

Over Christmas I will be allowed to go home for two days. The head nurse says: Just don't get sick! And if you should have an accident on the way, on no account let yourself be admitted to another hospital! You are not discharged. Otherwise there'll be difficulties. – Jack laughs and says: She can't of course be in two hospitals at the same time, poor thing. – On the way I ask him how things are with Rosie. He doesn't reply, seems to wait to see what else will come from me. I say: I could imagine you living with her on the first floor, for a while at least. I'm not going to leave our house, nothing has changed about that. – The road is slippery, Jack suddenly has difficulties keeping the car under control, we slide from one side of the road to the other, on the right side there is a gentle incline going down to the river, I consciously note the repeated back and forth, no oncoming traffic in these seconds, then the swings get shorter, Jack once again has the car under his control.

The yard, the barn, the light in the barn. The cats in front of the door, my boots in the hallway. I sit next to the stove, while Jack adds wood, gets the Christmas tree, asks me whether I would try to find the ornaments. I attach stars made of straw to the branches, little red apples, I don't ask where they came from, I put up gilded nuts, turn the tree a little, drape a white table cloth around its base. Jack gives me a little package, my present for him is not much bigger. We both give each other a watch. I spend the evening in bed wearing two pairs of pyjamas and covered with blankets, I'm cold, I'm afraid of catching a cold, I smell the raw air when Jack opens the window, I draw in the smells of the house, I find it hard to ward off the power with which the house captivates me. I love this house in which I've become ill.

The next day we take a little walk, then Jack does the cooking, I again sit by the stove, read distractedly, look out the window, look at the Christmas tree, think of the hospital, of Greta, who cried when I left, of Rosie, who remains silent and will continue with her presence. Jack had said nothing further to my suggestion. I don't even know whether he seriously considered it. In the kitchen I open the drawers, I walk through all the rooms, everywhere I open the drawers, open the doors of the wardrobes, rearrange the shoes in the hallway. I touch the dresses, the skirts, the sweaters, I smooth out the wrinkles in the underwear, the stockings, wipe the dust from my bedside table. There is dust everywhere, Jack has not cleaned once. Of course he has cleaned, he says. I sense how we need the good will of an illness and of the Christmas spirit. I have the feeling that our living together is a life-threatening machine.

After dinner the artist comes for a visit. I ask him about Friederike, she stayed in Switzerland this year. No one speaks of the past, but I sense how the artist, too, makes his comparisons. I lie in my bed as a loser, from the other room one can hear birds pecking at the window. – There's a rabbit in my garden, says the artist, before dusk it sits in the garden and muses. Then it gets dark and in the morning it's gone.

At the heavily barred window of the house opposite, says Kathleen, there was a little girl in a shawl reading a book. She had a small, oval face, with her hair parted down the middle. She was perfectly charming, as if set in the window with the shimmering white pages. It is as though God opened his hand and let you dance on it a little, and then shut it up tight – so tight that you couldn't even cry. – What is the meaning of the red shield on my bed, I ask her. Am I in danger, or the others? I don't have a sense of how things are with me. Whatever the doctors say gets translated to something else for me. I try to interpret their faces when they look at the X-rays, I keep repeating their observations to myself, I forget how I really feel. I lie here all alone under my eyelids, I'm afraid of no longer understanding myself. You, Kathleen, are the case history of someone else. I won't again know how I am doing until I close this room behind me, superstitiously having avoided the "See you," leaving in a taxi or in Jack's car. Away, away from the rituals, from the secure daily schedule, the friendly faces, the well-meaning jokes. I am still excused from all obligations, except for the task of getting healthy again. Hard work for someone who feels so worn out. Always feeling tired, too tired for reading, for writing, entirely awake, awake as if in the middle of life, as awake as one is while shoveling snow or chipping away at patches of ice or lugging loads of hay. Longing for the house, the garden, the animals, for one's own things, the things by which I once again recognize myself, which show me that I exist. Here, too, I have made myself such a stage, books, butterflies, like a child that takes its teddy bear to kindergarden as protection from strangers, as you do, Kathleen, with your doll Ribni.

I don't want to leave you, says Greta. – Don't be a fool, I say. You should be glad to get out of here. – Everything is getting so messed up, she says. You know my parents. Will I ever be entitled to decide what should happen with my child? I won't. They have custody. – She empties the drawer of her bedside table. Those who leave give their fruit and flowers to the nurses. Greta has nothing. You can keep my TV, she says then and beams. You can keep it as long as you can use it here. You're sweet, I say.

An old woman moves into Greta's bed. What can you say to someone who no longer wants to eat? She has a heavy, plump body, she has already lost twenty-five pounds and is still overweight. She can't get herself to eat anything, she screws up her mouth when the nurse puts the tray on her little table. Sit next to me, I say. Let's eat together, why don't you get up.

She says: I can't eat anything, I just can't. Try it, I say. The soup looks really good. If I were you, says the woman, I'd get myself sterilized. There's no point in having children when you're not healthy. You poor thing. – In the evening I read to her from the newspapers. At every accident and disaster she expresses her horror, hangs on to it, but I sense a certain satisfaction behind it all. No more stories? I ask. No, says Kathleen and shakes her head. No more stories.

When I begin to lose my hair so that only two thin braids remain behind my ears, they send for a dermatologist. He's an older man in street clothes under a white smock; he looks like a server at one of the fast food stands. He wears transparent gloves and with a thin wooden rod he parts the strands of my hair. He doesn't say anything, writes a prescription, makes a note of the visit on the chart. I ask him what the problem might be. He says: You'll get a biological shampoo and a herbal tonic. – On my bed there is the glove turned inside out and the wooden rod.

On New Year's Eve Franz is back. I didn't want to stay at home, he says. Everybody is celebrating, and I'm supposed to sit at home. I'm not that stupid. There's more going on here. – As a start, we play his favorite game, twenty questions. On the back of my laboratory reports we draw a grid for the categories: city, country, mountain, river, plant, animal, celebrity. We stop at the letter P, Franz is finished first. Plant! he cries out for the cue "plant." But you can't do that, I say. Franz yells: a plant is a plant! – His yelling awakens the old woman. Her labored breathing. I was in the ice cellar, she says.

Shortly before midnight Franz and I take the elevator up to the ninth floor. At the end of the hallway there are some young people in street clothes. We look out of the large windows, the dome of the closest church, the telecommunications building, the flat city, the tall sky. Then the first streamers write signs for us. Franz is excited. The clock in the hallway shows three minutes to twelve. Behind the monastery there's an eery green shimmer, bells ring, it is so important to just watch that we forget to wish all the best. All the best, health. I ask Franz how long he has been ill. Since birth, he says. – Back down on our floor he fetches a small bottle of lukewarm champagne from his room. We put Greta's TV in the hallway, there is a German variety show. We hardly hear what is sung and spoken, we've turned the volume down so low. The convent nurses keep coming by. At one o'clock we are in bed in the new year. I can hear the breathing of the old woman as it rattles with her through the night. No more stories. I have forgotten to wish her all the best. Her heavy, pale body that exerts itself so, that she drags into the bathroom in the mornings as if it were a second self. Can I walk? Only creep, says Kathleen. I feel that my whole chest is boiling. The notepad, the draft from the windows, a longing for home. Small things, passion; lonely, truthful. The doll Ribni. Sadness. A fur coat. Of what else am I reminded when I think of you?

Nothing is the way one thinks. Waiting turns into the mail that does not come, the silence of the telephone, the delayed visit; it is doing without the times in the garden, the quiet words with the sheep; it is being layed out under the X-ray apparatus; the searching for the face in the mirrored instruments; it is an unaccustomed longing for the artist, a listening for footsteps, again and again listening for footsteps.

Once a priest comes to the old woman, she complains to him about the bad life she has had, she submits to him her case about her bad luck. He admonishes her to be patient, to have faith in our Lord Jesus Christ, who has assumed the cross for all who have sinned. – When he is gone, she sends me for a church paper. She is not going to last long, the head nurse says outside. Full of metastases. I feel startled. All this time I hadn't once thought of the obvious. She wakes up three or four times during the night and changes her nightgown, which is drenched with perspiration. In the morning these gowns lie on the floor, the battle garments of the preceding night. Nobody explains to her the significance of these bouts of perspiration. Each night I keep watch over my fine perspiration, the symptom, and arrive in the morning, dry. No cause for alarm, we are at a safe distance, this tuberculosis and I and everything else. The name of a disease, and underneath there is a whole terrain of which these doctors know nothing. To dissolve, to transform into tissue that is compatible with my tissue, to quench the temperature, what do I know, to reverse the polarity of this deathly process.

Painting is nothing more than a greed for life, says the artist. What pedantic philistines we are, with our battles and passions and boredom deposited on canvas. This search for ever new forms of your life, your being, your materiality, of your matter, how else can I exist, again and again you try to get close to yourself, to seduce yourself, coax a confession out of yourself. And your hands, how they decode your madness! Sometimes I'm able to watch my hands as they paint. That is like meditation, I let myself fall into my hands and they know how to go on, know for a few seconds how much pressure to use, in which direction, they dab the brush into the paint, the brush caresses the canvas, applies a makeup extracted from anger, of which at that instant I may not even be aware.

The fire that feeds the smoldering heat in my lungs is being walled in, walled in to extinction. Shot at, confronted, encircled. It is to consume me no longer. I look into the mirror in the bathroom, search for the reflections of the fire in my cheeks, I look pale and have almost recovered. The urge to put up a good fight, what of it. The urge to drum on the wall of the sick room, to drum everybody together and to show them my pale, healthy, wild face. To prevent the old woman from dying, to contradict the doctors. Wanting to lie in a heated room and model for the artist, to tell him of a strange story which I have experienced and of which I was the protagonist. Wanting to evict Jack, to put him outside the door. Jack, outside the door, outside Rosie's door. To live alone, to be strong, and not to need his whistling when he comes home. What is it going to be like when I really do come home, sometime in a few weeks?

If I didn't have my walks, I would lie quietly on my bed, my head to one side, reduced to shallow breathing. I go through the unfamiliar city, know the few streets that lead to the hospital, pass a third-world store, see the nameplate of a club for migrant workers, try on clothes in a boutique, buy nothing. I think that in time the business people in the area must be getting to know me. I listen to myself, as I explain that I am in the hospital, permission to take walks, no contagious disease, just tedious, listen to myself reciting the litanies about patience, hoping that someone would tell me the story of their life, now I would have time for it. On a walk I once meet the chief of staff, we stare at each other, he too seems surprised that I exist.

What happened? I ask the artist. What happened with you? he asks. I now paint differently, he says. Everything has turned wild. I kiss you tenderly, but you really should see these pictures. Everything that I had done before, I took to the attic. Every time I visit you, I paint a picture. They are pictures with wounds, I inflict wounds on the canvas, I punch in nails, which I then pull out again, I glue on strips of canvas and then tear them off again, I injure, bandage up, doctor, remove the bandage. The painting then leans in front of me on the chair, its wounds healed; the traces of abrasion dry out, harden, drops can be chipped off, seams are smoothed. I continue to work on the paintings on the following days, they still yield something or other. – And you? he asks after a pause.

I do know that afterwards I will want to live again unmarked, with all the strength that I'm capable of and with all exertions, without sparing myself anything. I want to be able to yawn again in the afternoon, all because of my work. To be tired from what I've done, to stretch out my hands, arms, legs, watch how the injection scars fade, how the skin closes over the unfinished sentences, how I can take care of myself, rising early, taking the car; to know when to turn off, to pump gas at the service station, to put on the snow chains, send a telegram, decide when the light is to be turned off, keys, refrigerator, gas stove, perhaps visit a friend who is sick and who sits in her bed with a doll, mail letters, receive letters, breathe, inhale deeply past the scars that disfigure my upper body and make my shoulders sag, to have no more fear. No more fear.

I have fallen in love with you, I say to the artist. I want to be fully aware of it, this time I must do it more carefully. He sits beside my bed, caresses my forearm. In loops and circles he inscribes his feelings invisibly; on my skin he imagines stories about him and about me. We say very little, look at each other for a long time, only his hand draws its patterns on my arm, calms me, excites me, catches my excitement, inverts the calmness. I learn to read in his face, look at his lips, let my eyes suggest to my mouth what they see there of soft skin etched with tiny folds, white, how it feels, mouth on mouth, and the brief evasion, only to regain the touch. The few sentences are a contracting and tensing of the lips, are the tiny folds of the lips that have a part in speaking, revealing and concealing of the teeth, moistening, gasping for breath, sweet breath. Before these sentences can mean anything, they have already said so much. I just want to look at this mouth. You are not listening to me. I let myself sink into this soft deciphering, your incomprehensible secret speaking, your whispering.

My nightgown is sticking to my skin. I get up, take off my gown, dry my body, get dressed. I'm afraid for you, says the artist. How much longer do you still need for your illness? – We take a walk together. He has his arm around my waist, pushes, lifts me up by my side, presses me to his. We meet a man I know from before. He stops, greets me with wonder, asks what I'm doing here. I say: I've been living here for nine weeks. He doesn't believe it. In the hospital, I say. He promises to pay me a visit soon; after all, he is working in this city, purchased a house near the concert hall a year ago. He never comes, I don't miss him.

I have a craving for writing at length and without reserve, without regard for myself, without having to care whether there is someone asleep next to me, not to have to sit in bed with the notepad on my knees or to have to wait until the room over there is vacant. I observe myself, compare the slight apprehension, the shorter breath with what I feel when I sit at the typewriter and after intense concentration sink back into the feeling of my own body, apprehension, tension, the holding together of the ribs around something that makes me go on, my pulse, heartbeat, my machine, mysterious beating that keeps me alive.

I would like to paint you, says the artist. I have this fear that you won't come back, and I did not paint enough of you. Do you understand that? – I nod. I feel strong in his desire. It occurs to me that he has never been so tender and close. And how it is possible that a separation, which at one time one felt so clearly, can dissolve. I land in softness. It feels good there, it doesn't pull, there are not the distant sounds that could be interpreted in this way or that. I can surrender to my senses, they are at play without danger and in time I can recover. Your lips are narrow, dry, he says, the hospital air. His lips brush my cheeks, my throat, tenderly he lets me know that I'm his companion who still needs a bit of time.

When Kathleen comes in through the door for a last time, she is smaller than I remember, is taller when she gets up, has her hair styled differently in profile, looks at me with unfamiliar eyes, belies my fantasies. I say, let me do your makeup, Kathleen. She sits in my writing chair, slides it a little towards the window, holds out her face for me. I smooth the lotion over her cheeks, starting with her chin, down from her nose and up to her forehead, cover the blemishes with a cover stick, massage in the makeup. Powder over the cheeks, closed eyelids, on the lips too there is makeup. I say: Look at me, Kathleen, and she looks at me with her flat features, there are no black traces in them, a forelorn face with eyes that are too far apart. Blue shadow on the lids, blue in the corners, a darker blue, the darkness pulls the eyes closer together, brings her gaze together, the eyelids receive black strokes that are then smeared, now her eyes have a setting which holds the gaze, the gaze from within and the one that enters. Black on the eyelashes, the mascara on the eyelashes, above and below. Oh Kathleen, your Japanese face appears, and you resemble your doll which sits on the bed beside you when you are sick. The lip pencil follows the contours of her lips, fills in the shape of the lips, she presses her mouth on a handkerchief, a familiar gesture, apply some more color, slowly her mouth grows into a smile. Still missing, the blush on the cheeks to suggest the glow from within, the fire in you that indicates your fate. You are beautiful, Kathleen. Your hair style will be in fashion again one day, your dress with the long lapels. And anybody who claims that you derived your strength from your disease knows nothing of you.

The old woman is discharged against her will. Unhappy, she lets her things be packed up, she says that she is much too weak, she cries when her daughter ties the laces on her shoes. Her daughter has brought me a homemade doll, she stands fastened to some cardboard and is shrouded in a stiff coat made of different grains. You have taken such good care of her, says the daughter. If I can only come back to this room, says the old woman as she takes her leave. Then I'm alone and remain that way for two days. In the mornings time crawls by, until noon a new admission is possible, then the danger is passed and I can take my walk with relief. When I get home, all that I am missing is the key to my house where I live alone, looking at the window, which I could open without having to ask. I pinch my eyes shut, make some grimaces, spread some papers out on my bed. Next day I have a neighbor who feels sorry for me, because I have been here so long. During this night the old woman is admitted again and dies in a different room.

5

There has been a heavy snowfall, the director of the Red Cross, easily recognized by the paper hat with an inscribed cross, effortlessly pulls a sleigh behind him. I overtake him, to the sides the snowy mountains get ever higher. Along the way I see a woman on her back in the snow, making swimming motions, with every stroke the hair in her armpits is visible. Then I hear myself say the sentence: In my heart Celje makes an entry and I move on.

Do you still love Jack? asks the artist.

How are you going to paint me now? I ask him. He closes his eyes, his lower lip twitches, making it look as if he is receiving signals in Morse code that he first has to translate into images, colors – how to tell someone else? Don't know, he says and looks at me. A black wooden beam in the middle, above it, like a rainbow, a blue strip of the sky, something like the delicate blue of spring that is faintly drifting into green, coldness in it, not yet darkly heated up; then white strokes, that's where your body shimmers through, and this body I would stitch with brown jabs into this strip of sky, I would fasten you into the sky and into the spring and into an entire year. Then over it the varnish, which makes it gleam and endure. I would like to go away with you, to the south, not a big trip. A little time for us, we could have a room together, sense your breath during our walks, to cheer you up, to make you strong, to read to you and to recommend something from the menu. All little dreams.

How is Kathleen, the artist asks. – She's dead, I say. She has been dead for sixty years with all of her friends; only the dwellings, some of the many in which she lived, may still be there. Isn't it dreadful that a piece of furniture, a curtain, a picture may last longer than a human being?

I superstitiously avoid all words that might suggest a return. Those from whom I take leave say nothing but: See you, see you, see you. I look around to see if I've forgotten anything, I've given away the newspapers, the flowers, the stamps, I've returned the paper with the hospital letterhead. No shoes under the bed, the toilet articles quickly removed from the medicine cabinet on the wall and put into the bag. The dust in the medicine cabinet is already from me. A last glance at the little skeleton on the wall, in my bed there is already a newly admitted patient, a blond girl with tousled hair, black lacquered fingernails, she is no joy for the nurses this way. My gaze takes in the bed on which I have been lying for more than two months, this bed which the custodian pushed aside in the mornings. I sometimes let myself be pushed, sometimes the imposed movement drove me out. I say good-bye with an intimate tone in my voice, which is a little betrayal of the fact that I don't know anything about this new patient in my bed, about her fear, her anger. To tear myself away, I hear how the hallway door snaps shut, proudly intercepting the glance of the laboratory assistant to my bag, oh yes, they are letting me go. They let me go and outside in the no-parking zone there is the car of the artist, the seatbelt already holds me securely in this seat. Everything is happening much too fast, past the traffic lights we leave these streets, the post office that Franz likes so much disappears, the drivers in the cars around us have no idea what this is all about. I feel released, my detention is over, my police record clear and stowed in the bulging paper envelope with the X-rays. I put my hand on the hand of the artist, in this way I help to steer a little, like a child.

What about your story, he asks and briefly looks at me from the side. Are you going to finish it? – I don't know, I say. I can't imagine how that could ever work again. I don't have the strength for it, I very quickly lose the focus, the coherence. – Stupid, he says. What do you think happens with me when I stand there in my studio? Canvas, paints, brushes, turpentine, linseed oil – all of these things are there and ready, and I'm there too, we really could begin, but nothing happens. I can look at my hand as it reaches for a tube of paint, or my thumb, as it pokes through the palette, it's laughable, one could die laughing. In my head nothing but an emptiness, actually an emptiness filled with loose, drifting bad ideas, there's a jug, a fruit plate – always these pictures that have been painted to death over hundreds of years, as if in scorn, deer or moose, isn't that just idiotic? As if I had to start all over again, as if I had to experience everything over and over again. In between, at some point, a dab of color streaks by, that's the one, but I didn't even really see it, it's possible that it is nothing but the recollection of someone else's painting. There is a rage of emptiness and wrong ideas and impulses. At the same time I well know that the red is just waiting to be applied to the canvas, everything is waiting for me, sienna brown, black, they want to be joined, I'm supposed to bring them together and extract from them the single right shimmer for this instant, it lies in wait, bulging and ready to burst, ready to prostitute itself and be seen. Only my hands are needed for this, hands which give it a name and which organize it all, and it is quite all right for me to grow tired in the process. After that, while I lie on the old couch and feel the cold slowly creeping up my feverish body, the picture with its insolent smirk stands on the easel or on the chair. In its fullness it stands there, in its full extension, the nakedness of the canvas covered, but how! At first you can only touch it with your eyes, you can still feel the sharp scraping of the palette-knife, you see the scraping marks that you have made, feel how in one place the paint has thinned just right, feel the empty drag of the palette knife, there the background shimmers through. You know that it is now good this way, that you can see it with one glance and that its inner order is right. It is right. It is finished.

I wish that this trip would never end. I have written down for Kathleen what I would tell her. I miss her. I have such longing for her. Her warmth and her perceptiveness, her knowledge and her body. The artist puts on the turn signal to the right and drives onto the shoulder of the road. He bends towards me, kisses me on the neck, digs down with his head. Lips and teeth gently leave inscriptions on my body, I hold his head firmly all the while. He surfaces again, looks at me with eyes that are heavy, full, full to the brim, full of all that remains unspoken and rolls his face on my collar-bone, back and forth, so much tenderness – or is it just that his nose itches? Kathleen, Kathleen.

There is no feeling that compares with the joy of having written and finished a story, she then says. There it is, new and complete. – A story is not a child that one releases after months of patient work, I say. It is immediately an adult. And this adult leaves you right away, it's the first thing that it does. You are left behind. I'm afraid of this parting. The story scampers down the stairs, leaving behind a writing table stacked with papers, which you then bundle into folders. Now and then, of course, you hear from someone who has met your story and tells you of its effect. You tell yourself, it's part of me, this story, but you yourself never meet it again. While you are writing your story, you pretend that you are pulling something together, holding on to something. In truth, as you write, you are undoing ribbons, nothing more.

Afterword

Willy Riemer

In awarding a prestigious literary prize to Evelyn Schlag for her narrative *Die Kränkung* (1987, *Quotations of a Body*) the jury notes that her language approaches its subject matter with a reverence conveying a sense of intimacy seldom achieved in life or in literature.[1] The noted Austrian critic and literary scholar Wendelin Schmidt-Dengler regards her most recent book, *Unsichtbare Frauen* (1995, Invisible Women), as feminist prose in the very best sense, perspicacious and uncompromising in its detail.[2] Critical acumen and subtlety of expression indeed characterize all of her writings, but the reader also finds a finely textured humor and an imagination delightfully set free. To date, Schlag has published ten books, including narratives, three volumes of poetry, a collection of essays based on her poetics lectures delivered at the University of Graz, and a translation of the elegies by the Scottish poet Douglas Dunn. Schlag writes prose imbued with lyricism. Language and the bounds of expression thus form the basis of her work. And as she probes the limits of day-to-day experience, the protagonists, with very few exceptions, are women. Women with resilience and subtle irony, women who endure the projects and large visions of men, women who are rendered invisible by their association with such men. Some of the women are patterned on historical figures, such as Katherine Mansfield and the German baroque poetess

Catharina Regina von Greiffenberg. From an affinity to Peter Handke and Friederike Mayröcker in her early writings, Schlag has proceeded to forge her own style: lucid, strong, sometimes fragile words probing the peripheries of modern existence.

Evelyn Schlag was born in 1952 in Waidhofen/Ybbs. After completing an M.A. in English and German at the University of Vienna, she held a position at the Bundesrealgymnasium in Vienna and now teaches in Waidhofen. She began writing poetry in 1975, but soon also turned to prose. Her work has appeared in anthologies and in periodicals such as *Neue Rundschau*, *Literatur und Kritik*, *Protokolle*, and *manuskripte*. She has participated in major literary events, including the Ingeborg Bachmann competition (1984) and the "Harborfront International Festival of Authors" in Toronto (1987).

The main themes of all her work, as well as her keen interest in form and language are anticipated in *Nachhilfe* (1981, Private Lessons), Schlag's first book. In this narrative she explores the possibilities of self-fulfillment by experimenting with transactional relationships and with multiperspectival narration. Marianne, the dutiful wife and mother in the middle-class suburb of *Nachhilfe*, may be an unlikely match for the lonely and broken figures in Leonard Cohen's *Songs of Love and Hate*. But with her quotation from the song “Famous Blue Raincoat” – "yes, and thanks for the trouble you took from her eyes, I thought it was there for good, so I never tried" – Schlag suggests a similarly listless existence (N,87).[3] Settled into a comfortable household, Marianne cooks, darns, devotedly agrees with her husband, reads glossy magazines, and every once in a while indulges in chocolate. In the course of a few months and an ensuing intimate relationship she gains a tentative glimpse of possible self-realization, but also the sense that she is merely slipping from one dependency into yet another.

Schlag sets out to compensate for past prejudices; the narrator announces her partiality right off. Lingering in the background are familiar issues: the demand for autonomy and equal opportunity, a self-conscious sensibility, and a deep distrust of the analytical intellect. But the current adjustments occur in offices and public places, not in kitchens; they involve a program for the revaluation of status, not the individual consciousness alone. By contrast *Nachhilfe* quietly exposes the repressive structures endured in everyday life, the dual nature of Marianne's existence. For Marianne socialization turns out to be a highly restrictive process. Her self-concept is determined almost entirely by reference to her family, by functions that define the stereotype.

Consistent with her critique of restrictive paradigms, Schlag employs a multiperspectival structure that exposes the writing process itself. The narrator of *Nachhilfe* writes about the relationship between Marianne and her newly found friend Stefan (third-person), with interspersed jottings that are attributed to Stefan and that provide a highly subjective and unfiltered view of the events of the story (first-person). On yet another level the narrator in the first-person reflects on both of these positions, as well as on questions of narratology. These three relatively independent texts are typographically identified, distinct in mode of discourse and point of view. As the events unfold, this unusual strategy conveys different bracketings of the fictive reality, plainly revealing the attitude of the protagonists as well as the constraints of the narrative process. The vitality of *Nachhilfe* does not so much derive from a suspenseful plot as from the juxtaposition and tension between the different points of view.

The narrator with the superimposed perspective is a careful reader of Stefan's texts, a critic of his positions and attitudes, and a writer who self-consciously reflects on the process of narration. The most interesting questions considered by the metanarrator focus on the origin and function of the fictive characters. According to this view, fictionalizing involves a narrator poised between actual people and the figures of the narrative. In the guise of the narrator, Schlag thus suggests that all of the figures derive from real life. That she does not simply intend a transcription of life to art, a *roman à clef*, becomes evident when she notes: "What we lack in one life, we obtain from another"(N,5). The autobiographical component of Schlag's narratives thus involves the residue of actual encounters that is then redistributed and projected on invented characters, such as Marianne and Stefan. As the narrator makes clear, however, the figures are also shaped by the insights derived from working with each fictive character.

With the "normal" paradigms of social behavior thus in question, subsequent protagonists fall back on what they feel and know from their own experience. Amid an atmosphere of interpersonal tension they appear poignant, but also somewhat fretful and egocentric, a source of irritation to all who have found their conformable niche. Nowhere is this more evident than in Schlag's next work, *Beim Hüter des Schattens* (1984, Visiting the Custodian of the Shadow).

In this story of love and separation the point of view

is that of the narrator, a Viennese artist visiting Pflueger, the son of Austrian immigrants and himself an emigré from the USA. On one occasion she reflects, just this side of solipsism: "The whole world had its beginning right here where she stood and thought" (H,106) and reveals her self-centered temperament, ever apprehensive about possible infringements of her autonomy. Pflueger is an accomplished musician and craftsman in his forties. He is competent, fastidious in all he does, with an obsession for having control over his life. He represents the epitome of utilitarian rationality. Such a lifestyle is best realized in isolation, away from the unpredictable intrusions of urban life. Consequently, he has opted for a minimalist existence in a modest little house in a remote part of Quebec near the Maine border. It is a life about which the narrator aptly remarks: "How he lives here, on the stones!"(H,44).

In a series of episodes which render with insight the culture, politics, and landscape of Quebec the narrator considers their prospects and comes to a foreseeable conclusion: "There is something ineluctably alien on the way from one human being to another"(H,81). The narrator's metaphorical experience of reality contrasts sharply with Pflueger's obsession with factual knowledge and reason, with the referential dimension of language. As a favorite pastime he studies dictionary entries, searching for the etymology of words rather than their transactional force. One such word, periscian, becomes the leitmotif of the narrative and the origin of the title: as people isolated at the terrestrial poles can be thought to be encircled by their shadow in the course of the day, so ultimately all individuals are cloaked by the trappings of their personality, millstones that prevent them from engaging others at any but a superficial level.

With his insistence on self-sufficiency Pflueger becomes all but unapproachable. As Schlag observes in another publication: "A person who can console himself best of all cannot be helped."[4] The many attempts at mental intimacy fail. Sigrid Weigel considers this love impossible, "not for some external reason but rather because both partners have emotionally withdrawn out of fear of possessiveness, so that no intimacy can develop."[5] In the end, with her return to Vienna, the narrator fulfills the prediction of the epigraph taken from Margaret Atwood's controversial book on Canadian literature: "Endurance, survival, no victory"(H,5). The interpretation, however, is given a positive turn when the narrator concedes, "survival is enough of a victory"(H,82).[6]

The reference to Atwood, the most prominent figure in contemporary Canadian literature, suggests an affinity to her writings. In the last few lines of Atwood's novel *Surfacing* the narrator summarizes the lessons learned from her experiences and concludes: "This above all, to refuse to be a victim . . . The word games, the winning and losing games are finished."[7] After some harrowing events in a remote part of Quebec she decides, as does the narrator of Schlag's book, to return to the big city.

In both cases the narrator is a young woman artist who experiences a number of incidents that show the pervasiveness of certain attitudes associated with patriarchal society: the dominance games that involve factual knowledge, skill, and strength, the contrast of civilization and nature, the observation that women obtain their identity and social status not through their own achievement and profession but through association with a man. Some of these themes as well as the prevalence of a heightened awareness of body and emotion, to be sure, are frequently found in women's literature. However, Atwood's insistence on survival is specific particularly to her early work and refers both to individual and cultural survival. With this background Pflueger, in a kind of voluntary exile, does not appear nearly so heartless; after all, "In exile / survival / is the first necessity."[8] To some degree and certainly in accord with his disposition Pflueger's circumstance requires that he be competent and practical, that he exercise his mind with material at hand. Unlike the two narrators, who understand that change must come within society and therefore return to urban life, Pflueger chooses solitude. Both narrators look openly, if not optimistically, to the future; they have moved from a preoccupation with strategies for survival to one exploring change.

Pflueger's periscian syndrome finds its way into *Brandstetters Reise* (1985, Brandstetter's Journey) as well. Brandstetter is a mild-mannered dissident from the business world. Irritated by disagreements with his wife, he observes: "We are surrounded by our most delicate aversions, and it seems to me that these aversions have become boundless"(B,22). Where Pflueger withdraws to his millstone bulwark, Brandstetter allows his personal space to be absorbed into the role patterns of his relatives, friends and colleagues. With little regard for the subtle uncertainties of his self-image they determine his persona. Their every gesture of uncaring familiarity then provokes a little resentment at the foreshortened encounter, a little antipathy that spreads finally to taint all that Brandstetter thinks and feels.

Brandstetter's journey then deals with the stages of his disentanglement from deadening relationships so that in the end he can claim: "Cut free from friends and acquaintances, that is sad, but now there is space"(B:156). In her third narrative Schlag thus returns to the central theme of *Nachhilfe* and a similar, though gender-reversed, constellation of characters.

Where Pflueger accepts frugality for its rational control, Brandstetter simplifies his life by withdrawing to a sentimental shelter. Neither alternative has much social relevance. More promising is the path that is suggested by the narrator of Pflueger's retreat, an approach that is further developed in *Quotations of a Body*.

Quotations of a Body begins with the same strained atmosphere and scabrous relationship that pervades *Beim Hüter des Schattens*. The narrator and Jack, her intimate friend, attempt to salvage their relationship by moving to an old house in the country. But instead of restoring their tender intimacy the solitude of the pastoral setting accentuates their separation.Yet neither of them is willing to invalidate the years spent together. The relationship is further strained when Jack falls in love with Rosie, the young and attractive neighbor. The events at the manor and new acquaintances fill each hour but not the narrator's day.Faced with this unendurable situation, she begins to regard their relationship as a dangerous machine. The predicament is resolved for the narrator not by a conscious decision but by the response of her body: she becomes ill with tuberculosis. At the hospital she is exposed to the impersonal procedures and rational discourse of modern medical practice, but she also finds the love and affection of an acquaintance; thus recovery is paired with a joyful optimism for their future.

In the quest for representing the transactional self Schlag employs an ingenious device. Instead of the interspliced divergent texts of *Nachhilfe*, *Quotations of a Body* merges first-person narration with the perspective provided by an imagined character called Kathleen. The events at the manor thus are retrospectively interpreted and written down from a point of view that is centered on the narrator and that at the same time provides for the peripheral perspective of Kathleen, who is patterned after Katherine Mansfield.

As snow gives a different aspect to a landscape, so Mansfield's biography provides a rich overlay for the events and relationships of *Quotations of a Body*. Details from her life are absorbed into the text in a way that distinguishes her presence, but also clearly suggests an act of identification for the narrator: both are writers, both suffer protracted ill health that ultimately manifests itself as tuberculosis, and neither is able to resolve a problematic relationships. For the narrator the fictive Mansfield is an imagined companion, literary mentor, and alter ego all in one. She compensates for the lack of affection, lightens the self-doubt of the writer, and reveals the dark regions of her subconscious: in the text Kathleen is explicitly linked with Jack's affair with Rosie and with the repressed knowledge of the narrator's disease. At the same time Mansfield's short and troubled life lingers in the background as a threatening alternative.

Katherine Mansfield's journals and correspondence give ample evidence of her volatile temperament, her dark moods, and ebulliently joyful moments. She was wary, sometimes manipulative in her encounters, and yet desperately in need of unrestrained affection. In a letter to her husband John Middleton Murry she confides: ". . . somehow I do always have to be 'needed' to be happy."[9] The emotional self-sufficiency of Murry and that of the narrator's friend, both called Jack, therefore makes for an unpromising relationship.[10] As Mansfield's health deteriorated and her ambitions as a writer failed to bring the expected rewards, Murry was apparently too preoccupied with his career to extend much compassion. Similarly the narrator finds reasonable care with her Jack but not a commitment of intimacy.

The characters of Schlag's narratives primarily express dispositions and insights. Consequently they are not depicted in their appearance but rather in their transactions and in their use of language. While Jack thus represents the attitudes and discourse of utilitarian rationality, Kathleen is ever present in the numerous biographical details as an alternative that acknowledges the intellect, but also respects the domain beyond reason, the sensuous language of her body.

By some psychosomatic process, so the book suggests, the body responds to deprivation and neglect with a manifest disease. The cumulative effect of Mansfield's presence and the narrator's empathy and illness establish a point of view that is at the periphery of normalcy. The impressions and observations of the narrator thus are depicted in a conventional first-person narration, but always in an atmosphere that prompts alternative interpretations.

The four narratives display a refinement of technique and elucidation of theme. In *Nachhilfe* the multiperspectival narration addresses the restrictive nature of the point of view, and Marianne experiences all the self-doubts and alienation depicted in subsequent narratives without finding a consistent solution. *Beim Hüter des Schattens* shows the central role of the transactional self and the destructive aspect of utilitarian rationality. With a role reversal in *Brandstetters Reise* Schlag suggests that the issue is not necessarily endemic to patriarchal society; rather it is an attitude that is engrained in modern thinking. *Quotations of a Body* provides both an elegant solution to the problem of narrative perspective and an ending whose potential is more fully expressed in Schlag's poetry and later narratives.

Notes

1. *Verleihung der Bremer Literaturpreise 1988 an Peter Handke, Evelyn Schlag. Laudationes und Dankesworte* (Bremen: Rudolf-Alexander-Schröder-Stiftung, 1988), p. 7.

2. Wendelin Schmidt-Dengler, Review of *Unsichtbare Frauen* by Evelyn Schlag, *ORF ex libris*, 27. September 1995.

3. References to Schlag's first four works will be given parenthetically as N= Nachhilfe; H= Beim Hüter des Schattens; B= Brandstetters Reise; and K= Die Kränkung. Translations are by Willy Riemer.

4. "Trost," in *Was mich tröstet. Literaturalmanach 1988*, ed. Jochen Jung (Salzburg: Residenz, 1988), p. 103.

5. Sigrid Weigel, *Die Stimme der Medusa. Schreibweisen in der Gegenwartsliteratur von Frauen* (Dülmen-Hiddingsel: tende, 1987), p. 244.

6. Margaret Atwood, *Survival. A Thematic Guide to Canadian Literature* (Toronto: Anansi, 1972), p. 158.

7. Margaret Atwood, *Surfacing* (New York: Simon and Schuster, 1972), p. 222.

8. Margaret Atwood, *The Animals in That Country* (New York: Simon and Schuster, 1969), p. 29.

9. *The Collected Letters of Katherine Mansfield. Vol. I: 1903-1917*, ed. Vincent O'Sullivan and Margaret Scott (Oxford: OUP, 1984), p. 189.

10. Mansfield appraises Jack: "There never was a creature less fitted by nature for life with a woman." *Journal of Katherine Mansfield*, ed. J. Middleton Murry (London: Constable, 1954), p. 166.

CW00745887

LET'S COOK!

Also by Mary Danby in Piccolo Books:

Fun for Five Year Olds

Fun for Six Year Olds

Fun for Seven Year Olds

Fun for Eight Year Olds

Mary Danby

LET'S COOK!

A First Cookery Book

Illustrated by Ray Mutimer

Design by Sarah Fretwell

A Piccolo Original

First published in Piccolo 1990 by Pan Books Ltd,
Cavaye Place, London SW10 9PG
9 8 7 6 5 4 3 2 1
© Mary Danby
Illustrations © Ray Mutimer
ISBN 0 330 31258 8
Phototypeset by Input Typesetting Ltd, London
Printed and bound in Great Britain by
Richard Clay Ltd, Bungay, Suffolk

This book is sold subject to the condition that it shall not, by way of trade or otherwise, be lent, re-sold, hired out, or otherwise circulated without the publisher's prior consent in any form of binding or cover other than that in which it is published and without a similar condition including this condition being imposed on the subsequent purchaser

CONTENTS

	Page No.
Let's Cook!	9
Danger – Cook at Work	10
Clean – and Safe	11
Weights and Measures	12
What Do I Need?	14
Cooking Know-How	16
Cooks' Words – and what they mean	18
Before You Begin	19
VERY EASY RECIPES	
Baked Tomatoes	20
Frozen Bananas	22
Home-Made Muesli	24
Raspberry and Lemon Cooler	26
Cheesy Hedgehogs	28
Heavenly Pud	30
Stuffed Dates	32

Fruit Fool 34
Party Sandwiches 36
Yogurt Lollies 38
Pineapple Punch 40
Chocolate Cream Biscuits 42
Jacket Potato 44
Fillings for Jacket Potatoes 46
Chocolate Milkshake 48
Topsy-Turvy Eggs 50

FAIRLY EASY RECIPES
Hard-boiled Eggs 52
Welsh Rarebit 54
Sausage Casserole 56
Tuna Scramble 58
Frosted Fruit 60
Teatime Treat 62
Cheese 'n' Nut Salad 64
Sesame and Sunflower Seed Snack 66
Banana Boats 68

Toasted Ham and Cheese
Sandwich 70
Chocolate Crispies 72
Fruit Salad 74
Celery Dip 76
Crunchy Munchies 78

NOT QUITE SO EASY RECIPES

Meatballs 80
Spicy Apple Buns 82
Tea Loaf 84
Stained Glass Jelly 86
Gingerbread Men 88
Energy Bars 90
Potato Pastry 92
Chocolate Pieces 94

LET'S CLEAN UP 96

LET'S COOK

The Greeks have a saying, 'You eat with your eyes.' You may prepare food that smells and tastes good, but to make it really tempting you should do everything you can to make it *look* good, too.

- Arrange it carefully on pretty dishes and decorate it with whatever looks right – parsley, perhaps, or a slice of lemon. Everyone will be queuing up to try your exciting food!
- Nearly all children like treats in the form of sweets, chocolate, crisps, fizzy drinks and chips, but although these foods fill you up, they don't do you much good.
- Make sure you leave room for the kind of food that will help you to be strong and healthy – and look good – such as vegetables and salads, fresh fruit, fish, brown bread, beans, eggs, cheese and milk.
- A good cook will always think about the health of the people he or she is cooking for, and try to give them a good, balanced meal.

DANGER – COOK AT WORK!

A kitchen can be full of dangers, so be sure to learn these basic rules.

- Sharp knives, used very carefully, are safer than blunt ones.

- Never use a cooker without permission from an adult.

- Don't try to cram too much into a small pan.

- Be specially careful when cooking sugar, syrup, hot fat or oil – they can burn your skin very badly.

- Turn pan handles to the sides of the cooker so that you don't knock them.

- Always use oven-gloves when handling anything hot or putting something into a hot oven.

- Anything spilt on the floor should be wiped up straight away, so that you don't slip on it.

- When you use any ingredient, always be sure that it's what it says on the bottle or packet. Thoughtless people sometimes store poisonous goods in food containers.

CLEAN AND SAFE

There's an unseen danger in the kitchen – germs. These tiny bugs can make you very ill, and are easily passed on through food.

To make sure that everything you cook is germ free, always remember:

- Wash your hands with warm water and soap before you start.

- Dry them on a clean towel – not your drying-up cloth.

- Make sure your nails are clean.

- Wipe down your work surface before you start, and after you finish.
- Never use food that doesn't look or smell absolutely fresh.
- Don't leave food sitting about in the kitchen for longer than necessary. Put it in the fridge. This is specially important with meat and fish.
- Unused tinned food should not be left in the tin. Tip it into another container and put it in the fridge.
- Wear a clean apron.
- Avoid coughing and sneezing over food.
- Be very careful with uncooked meat. Keep it away from other food.
- A knife or chopping board that's been used for cutting raw meat should not be used for anything else.

WEIGHTS AND MEASURES

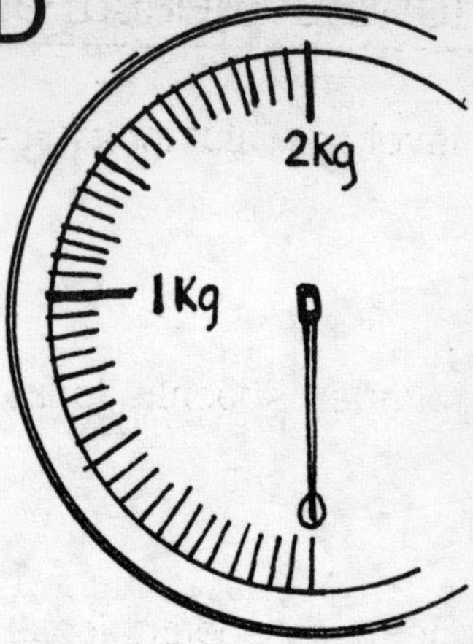

How to weigh dry food

Place the bowl on the scales and make sure the needle points to '0'.

Put the food bit by bit into the bowl until the needle points to the amount you require.

Most scales have measurements that look like this:

Each small line is 25 grams (25g.). Each tall line is 1 kilogram. 150 grams would look like this:

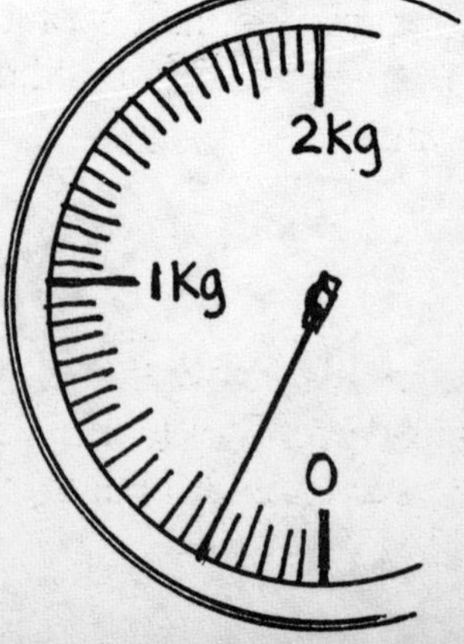

How to measure in spoonfuls

1 level spoonful looks like this:

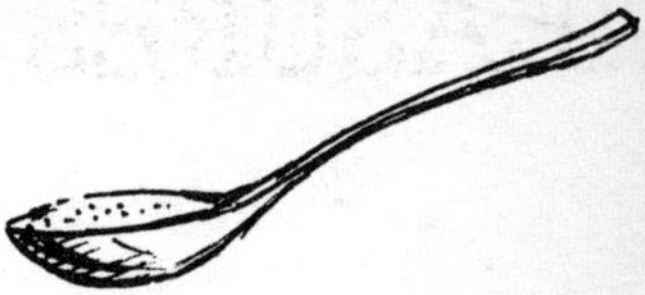

1 rounded spoonful looks like this:

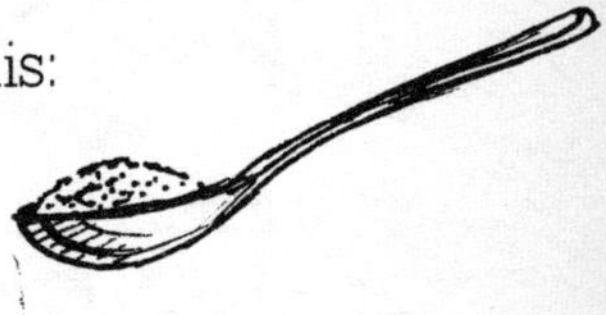

A heaped spoonful looks like this:

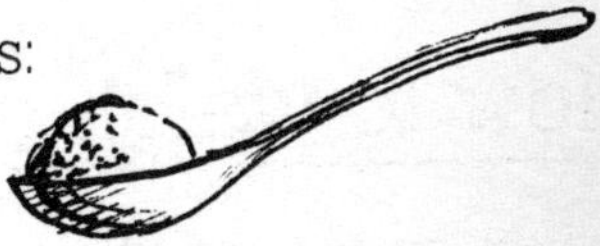

If a recipe just says 'a spoonful', it usually means a level spoonful.

How to measure liquids

Use a measuring jug and slowly add the liquid until it reaches the right level.

For instance, half a pint (which is also 10 fluid ounces or 284 millilitres) would look like this:

It's useful to know that a small yogurt or cream carton holds a quarter of a pint (5 fluid ounces/142 millilitres).

WHAT DO I NEED?

Each recipe in this book tells you what equipment you will need. This is what some of the items look like:

BEFORE YOU BEGIN

① Ask an adult if you may use the kitchen (and the cooker, if necessary).

② Wash and dry your hands.

③ Put on an apron.

④ Rinse out a cloth in warm soapy water and wipe over your work surface.

⑤ Read right through the recipe and get out everything you need.

⑥ If you're making something that needs cooking, make sure you have somewhere heatproof to put down the hot pan or dish (*not* straight on to the worktop).

⑦ Remember that an oven takes about 15 minutes to reach the right temperature, so you may want to switch it on before you begin preparing the food.

BAKED TOMATOES

What you need

- 1 tomato for each person
- Small kitchen knife
- Chopping board

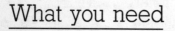

- Shallow ovenproof dish
- Salt and pepper

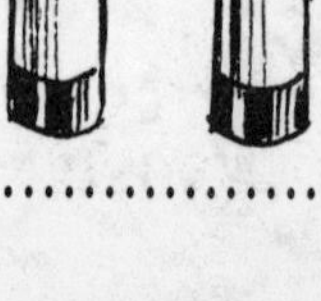

What you do

① Turn on the oven and set it to 190°C (375°F, gas mark 5).

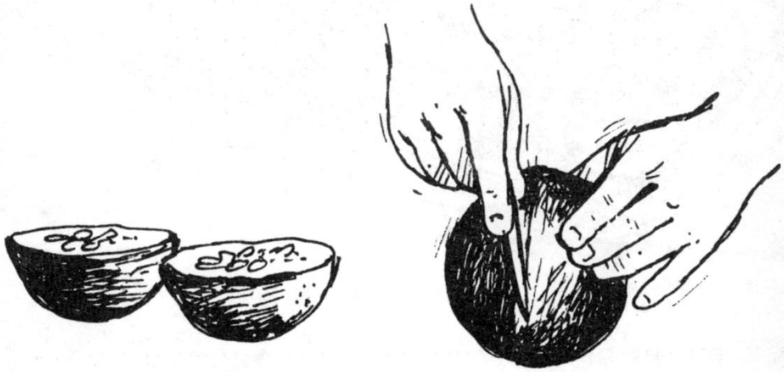

② Cut each tomato in half.
③ Stand the tomato halves in the dish.
④ Sprinkle them with salt and pepper.

⑤ Bake in the oven for about 15 minutes.

FROZEN BANANAS

What you need

- 1 firm, ripe banana
- Runny honey
- Crunchy breakfast cereal

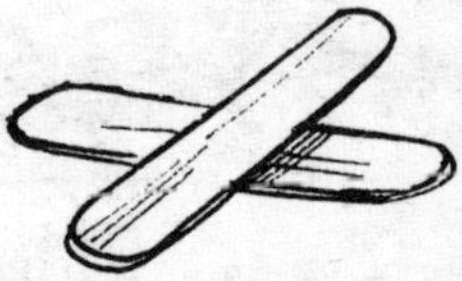

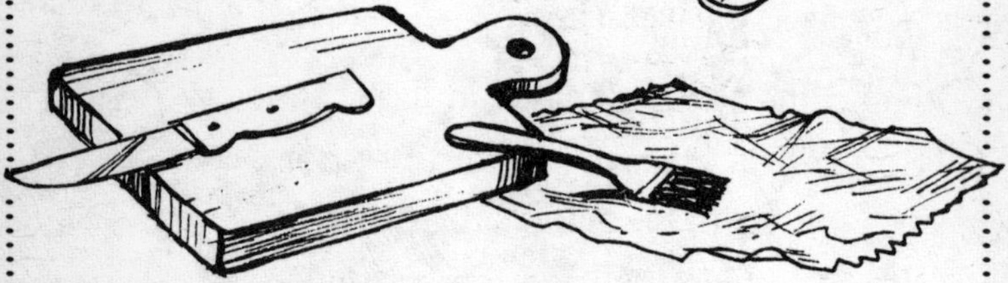

- Small knife
- 2 used lolly sticks, well scrubbed
- Chopping board
- Pastry brush
- 2 pieces of tin foil

Servings: enough for 2 people

What you do

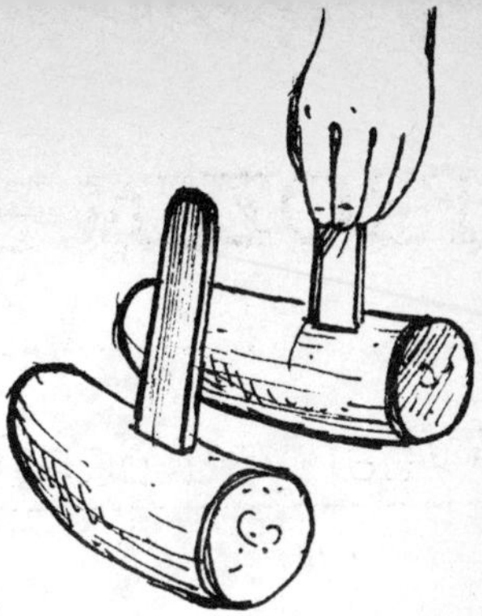

① Peel the banana, and cut it in half.

② Push a lolly stick into the cut end of each banana half.

③ Put each banana-half on to a square of foil.

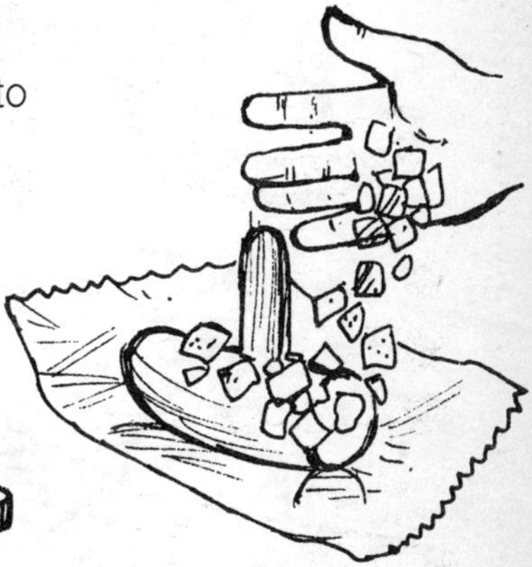

④ Brush the bananas with honey.

⑤ Sprinkle them all over with cereal.

⑥ Wrap the tinfoil around the bananas.

⑦ Put the banana parcels into the freezer and leave them until the next day.

HOME-MADE MUESLI

What you do

① Measure all the ingredients and tip them into the bowl.

② Give everything a good stir with the spoon.

What you need

- 4 cups porridge oats
- 1 cup bran
- 1 cup dried fruit
- 2 cups wheatflakes
- 1 cup wheatgerm
- 1 cup unsalted nuts
- Teacup for measuring
- Big mixing bowl

- Wooden spoon
- Airtight storage jar

Servings: enough for 4 people

③ Tip or spoon the mixture into the storage jar.

This is good for breakfast, with fresh fruit and milk or yogurt.

RASPBERRY AND LEMON COOLER

What you need

- 1 carton of raspberry yogurt
- ¼ pint (5 fluid oz.) fizzy lemonade
- Vanilla ice-cream

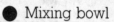

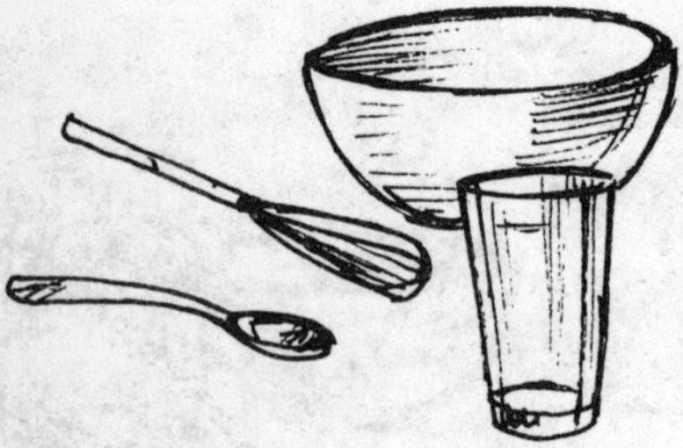

- Mixing bowl
- Whisk
- Dessert spoon
- Tall tumbler

Servings: enough for 1 person

What you do

① Tip the yogurt into a bowl.

(2) Fill the empty carton with lemonade and tip that in, too.

(3) Whisk the yogurt and lemonade together (being careful not to splash too much).

(4) Place a spoonful of ice-cream in the tumbler.

(5) Pour the yogurt and lemonade mixture over the ice-cream.

CHEESY HEDGEHOGS

What you do

① Cut the grapefruit in half and place each half on a plate.

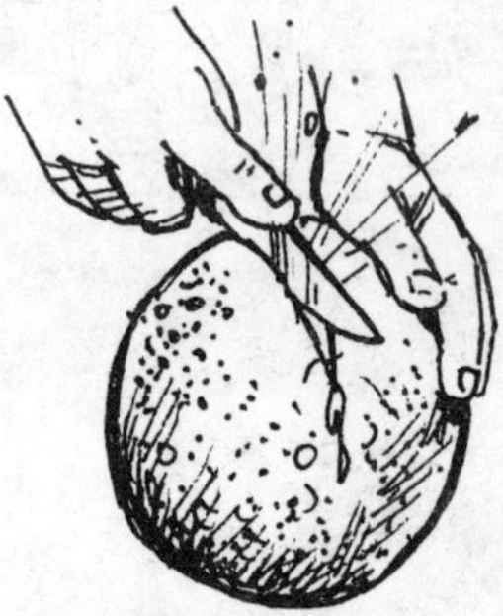

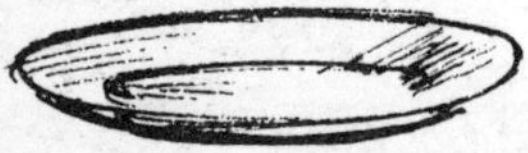

What you need

- 1 grapefruit
- 150g. (150 grams) of cheddar cheese
- A large tin of pineapple chunks
- 2 glacé cherries
- 4 sultanas

- Cocktail sticks
- Small kitchen knife
- Chopping board
- 2 small plates

(2) Cut the cheese into pieces, roughly the same size as the pineapple chunks.

(3) Push one piece of cheese and one piece of pineapple on to each cocktail stick.

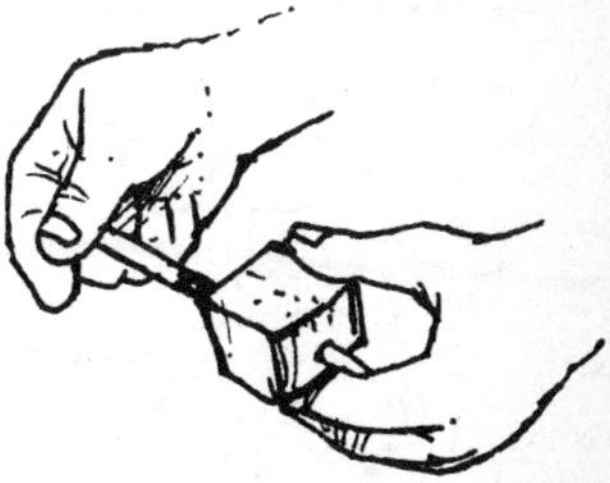

(4) Push the cocktail sticks into the grapefruit halves so that they look like the prickles on a hedgehog.

(5) Push the cherries on to cocktail sticks and use them for the hedgehogs' noses.

(6) Push each sultana on to a cocktail stick and use them for the eyes.

HEAVENLY PUD

What you do

① Tip the cream and yogurt into the mixing bowl.

② Whisk them together until they become light and fairly thick.

③ Pour the mixture into the serving dishes. Spread a fairly thick layer of sugar on top of the mixture in each dish.

What you need

- Small carton of double cream
- Small carton of plain yogurt (unsweetened)
- Brown sugar (any kind)

- Mixing bowl
- Whisk
- Small serving dishes

Servings: enough for 4 people

④ Put into the fridge and leave overnight.

The sugar will dissolve, making a lovely, rich syrup on top of the creamy mixture.

STUFFED DATES

What you need

- 1 box of dates
- 2 or 3 satsumas
- Small kitchen knife
- Chopping board
- 24 small paper cases

What you do

① Cut each date along the top and take out the stone.

② Peel the satsumas and break them into segments.

③ Put a satsuma segment in place of each date stone and press the date together again.

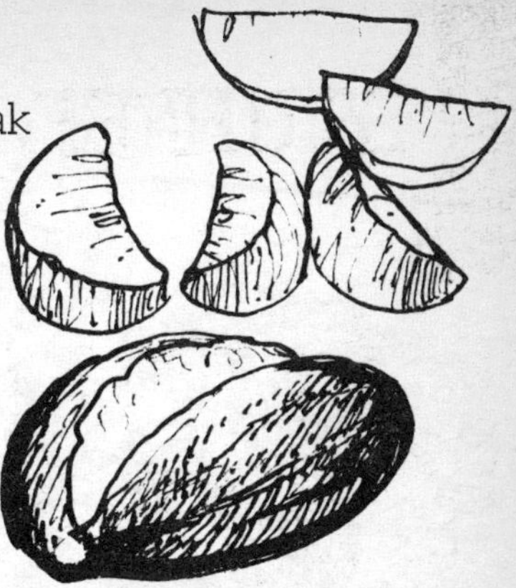

④ Put the finished dates into the paper cases and serve them on a pretty plate.

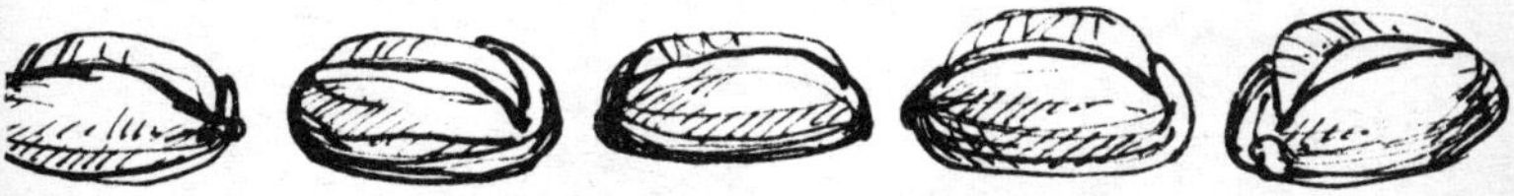

These are nice to make at Christmas.
You could arrange them in boxes or baskets to give as presents.
You could also try stuffing the dates with marzipan or nuts.

FRUIT FOOL

What you do

① Open the tin and pour the fruit into the mixing bowl.

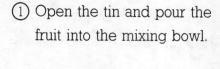

② Add the yogurt.

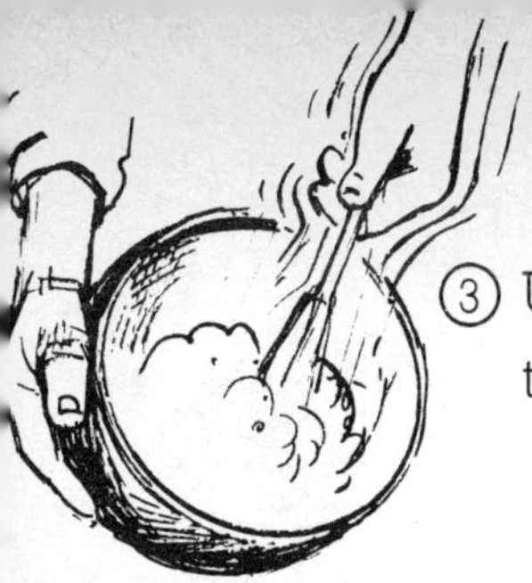

③ Use the whisk to mix them together.

④ Spoon the fruit fool into a serving bowl.

⑤ Decorate the top with 'hundreds and thousands'.

Servings: enough for 2 people

What you need

- 1 tin of stewed fruit-pie filling
- 1 small carton of natural yogurt (unsweetened)
- 'Hundreds and thousands'

- Tin-opener
- Mixing bowl
- Tablespoon
- Whisk
- Serving bowl

PARTY SANDWICHES

Sandwich-making is very easy, especially if you remember a few rules.

① The bread must be cut thinly, so it's probably best to use ready-sliced bread.
② Use soft margarine for easy spreading.
③ Make sure that the filling isn't too runny.

Fancy sandwiches can be made by cutting the bread with different shaped pastry cutters, or by using brown bread for the bottom layer and white for the top. Or you could try making 3-decker sandwiches – again using white and brown bread.

Open sandwiches can be made using different kinds and shapes of crispbread or cheese crackers for their bases.

Here are some ideas for fillings:

- Chopped hard-boiled egg mixed with mayonnaise (remember rule 3!)
- Marmite and lettuce
- Tuna fish and cucumber
- Cheddar cheese and strawberry jam (This sounds awful, but tastes nice if you like a mixture of sweet and savoury food)
- Cottage cheese and pineapple
- Sliced banana and honey

A plate of sandwiches looks very inviting if you garnish it with sprigs of watercress or parsley.

YOGURT LOLLIES

What you need

- 1 small carton of plain yogurt
- 1 carton of frozen concentrated orange juice

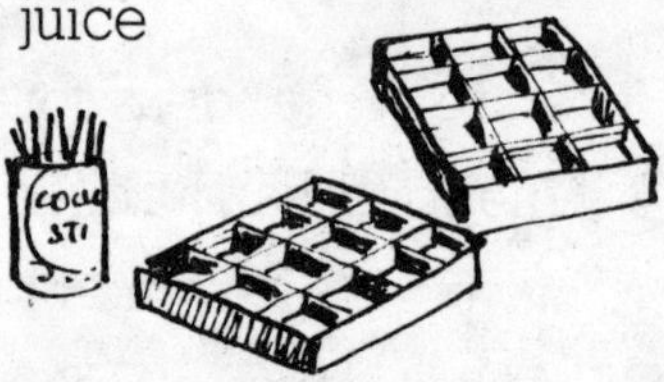

- Ice-cube trays
- Mixing bowl
- Fork
- Teaspoon
- Cocktail sticks

What you do

1. Take the orange juice out of the freezer one hour before you need it.
2. Tip the yogurt and orange juice into the mixing bowl and stir the mixture well.
3. Spoon the mixture into the ice-cube trays.

(4) Put the trays in the freezer until the mixture is almost firm.

(5) Take them out of the freezer and push in the cocktail sticks.

(6) Put the trays back in the freezer and leave until the lollies are frozen solid.

PINEAPPLE PUNCH

What you do

① Open the tin of pineapple.
② Put the sieve over the bowl and empty the pineapple into the sieve.
③ Cut the pineapple pieces in half once, then in half again.
④ Do the same with the glacé cherries.

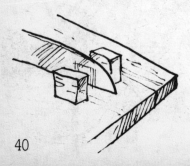

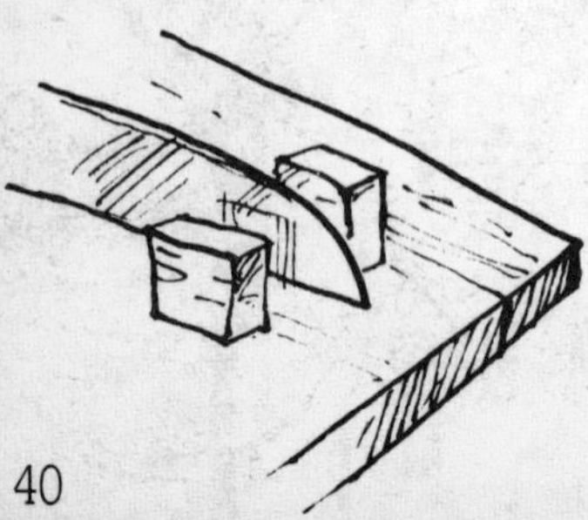

What you need

- 1 bottle of fizzy mineral water
- 1 large tin of pineapple pieces in natural juice

- A few glacé cherries
- Small kitchen knife
- Large bowl
- Tin opener
- Sieve
- Glasses
- Ladle
- Chopping board

⑤ Fill the empty tin with mineral water.

⑥ Add the mineral water to the pineapple juice.

⑦ Add the pineapple pieces and the cherries.

⑧ To serve, pour the punch into small glasses, using a ladle. Make sure that some fruit is served with each drink.

Servings: enough for 6 people

CHOCOLATE CREAM BISCUITS

What you need

- 2 tablespoons thick honey
- 50g. soft margarine
- 4 tablespoons of drinking chocolate
- 1 packet of plain biscuits

- Scales
- Mixing bowl
- Wooden spoon

What you do

① Put the honey and margarine into the mixing bowl. Mix them together with the spoon.

② Add the drinking chocolate and stir everything together until the mixture is an even colour.

③ Spread the mixture on the biscuits and sandwich them together.

This mixture also makes a good cake topping.

JACKET POTATO

What you need

- 1 potato for each person
- Square of baking foil
- Small kitchen knife

What you do

① Turn on the oven and set the temperature to 190°C (375°F, gas mark 5).

② Wash the potato well to remove any dirt. Prick the skin a couple of times with the knife to prevent it bursting.

③ Wrap the potato in foil, so that the 'parcel' can be opened from the top.

④ Put the potato in the oven and cook it for about an hour, or until the potato is soft. (To test, push the knife through the foil into the potato.)

⑤ Remove the potato from the oven. Open the foil and cut a cross on top of the potato.

⑥ Gently squeeze the potato at the sides to make the cross open out.

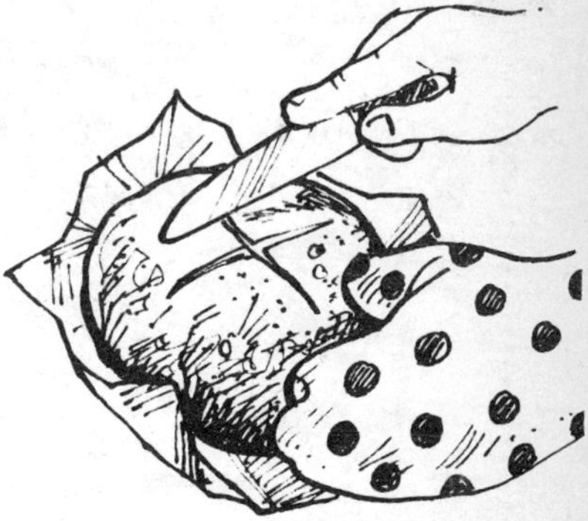

⑦ Put a piece of butter into the open cross and leave it to melt.

The potato will taste good just as it is, but to make it even better, try it with one of the yummy fillings on the next page.

FILLINGS FOR JACKET POTATOES

Try your potato with one of these fillings:

- Grated cheese
- Pickle and grated cheese
- Prawns
- Cream cheese and chopped chives
- Tuna (see page 58 for how to drain it)

As well as your chosen ingredients, you'll need these:

- Knife
- Spoon
- Mixing bowl

What you do

① Instead of cutting a cross on the top of the cooked potato, cut it in half.

② Using a large spoon, scoop out the soft potato and put it in the mixing bowl.

③ Add your chosen filling, together with a little salt and pepper, and mix well.

④ Spoon the mixture back into the potato shell.

If you've taken a long time to do the mixing, you may find that your potato is cold. To warm it up again, put it back into the foil, close the foil loosely over the top and put the potato back into the oven for about 5 minutes.

CHOCOLATE MILKSHAKE

What you need

- 1 pint of cold milk
- 2 scoops of vanilla ice-cream
- 4 teaspoonfuls of drinking chocolate
- 1 small chocolate-flake bar

- Large basin
- Whisk
- Tablespoon
- 2 tall glasses

Servings: enough for 2 people

What you do

1. Put the drinking chocolate into the basin and add 2 tablespoons of milk (taken from the pint).
2. Mix well to make a smooth paste.

③ Add the ice-cream and whisk the mixture until it's thick and bubbly

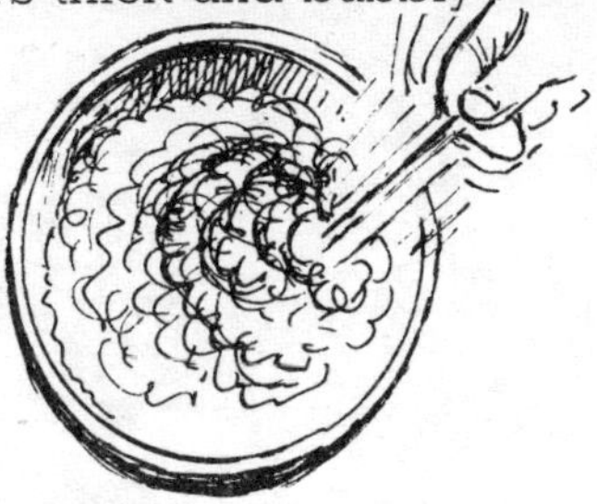

④ Add the rest of the milk and whisk slowly to mix everything together.

⑤ Tip the mixture into tall glasses.

⑥ Break up the flaky bar and scatter some of it on the top of each milkshake. (Eat the rest!)

TOPSY-TURVY EGGS

What you do

1. Make sure the eggs are absolutely dry.
2. Put an egg into the egg cup and draw a face on it, with hair on the top and sides.
3. Turn the egg around and draw another face on the other side.
4. Now turn the egg upside down and draw two more faces.

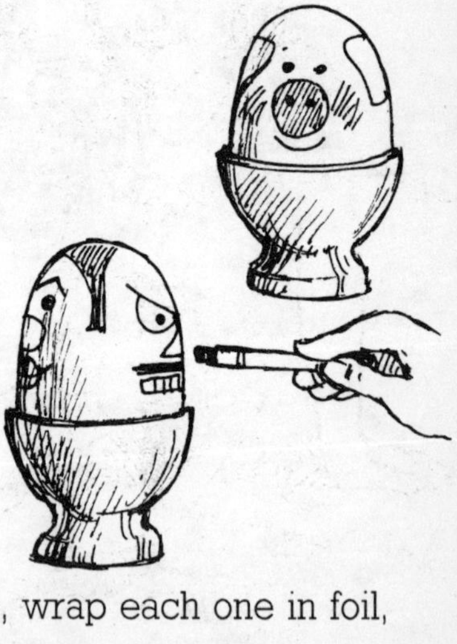

Your egg now has four different faces on it.

To pack the eggs for a picnic, wrap each one in foil, and take along a dip made of mayonnaise and tomato ketchup mixed together.

What you need

- Hard-boiled eggs (see page 52)
- 1 egg cup
- Felt-tipped pens

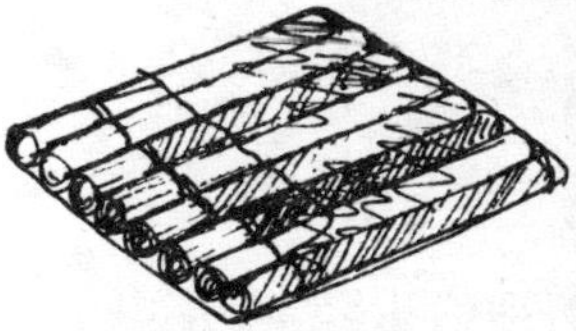

HARD-BOILED EGGS

What you need

- 1 egg for each person
- Cold water
- Small saucepan

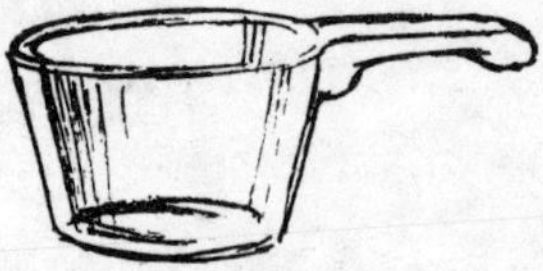

What you do

① Half fill the saucepan with water.

② Put the eggs gently into the water.

③ Put the saucepan on the cooker on a fairly high heat, until the water bubbles.

④ Turn the heat down a little, so that the water continues to boil gently. After 15 minutes, the eggs should be ready.

⑤ Take the saucepan to the sink. (Be very careful. Use an oven mitt if the handle is hot, and move slowly so as not to spill the water.)

⑥ Run cold water into the pan for a few minutes, to cool the eggs.

⑦ To peel the eggs, hit them gently in several places against something hard, then remove the shells bit by bit.

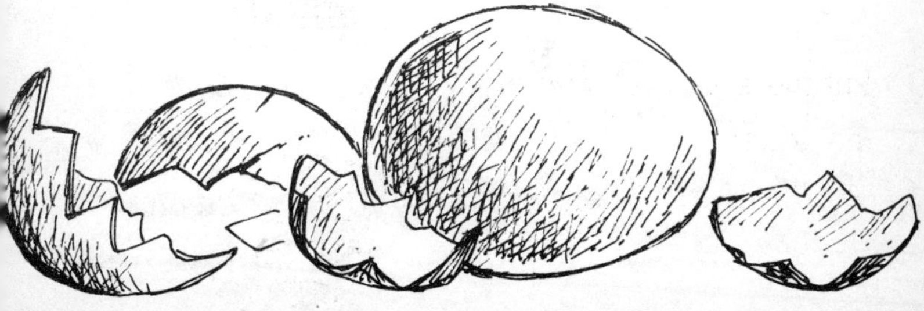

WELSH RAREBIT

What you need

- A slice of bread
- Grated cheese

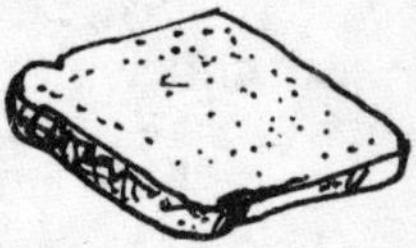

- Grater
- Grill pan
- Spatula

Servings: enough for 1 person

What you do

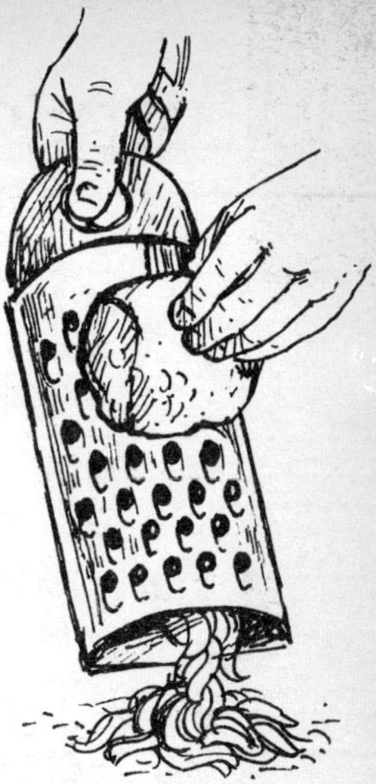

① Grate the cheese.
② Turn on the grill.
③ Put the bread on the grill pan, put it under the grill and toast the bread on one side only.

④ Remove the pan from under the grill and take the toast off the grill pan with the spatula.

⑤ Sprinkle some cheese on the untoasted side of the bread, making sure it goes right to the edges.
⑥ Put the toast back under the grill until the cheese melts.

If you spread pickle on the toast before adding the cheese, you've made PICKLED RAREBIT.

SAUSAGE CASSEROLE

What you need

- 8 large sausages
- 1 tin of baked beans
- 1 small packet of frozen, mixed vegetables
- Salt and pepper

- Small, sharp knife
- Chopping board
- Ovenproof dish, with a lid
- Tin-opener
- Spoon

Servings: enough for 4 people

What you do

① Turn on the oven and set it to 170°C (325°F, gas mark 3).

② Cut each sausage into 4 pieces.

③ Put them in the dish.

④ Cook them in the oven for half an hour (with no lid on the dish.)

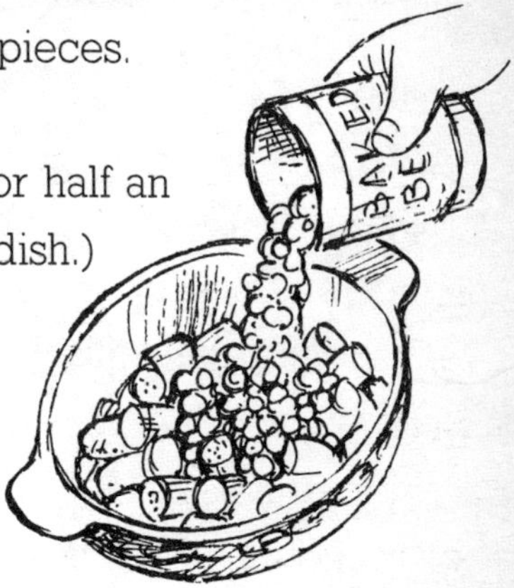

⑤ Open the tin of baked beans and pour them over the sausages.

⑥ Add the frozen vegetables and a little salt and pepper, and stir everything together.

⑦ Put the lid on the dish and cook in the oven for a further half-hour.

TUNA SCRAMBLE

What you do

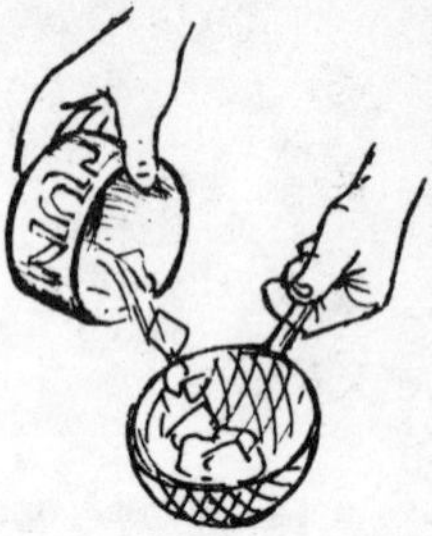

① Open the tin of tuna and tip the contents into the sieve (held over the sink, so that the oil or brine goes down the plughole).

② Tip the tuna from the sieve into the saucepan.

③ Break the egg (see page 16) into the mixing bowl and beat it with the fork until the yolk and white are thoroughly mixed.

④ Add a little salt and pepper.

⑤ Toast the bread in a toaster or under the grill. Put it on a plate and keep it warm.

⑥ Put the pan on the cooker on a medium heat and warm the tuna. Stir it with a wooden spoon to be sure it doesn't stick. Add the egg and stir the mixture until the egg is slightly firm.

What you need

- 1 small tin of tuna fish
- 1 egg
- Salt and pepper
- 1 slice of bread

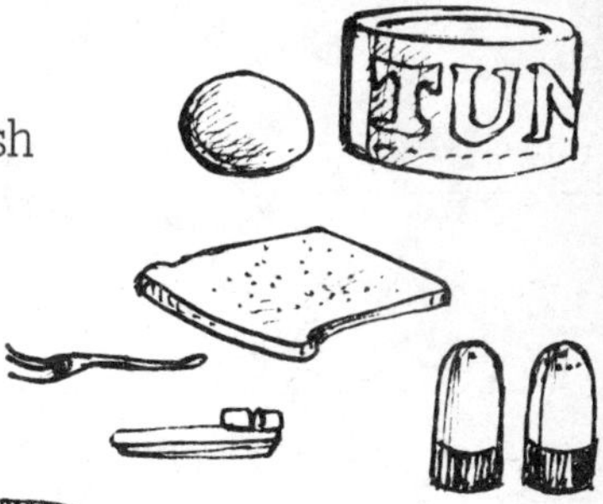

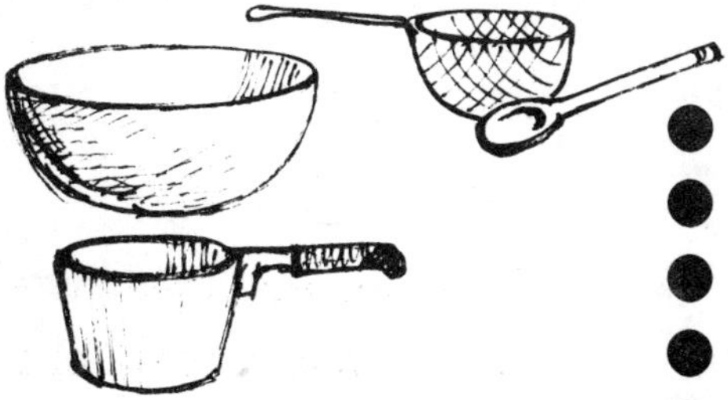

- Tin-opener
- Sieve
- Wooden spoon
- Fork
- Mixing bowl
- Small saucepan

Servings: enough for 1 person

Tinned tuna is packed in oil or brine (salt water), which you need to get rid of.

⑦ Spoon the tuna scramble on to the toast.

FROSTED FRUIT

What you need

- A selection of fruit: try grapes, orange segments, strawberries, cherries, etc.
- 1 egg white
- Caster sugar
- 2 tablespoons of water
- Mixing bowl
- Whisk
- Fine paint brush
- Greaseproof paper

What you do

① Wash and dry the fruit.

② Separate the egg yolk from the white (see page 16). (Keep the yolk in the fridge and use it for something else. It's great mixed into mashed potato.)

③ Put the egg white into the mixing bowl. Add the water, then whisk until the mixture is frothy.

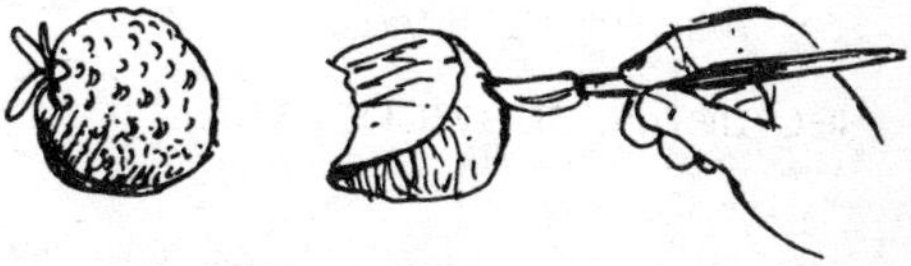

④ Brush the egg-and-water mixture on to your chosen fruit.

⑤ Dip each piece of fruit into the caster sugar and then put it to dry on the greaseproof paper.

TEATIME TREAT

What you need

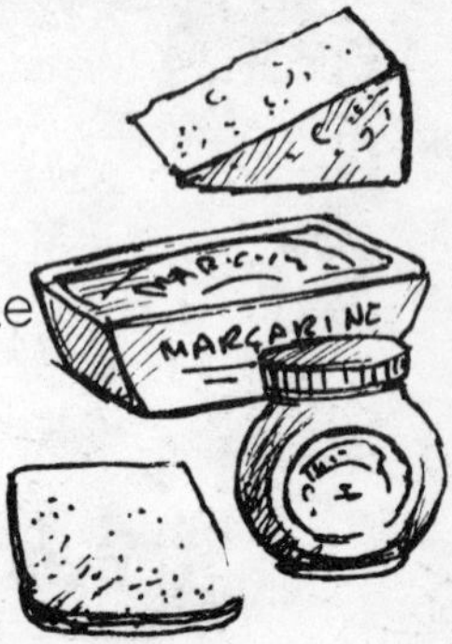

- About 50g. cheddar cheese
- 1 teaspoon butter or margarine
- 1 teaspoon Marmite
- 1 slice of bread

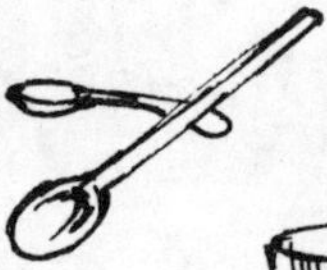

- Grater
- Teaspoon
- Wooden spoon
- Small saucepan
- Table knife

Servings: enough for 1 person

What you do

① Grate the cheese into the saucepan.

② Add the butter and Marmite.

③ Put the saucepan on the cooker and heat gently until the cheese has melted. Stir with the wooden spoon.

④ Toast the bread on both sides, in a toaster or under the grill.

⑤ Cut the toast into fingers.

⑥ Spread the mixture on the toast fingers.

(Before you tuck in, fill the saucepan with water – it'll be easier to wash up later.)

CHEESE 'N' NUT SALAD

What you do

1. Cut the cheese into small cubes.
2. Wash the celery and cut off any leaves. Chop the stalks into small pieces.
3. Wash the apples and cut each one into four quarters.
4. Cut the core from each quarter.
5. Chop the apple into small pieces.

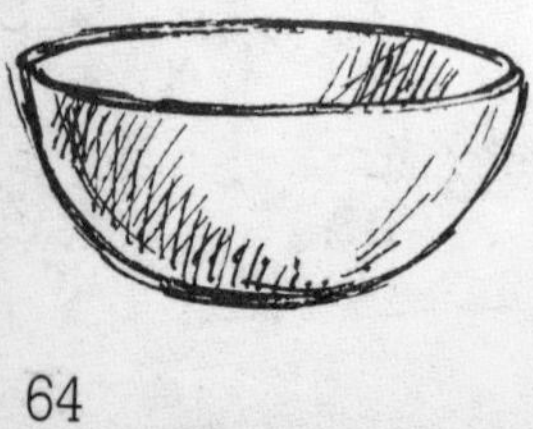

⑥ Put the apple and celery pieces into the bowl and sprinkle them with the lemon juice.

⑦ Add the cheese, nuts and sultanas and stir everything round.

⑧ Add the mayonnaise and yogurt, and mix well.

What you need

- 100g. cheese
- 2 eating apples
- 4 sticks of celery
- 4 teaspoons lemon juice
- 50g. chopped walnuts
- 50g. sultanas
- 2 tablespoons mayonnaise
- 2 tablespoons natural (unsweetened) yogurt

- Scales
- Kitchen knife
- Chopping board
- Large mixing bowl
- Large spoon

Servings: enough for 2 people

SESAME & SUNFLOWER SEED SNACK

What you need

- 1 tablespoon sesame seeds
- 1 tablespoon sunflower seeds
- Soy sauce
- Grill-pan

What you do

① Turn on the grill.
② Spread all the seeds over the bottom of the grill-pan.

③ Sprinkle them with soy sauce.

④ Put the grill-pan under the grill and toast the seeds until they're light brown. (You need to watch them carefully, to make sure they don't burn.)

⑤ When the seeds are cool, store them in an airtight container.

Use them as party nibbles, or as a delicious sandwich filling.

BANANA BOATS

What you do

① Peel the banana and cut it in half lengthways.
② Put the two halves on the dish side by side.
③ Spoon the ice-cream along the banana.

④ Pour the cream over the ice-cream.
⑤ Squeeze some chocolate sauce over the cream.

What you need (for each person)

- 1 banana
- 1 scoop of vanilla ice-cream
- 1 scoop of chocolate ice-cream
- 1 scoop of strawberry ice-cream
- 1 tablespoon of double cream
- A tube (or bottle) of chocolate sauce

- A packet of chopped nuts
- 1 slice cut from an orange
- Small kitchen knife
- Chopping board
- Serving dish
- 2 cocktail sticks

⑥ Scatter some nuts over the top.
⑦ Cut the orange slice in half.
⑧ Push a cocktail stick through each half slice to make the boat's sails.
⑨ Push the cocktail sticks into the banana.

TOASTED HAM & CHEESE SANDWICH

What you need

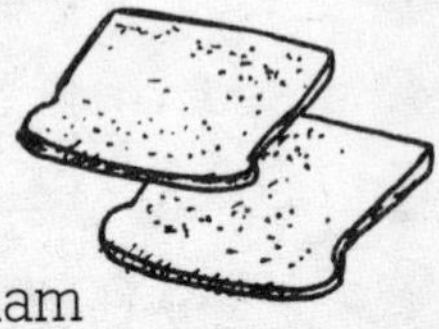

- 2 slices of bread
- Cheddar cheese
- Slice of ham

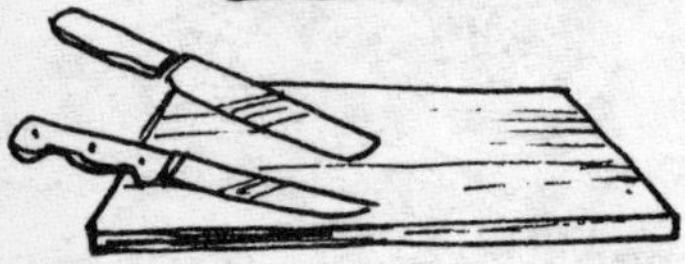

- Grill-pan
- Spatula
- Kitchen knife
- Chopping board

What you do

① Turn on the grill.

② Put both slices of bread under the grill. Toast one side of each slice.

③ Remove the bread from the grill-pan.

④ Put the ham on the toasted side of one piece of bread.

⑤ Cut a slice of cheese and put it on top of the ham.

⑥ Put the other piece of bread *toasted side down* on top of the cheese.

⑦ Put the completed sandwich back under the grill and toast the top.

⑧ Carefully turn the sandwich over, and toast the other side.

⑨ Cut the sandwich in half and serve it right away.

CHOCOLATE CRISPIES

What you do

① Arrange the paper cases on the baking tray.

② Measure the margarine and syrup into the saucepan.

③ Heat them *gently*, until the margarine has melted.

What you need

- 50g. Rice Krispies (about 8 heaped tablespoons)
- 25g. margarine (about 1 tablespoon)
- 1 tablespoon drinking chocolate

- 1 tablespoon golden syrup
- Paper-cases
- Baking tray
- Saucepan
- Wooden spoon
- Teaspoon

④ Take the pan away from the cooker and stir in the drinking chocolate.

⑤ Add the Rice Krispies and mix well.

⑥ Spoon the mixture into the paper-cases and put them in the fridge to set.

FRUIT SALAD

What you do

① Peel the orange and divide it into segments. Pull off any white pith. Cut each segment in half. Put them in the serving bowl.

② Wash the apple and cut it in half. Cut each half in half again. Cut out the core. Chop the apple into small pieces.

What you need

- 1 orange
- 1 apple
- 1 pear
- 1 small tin of pineapple pieces
- 1 banana
- Lemon juice

- Tin-opener
- Small kitchen knife
- Chopping board
- Wooden spoon

Servings: enough for 4 people

③ Put the apple in the bowl and sprinkle lemon juice over, to stop it going brown.

④ Wash, slice, core and chop the pear, in the same way.

⑤ Add the pear pieces to the serving bowl. Stir gently.

⑥ Open the tin of pineapple pieces, then pour the pineapple and its juice into the serving bowl. Stir gently.

⑦ Peel the banana, cut it into slices and add them to the serving bowl. Mix well.

CELERY DIP

What you do

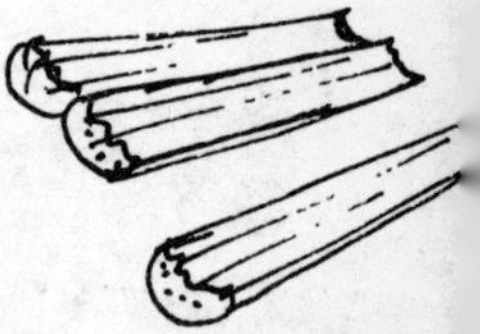

① Pull the celery stalks apart and wash each one separately. Cut off any leaves.

② Cut the celery into sticks.

③ To make the dip, mix the cream cheese and mayonnaise very thoroughly in the bowl. If the mixture seems too stiff, add milk very carefully, drop by drop, until it feels right (soft enough to pick up with the celery, but not so runny that it drips).

What you need

- Celery
- A small packet of cream cheese
- 2 tablespoons mayonnaise
- Milk
- A few peanuts
- Salt and pepper

- Small knife
- Chopping board
- Mixing bowl
- Wooden spoon
- Plastic bag
- Rolling pin
- Plate and bowl for serving

④ Put the peanuts in the plastic bag and crush them with the rolling pin. Add them to the dip, with a little salt and pepper, and mix well.

⑤ Spoon the dip into the serving bowl, place the bowl in the middle of the plate and surround it with the celery sticks.

CRUNCHY MUNCHIES

What you do

① Put the muesli, raisins and chopped nuts in the mixing bowl.

② Add the honey.

③ Mix it all up with the fork.

④ Put the bowl in the fridge for about half an hour.

⑤ To make each Crunchy Munchy, take a teaspoonful of the mixture and press it between your fingers. Now roll it into a small ball.

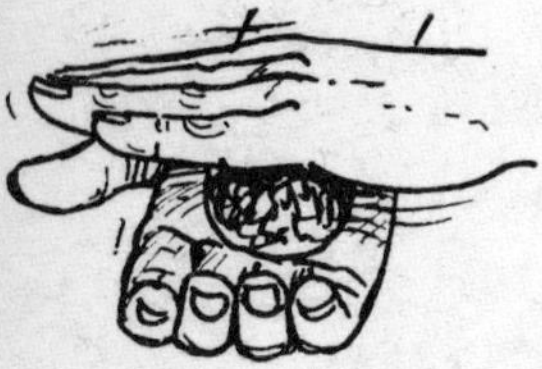

⑥ Put the coconut on to a plate. Roll each ball in it until it's covered in coconut.

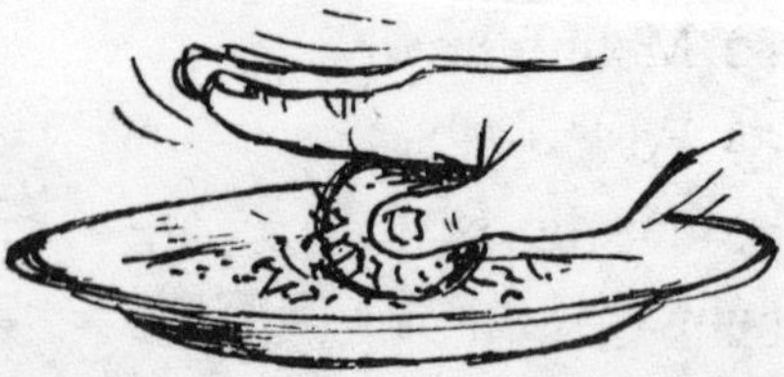

⑦ Arrange the Crunchy Munchies on a clean plate, then put them in the fridge for about an hour, to make them nice and firm.

What you need

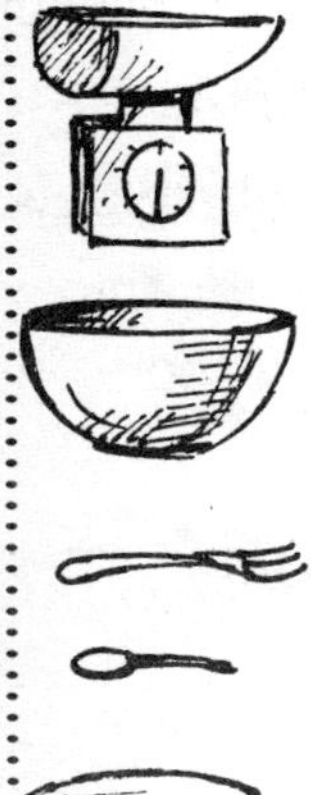

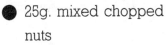

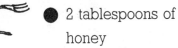

- 50g. muesli
- 50g. desiccated coconut
- 25g. raisins
- 25g. mixed chopped nuts
- 2 tablespoons of honey
- Scales
- Mixing bowl
- Fork
- Teaspoon
- 2 plates

MEATBALLS

What you need

- 1 onion
- 500g. sausagemeat
- 25g. porridge oats
- ½ tablespoon of Worcester sauce
- 2 tablespoons of tomato ketchup
- ½ teaspoon of mixed herbs
- ½ teaspoon of salt
- Pepper
- Margarine
- Small kitchen knife

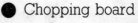

- Chopping board
- Mixing bowl
- Scales
- Dessert spoon
- Wooden spoon
- Baking tray
- Kitchen paper

Servings: enough for 4 people

What you do

① Turn on the oven and set it to 200°C (400°F, gas mark 6).

② Peel the onion (see page 17), chop it into small pieces and put it in the bowl.

③ Measure the other ingredients and add them to the onion. Mix well with the wooden spoon.

④ Grease the baking tray, using the margarine and kitchen paper (see page 17).

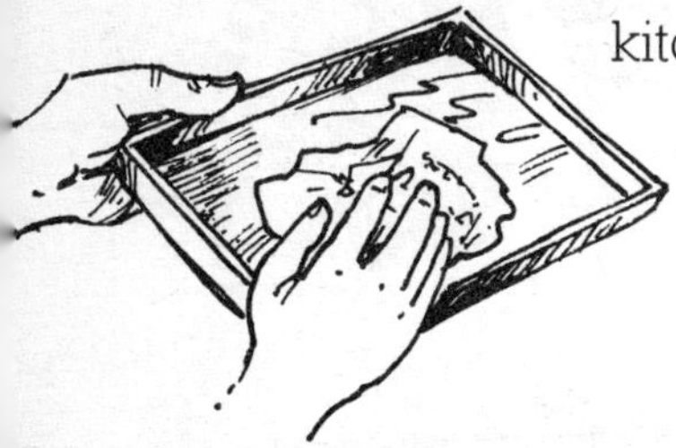

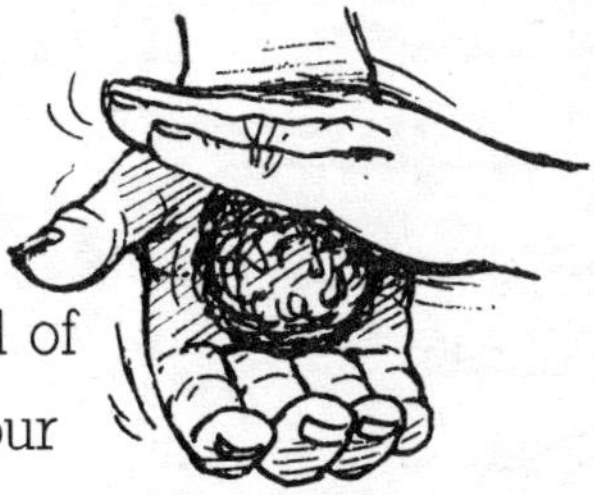

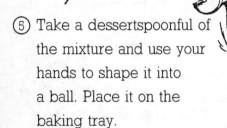

⑤ Take a dessertspoonful of the mixture and use your hands to shape it into a ball. Place it on the baking tray.

⑥ Continue doing this until all the mixture is used up.

⑦ Put the tray in the oven and bake for 50 minutes.

If you like spicy food, you could use a level teaspoon of curry powder instead of the herbs.

SPICY APPLE BUNS

What you do

① Turn on the oven and set it to 220°C (425°F, gas mark 7).

② Put one paper case in each section of the bun-tin.

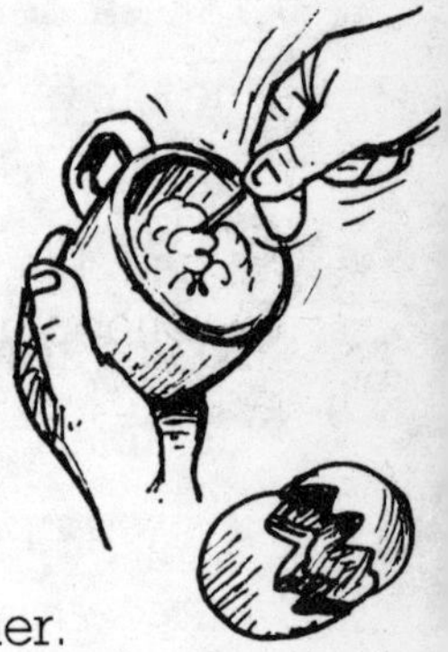

③ Break the egg into a teacup and beat it with the fork.

④ Put the margarine and sugar into the mixing bowl. Use the wooden spoon to cream them together.

⑤ Add the beaten egg to the creamy mixture. Stir well.

⑥ Cut the apple into quarters and remove the core. Chop the apple into small pieces and add them to the bowl. Stir well.

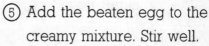

⑦ Add the flour and spices (cinnamon and nutmeg). Stir well.

What you need

- 50g. self-raising flour
- 25g. margarine
- 25g. caster sugar
- 1 apple
- 1 egg
- ½ teaspoon cinnamon
- ½ teaspoon nutmeg

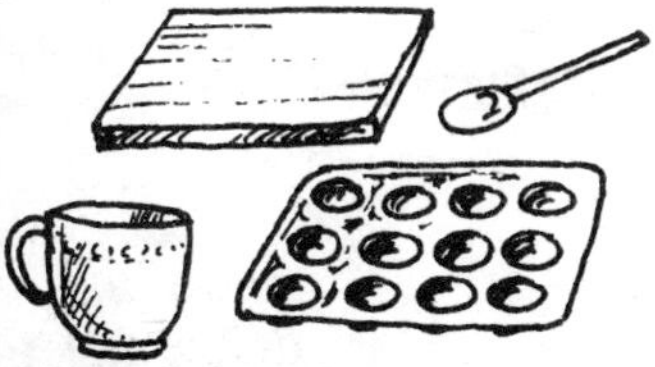

- Small kitchen knife
- Chopping board
- Teaspoon
- 6 paper baking-cases
- Bun-tin
- Teacup
- Mixing bowl
- Wooden spoon
- Fork

⑧ Put a heaped teaspoonful of the mixture into each paper-case. Try to get the same amount in each case.

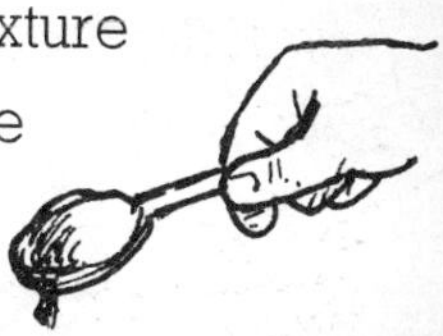

⑨ Put the bun-tin in the oven and bake for about 15 minutes, until the buns are a golden colour.

TEA LOAF

What you do

1. Put the mixed fruit, sugar and orange juice into the mixing bowl. Cover the bowl and leave it overnight.
2. Next day turn on the oven and set it to 180°C (350°F, gas mark 4.)
3. Break the egg into the small bowl (see page 16). Beat it with the fork and pour it into the mixing bowl.

What you need

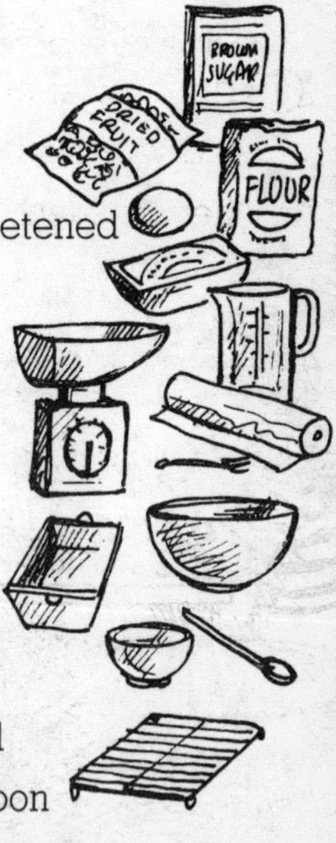

- 200g. mixed dried fruit
- 100g. brown sugar
- ¼ pint (5 fluid ounces) unsweetened orange juice
- 1 egg
- 150g. self-raising flour
- A little margarine

- Scales
- Measuring jug
- Clingfilm
- Fork
- Small bowl
- Small loaf-tin
- Mixing bowl
- Wooden spoon
- Wire cooling tray

④ Weigh the flour and add it to the mixture in the mixing bowl.

⑤ Stir everything together.

⑥ Grease the loaf-tin, using the margarine and kitchen paper (see page 17).

⑦ Spoon the mixture into the loaf-tin.

⑧ Put the tin into the oven and bake for an hour. (To test when the loaf is cooked, see page 17).

⑨ Tip the loaf out on to the wire tray and wait for it to become cool, then slice and butter it for tea.

STAINED GLASS JELLY

Make sure you allow plenty of time to make this, because you need to leave each jelly colour to set before adding the next.

What you do

1. Choose the first colour jelly and make it in the measuring jug, following the instructions on the packet.
2. Stir it well with the fork.

3. Pour a shallow layer of jelly into each glass dish.
4. Put a wedge (such as a pencil, rubber or thin book – anything to tip the dish) under one side of it, to make the jelly slanted. Leave in a cool place to set.

What you need

- 1 packet of red jelly
- 1 packet of green jelly
- 1 packet of yellow jelly
- Measuring jug
- Fork
- 4 glass dishes

Servings: enough for 4 people

⑤ Make up your second colour jelly and pour it on top of the first colour in the dishes. This time put the wedge on the opposite side of the bowl so that the jelly tips the other way. Leave to set.

⑥ Make up the last jelly and pour it on top of the other two. This time leave the dishes flat. Leave to set.

Serve your stained glass jellies topped with cream or ice-cream.

GINGERBREAD MEN

What you do

① Turn on the oven and set it to 180°C (350°F, gas mark 4).

② Put the flour, ginger and cinnamon into the bowl.

③ Put the margarine, sugar and syrup into the saucepan. Place the pan over a low heat and

What you need

- 200g. self-raising flour (and a little extra)
- 2 level teaspoons ground ginger
- 1 level teaspoon ground cinnamon
- 50g. soft margarine (and a little extra)
- 50g. soft brown sugar
- 2 heaped tablespoons golden syrup
- A few currants for decoration

- Scales Mixing bowl
- Saucepan Wooden spoon
- Pastry board
- Knife Spatula Kitchen paper
- Large baking tray
- Wire cooling tray

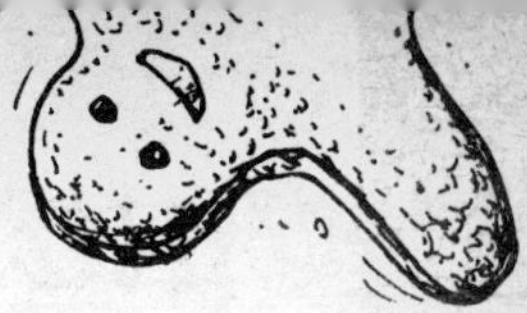

stir until everything has melted.
Don't let it get too hot.

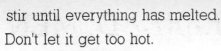

④ Pour the melted mixture into the mixing bowl.

⑤ Mix everything together, then sprinkle a little flour on to the pastry board and tip the mixture on to it. Roll the mixture into a ball and cut it into twelve equal pieces.

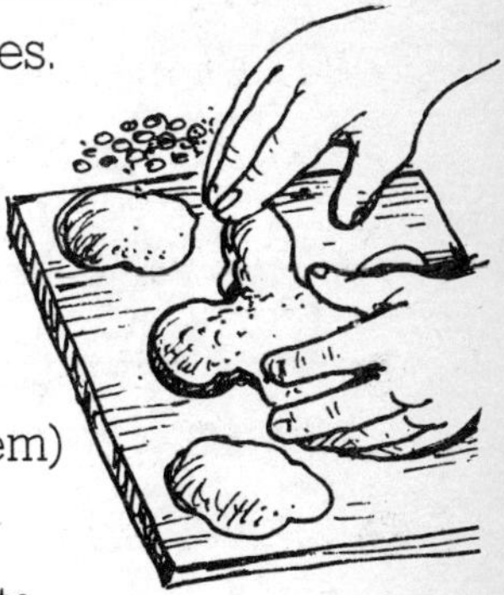

⑥ Grease the baking tray with margarine and kitchen paper (see page 17).

⑦ Put some flour on your hands (to stop the dough sticking to them) and pinch a piece of dough into the shape of a man. Pat it down to make it flat.

⑧ Lift it with the spatula and place it on the baking tray. Make the eleven other gingerbread men in the same way.

⑨ Make the faces with the currants. Press some more currants down the bodies for buttons.

⑩ Bake in the centre of the oven for 10–12 minutes, or until the gingerbread men are golden brown.

⑪ Remove the baking tray from the oven and carefully lift each gingerbread man on to the wire cooling tray.

ENERGY BARS

What you do

① Chop the apricots into small pieces.

② Put them into the saucepan. Add the water. Cook gently until the apricots are soft and all the water has been absorbed. (This will take about 5 minutes).

③ Put all the other ingredients (except the honey) into the mixing bowl.

④ Add the apricots to the mixing bowl and stir well.

⑤ Add the honey and stir to make a firm paste.

⑥ Tip the mixture on to the chopping board and divide it roughly in half.

⑦ Wet your hands and use them to roll the mixture into two sausage shapes.

What you need

- 50g. dried apricots
- 100 millilitres (4 fluid ounces) water
- 50g. chopped mixed nuts
- 1 dessertspoon lemon juice
- 2 tablespoons honey
- 25g. skimmed milk powder
- 25g. desiccated coconut
- Small kitchen knife
- 40g. sultanas
- Chopping board
- Small saucepan
- Measuring jug
- Scales
- Mixing bowl
- Wooden spoon
- Clingfilm

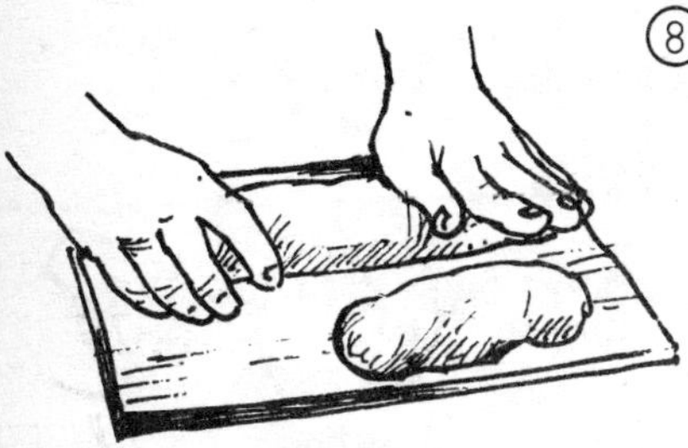

⑧ Wrap each 'sausage' in a piece of clingfilm.

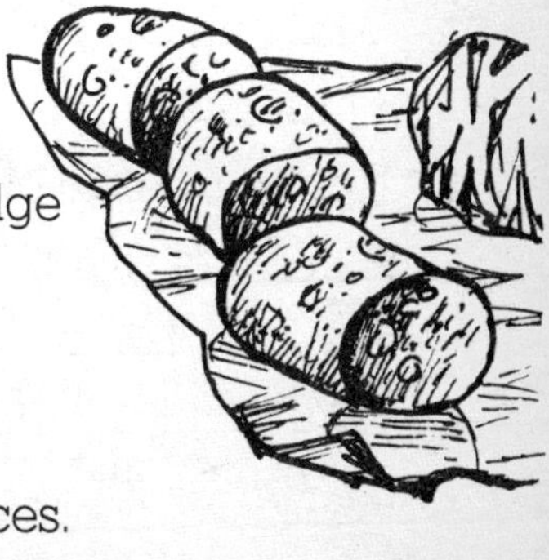

⑨ Put the 'sausages' into the fridge and leave them overnight.

⑩ To serve the Energy Bars, take off the clingfilm and cut each sausage into slices.

POTATO PASTRY

What you do

1. Peel the potatoes and chop them into even-sized pieces.
2. Put them in the saucepan and add enough cold water to cover them. Heat the pan until the water bubbles (which means it's boiling). Turn down the heat so that the water is only just bubbling, and cook the potatoes until they are soft. (This will take about 15–20 minutes.)
3. Tip the potatoes into the colander and drain them over the sink.
4. Put them in the mixing bowl and mash them. Add the margarine and flour and mash a bit more. Leave the mixture to get cold.

What you need

- 500g. potatoes
- 25g. soft margarine
- 250g. plain flour
  (and a little extra)

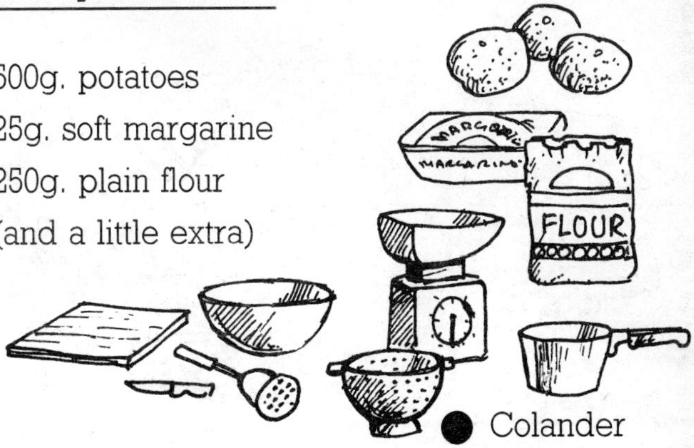

- Scales
- Potato peeler
- Saucepan
- Colander
- Mixing bowl
- Potato masher
- Pastry board

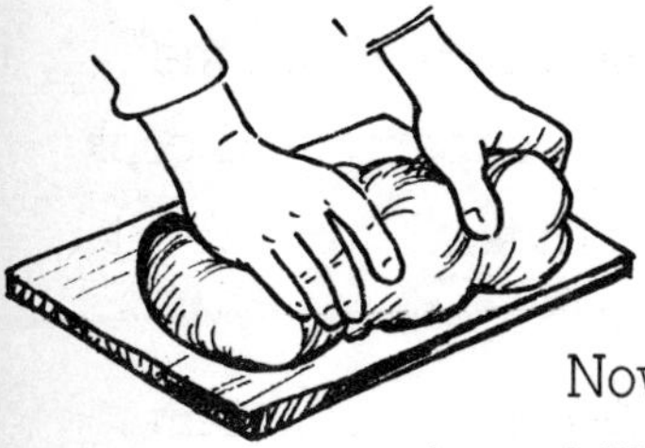

⑤ Tip the mixture out on to the floured pastry board and knead it with your hands until it's smooth.

Now the mixture can be rolled out and used like ordinary pastry. You can use it to make pies and pasties, or you can simply roll it out, cut out bite-sized shapes, bake them on a baking tray and serve them as snacks.

CHOCOLATE PIECES

What you need

- 150g. soft margarine (and a little extra)
- 100g. flour (plain or self-raising)
- 50g. sugar
- 100g. desiccated coconut
- 50g. crushed cornflakes
- 1 tablespoon of drinking chocolate
- Scales
- Plastic bag
- Large mixing bowl
- Wooden spoon
- Shallow baking tin (about 20 cm × 20 cm)
- Kitchen paper
- Palette knife
- Small saucepan

What you do

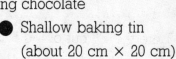

① Turn on the oven and set it to 200°C (400°F, gas mark 6).

② Crush the cornflakes by putting them into the plastic bag and squeezing it.

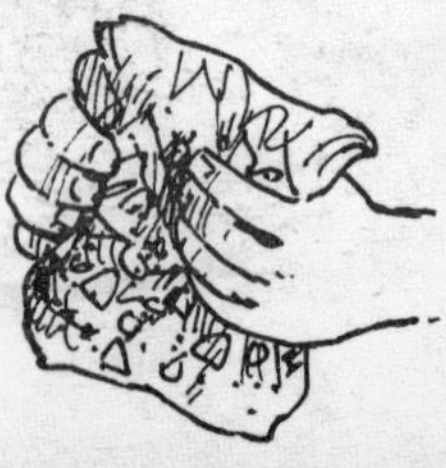

(3) Put the flour, sugar, coconut, cornflakes and drinking chocolate into the mixing bowl and stir well.

(4) Put the margarine in the saucepan and melt it over a low heat.

(5) Add it to the mixture in the bowl. Stir well.

(6) Grease the baking tin, using the margarine and kitchen paper (see page 17).

(7) Spoon the mixture into the baking tin, and press it down evenly.

(8) Put the tin in the oven for 20 minutes.

(9) Take the tin out of the oven and, before it cools, cut the mixture into squares.

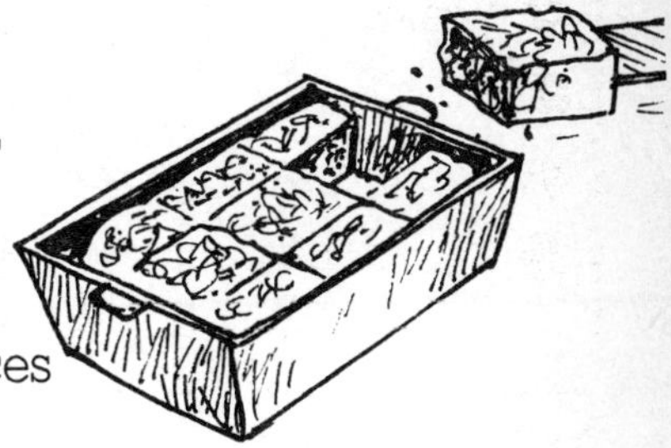

(10) When the chocolate pieces are cold, use the palette knife to help you lift them from the tin.

LET'S CLEAN UP

① If your hands are messy from cooking, wash them again.
② Put away all unused food and equipment.
③ Wash up in warm, soapy water. Wash the cleanest things first. (This will all be much easier if you have put each item to soak in the sink after you have used it.)
④ Dry up and put everything away.
⑤ Wipe down the work surface with a squeezed-out, soapy cloth.
⑥ Check that you have turned off the oven, grill and hotplates.

If you clear up properly, you're always sure to be welcome in a kitchen.